The Big Wide Calm

The Big Wide Calm

A Novel

Rich Marcello

LANGDON STREET PRESS // MINNEAPOLIS, MN

Langdon Street Press
322 First Avenue N, 5th floor
Minneapolis, MN 55401
612.455.2293
www.langdonstreetpress.com

ISBN-13: 978-1-62652-795-9
LCCN: 2014935817

Distributed by Itasca Books

Edited by Michelle Josette and Erin Roof
Cover Design by Sophie Chi
Typeset by Jenni Wheeler

Printed in the United States of America

For Matt

HARTON WOODS

My name is Paige Plant, and I'm a singer-songwriter. I have fourteen paintings to prove it—one for each song I've written. Thirteen Möbius strip watercolors where I painted the song's story on the strip. What can I say? I was good at science back in the day. The fourteenth, done in oil and not on a Möbius strip, depicts the only love song I've ever written. Not that I've had only one lover or anything—I'm quite attractive in a B+ kind of way—but only one worth an oil painting. Plus, oil makes the other guys, and an occasional girl, work a little harder at pleasing me. Everybody wants a love song written about them; almost everyone wants to see their song in oil.

Today, I'm going to meet this guy named John Bustin. He's older, like pensioned, and, well, from the whisper-whisper out there, he was a decent songwriter in his time. No one that most people would know, but he's well respected in a few east coast music circles. A buddy of mine saw John's ad online and set us up. I guess John has this million-dollar recording studio in the woods forty miles west of Boston, and he lets singer-songwriters use it for free if he vibes on their stuff. Who knows, maybe I'll get a few paintings out of the place if things go well.

Watercolors. Not oils. I don't do the daddy thing. Already have one of those, and he's great. When I was five, he told me I would front the next Led Zeppelin. Even legally changed my last name to prove he was serious. "Paige Plant" he would sing over and over to a little nursery rhyme of a tune he'd written for me. I still play it every now and then as a reminder, as a future eulogy.

Main Street in Harton, the town where John lives, is a throwback to a different era. Boutique shops line both sides of the extra-wide street. A

1

general store. A potter's showcase. A cucina. A coffeehouse. An old marquee cinema. Too many churches and a small inn surround a large green. On any given weekend, I bet the sidewalks fill equally with townies and tourists, though there's hardly anyone around today.

After coffee at The General, as the townies like to call it, I make my way out of the center and down country roads with sickeningly panoramic Mount Wachusett views toward John's. Nature girl I am not. Almost miss my turn onto this long private gravel road that splits a field in two. Probably a cornfield, which is a common crop in this part of Massachusetts, though now all you can see are snowmobile tracks. After about a mile, I'm swallowed by a deep oak and evergreen forest. Inside, I wind through trees, which occasionally give way to fifty-foot-high rock formations that must be thousands, if not millions, of years old. I'm back in the time before humans—at any moment, a giant raptor might jump out from behind the rocks and keep me from my destiny. Finally, the road stops at a large clearing with a wooden building, the studio I'm guessing, which looks like a modern version of a barn. Big doors in the front. A high angled roof with solar panels. Lots of glass. A large silver-backed dog, or maybe a wolf, circles my car as if it's searching for its next meal. A moment later, the barn doors open.

"Hi, I'm John. That's Solly. He's harmless." Almost on cue, Solly wags his tail for a bit, then sits in front of my car door.

I slip out. Palm up, I reach forward and pet Solly under his chin. "Paige. Nice to meet you. I like your dog's name."

"Short for Solidarity."

John is tall and wears a charcoal-gray suit with a red silk tie. He's in relatively good shape for his age, which I guess is around sixty. Brown hair with just a touch of gray on the sides. Not much of anything on the top. Probably was a B+ himself in his prime. But none of that stuff much matters—it's his face that grabs me. John's playing tour guide and showing me around the place, talking about this and that capable-of-sonic-wonder black box, but all I can think about is his face. It's a steady state of sadness, like he's seen too much, read too much, like he's touched the big wide calm from only a few parts of his life. Maybe his children, if he has any. Or work. Yeah, work for sure. Probably a big executive for years, he's using the money he made to do the frustrated-artist-who-is-now-a-patron-of-the-arts thing. For sure, he hasn't reached the big wide calm with a woman. At least not for long. They've left him. Or he drove them away. Those deep grooves on his face are all that remain of his loves.

In the span of a few minutes, while he's talking about Pro Tools or an Avalon preamp or his rack of reverbs, his face morphs a few times like he's judging me, himself, or the entire world for crimes against, well, I don't know what yet. His eyebrows scrunch down, or one side of his mouth flashes up, or his face pales. I don't even think he knows he's doing it. Slips into his judgment robes, does the thumbs-down thing, slips back out into sadness. I bet he turns a lot of people off when the robes are on. I bet that's why he lives by himself out in the middle of Harton Woods.

But here's the thing. Yeah, yeah, his face is all old and brown-spotted, and when he smiles, the wrinkles around his eyes are like Grand Canyon deep, but his eyes could heal the planet if he would let them. When he looks at me and isn't judging, even for a short time, I have to look away. It's too much. Too much power. Too much x-ray vision. Too much something-that-scares-the-Zep-out-of-me, and at the same time makes me want more. That's probably why one of his eyes is lazy. I mean, who wants that much responsibility? Better not to see so much. An occasional half-glimpse of something real, but mostly a view thriving on distraction. What a good title for a song.

Today, I'm dressed in layers, as the fashion girls would say, not because I care about that stuff, but because there's two feet of snow on the ground and it's freezing, and, at the same time, I tend to get really hot indoors, especially in recording studios, which are gateways to my greater-than-Zep future. Part of me wants to take my leather jacket off, my Ani DiFranco *Dilate* sweatshirt, but I already feel naked around this guy, so I keep them both on and bake a little. Baking in John's studio. Three hundred fifty degrees for a time, then—Pop!—I'm a rock star.

"So, what do you think?" John asks.

"It's cool."

"Do you want to play one of your songs?"

I set up in his plush, wood-paneled studio that smells like a just-cut Christmas tree and guitar polish. My old beat-up 1968 Martin D-28 has so many cracks in it that sometimes I wonder why it plays at all. I doodle a bit up and down the neck. She's still a siren. I'll never give her up because she was the first real guitar Dad gave me after I outgrew the baby ones.

When my fingers touch metal in chord formation, John looks up from the mixing console through the control room glass. At first I can't hear him through the glass, but he catches himself and pushes a button.

"That guitar sounds fantastic! I've never heard one with such a rich tone."

I nod once. Through the speakers, he sounds like the wizard from Oz. Though I'm certainly no Dorothy, I'm grateful I've passed the whiz-bang instrument test. All of us songwriters give each other the test, since a musician's choice of guitar says so much about them. Like mine is all about the sound and the tradition, not about the cracks on the outside, not about a pick guard that's almost worn away, not about so many scratches that the finish seems more matted than glossed.

Anyway, I better cut right to it and play my best watercolor. I ad-lib for a bit off the intro to "Latecomer." One night I woke from this nightmare where I was old instead of twenty-five, where I never caught a wave, where I never passed Zep. Scared me so much that I had to create something on the spot, so I reached for my guitar and notepad, both stationed right next to my bed for moments just like that one, and wrote "Latecomer" in one pass. *I'm a latecomer / You're a latecomer, too / We have waited long enough.* That's the main gist. I must admit it's my only as-good-as-Zep watercolor. But here's the thing: each time, right before I play it, there's an uneasiness in my back and right below my heart, a tightening, a knot. I have no idea why. Each time I

4

try to squash it. Push it down. Figure out some way to kill it. I never have any luck. If I could unwrap it now, I'm sure it would tell me something, but I can't, so I tap the soundboard of my guitar four times and launch into "Latecomer."

Four fast minutes later, the last chord rings out, and—abracadabra—poof goes the tightening. Before I look to get John's reaction, I sync-up that the tightness I'm experiencing during "Latecomer" serenades is the same tightness I saw earlier on John's face, except his has an unending quality to it. How does that happen? I mean, no one aspires to grow up permanently tight. Do they? You know, there's a lot underneath his tightness. Emotionally, he's Stephen Hawking. Where's the software program to interface with those eyes and figure out what's on the inside? Maybe I'll put my college education to use for a change and write one. After all, he seems to be a songwriting treasure trove, and I'm a songwriter; the inside story is what I'm all about.

I look up at John, and from a distance, I'm convinced his eyes have teared over. Pretty good. I untangle myself from my guitar, the wires, the headphones. Must be ninety, so I take off my leather jacket. A moment later, I join him in the control room. The tears in his eyes have drained, if they were even there in the first place.

"Great song."

"Thank you."

"You're very talented."

"Thank you." Modesty isn't my thing, but it seems like the best way with John. He's fumbling with the controls on his mixing board, like he's doing something important, but we both know he's just figuring out the big yes or the big no. He fumbles for a long time. Normally, I have little respect for people, guys especially, who hesitate. With John, though, I'll make an exception. I mean, the eyes, the recording studio, the sadness trump the fence sitting.

"I'd like to work with you, if you're interested," John says.

"That would be fantastic."

"Would you like to have a cup of coffee up at the house?"

"Sure."

"I live by myself, so please excuse the messiness."

"No problem."

We leave the recording studio and follow a snow-covered walkway a long way up to the main house. The front of the house is all glass, one of those super modern designs you sometimes see in *Architectural Digest* when you're waiting for your semiannual cleaning in the dentist's office. Does anyone other than dentists, doctors, and therapists subscribe to that magazine? Anyway, here's this guy living by himself in an all-glass house in the middle of the woods without another house or road or anything manmade visible in any direction. It's scary beautiful. Maybe it would be better to take my songs elsewhere. Maybe he's some psycho killer and I'm never going to pass Zep, never mind leave Harton Woods alive. Okay, Paige, genius, goddess, use some of that innate wisdom you have and get the frack out of John's woods. But then, as he holds open the front door, those magnetic eyes do their pull thing. I go in.

#

The inside isn't at all what I expect. Books are everywhere. In floor-to-ceiling cases along the walls of the living room. On the floors. On tables. Except for the books, it's not that messy. I notice a pile on the floor, maybe ten hardcovers, with a yellow sticky on top that says, "Happiness."

"All of my books are grouped by topic," John says.

"You've read them all?"

"I have a lot of time."

I look around the room at all of the yellow stickies. Death. Star Wars. Love. Quantum physics. The Beatles. Peace. Charnel grounds. What the . . . ? "What are charnel grounds?"

"Buddhist burial sites. In Nepal, the ground is frozen, so the custom is to chop up the bodies of the deceased and put them in a charnel ground until the vultures eat the dead body parts. Needless to say, they're very scary places for most."

6

I nod, swallow dryness. Okay, so now I'm convinced I'm going to die, but instead of freaking out, I walk around the living room, head down, and study the other towers of topics. Guitar making. Alice Walker. Soccer. Best to appear calm in these situations. Best not to let him see my face. Best to . . . ah, fuck it. Just ask him. "You're not one of these guys who abducts young women and chops them up, are you?"

A flash of I-would-never horror consumes John's face until he can steady it. "No. No. Sorry. I didn't mean to . . . I'm more interested in emotional charnel grounds. We all do a pretty good job of creating them."

"Ah." Okay, so I have no idea what that means, but there is a story here, and at least a few songs. Fact: John eats knowledge for breakfast. Fact: he's wealthy and alone. Potential fact: he may be able save the world. What else is under the covers? Every great songwriter has a muse. Mine's going to be a lonely guy in the woods who seems to have pieced together all human knowledge for some unknown purpose. No wonder his face is sad; it's too much. "How about that coffee?"

John moves a few stacks of books from his dining room table and chairs and eye-directs me to one of the open seats. A moment later, he's back with the coffee and a box of Dunkin' Donuts Holes.

"You eat that stuff?"

"Yes. Holes are one of the great American treasures. I have fruit if you prefer."

"Just coffee. Thanks."

"Do you live in Boston?"

"Yeah. In a studio, if you can call it that, in the North End."

"And work?"

"I'm still trying to make it. It's been hard. I play a few gigs around town when I get them. Sometimes I play on the street in Harvard Square. And I waitress, which pays the rent."

"Ah."

So this time, instead of dialing knobs on his mixing board, John is playing with his spoon and popping Holes in his mouth at a heart-attack rate. How can such a smart guy not know the nutritional value of donuts? And does he always fidget when he decides something important?

"How seriously do you want to do your music?"

"It's my life."

"Are you sure?"

"More than sure."

"I see."

John pops up from his chair and disappears into another part of the house. Two cups of coffee later, just when I'm about to cave and end my little prehistoric adventure, he returns. His hair is all wet and slicked back, like he just got out of the shower. What the . . . ?

"How about this? Why don't you quit your job and move out here for a year? I have a spare bedroom in the house or another one in the studio if you prefer more privacy. You can live and eat here for free. I'll pay you a generous monthly stipend so you have spending money. Over the year, we'll record all of your songs, and maybe write a few new ones. Then I'll help you get them out into the world when they're done."

Okay, who does something like this? All of my songs? Free room and board? And free money? Dad is whispering in my ear to walk away. Hell, all of the relatives are whispering in my ear to walk away. Instead, I reach over and pop a Hole. Surprisingly good. I study every inch of my coffee cup for clues on how to answer. Is he for real? Is it safe out here? After two frustrating years, is this finally my big break? I look up and there's John with those eyes, those big calm eyes that somehow hold the keys to everything I've ever longed for, wanted, needed. I rise out of my body and hover above the table like I'm watching a movie from a distance, like I somehow know this is my first big life decision and I need to observe it from far away. From there, I watch myself say, "I'll move into the studio tomorrow."

THE STORY OF P

The move takes most of the day. My buddy, Z, the one who found the online ad, lets me borrow his car again and helps me move my stuff. Not much of anything really, but still enough for two loads. My clothes, my paintings, pictures of my family back in New Mexico, my guitar, books, music, a laptop. That's about it. Z agrees to sell or get rid of everything else for me. No need for furniture in John's woods.

Late afternoon, John and I wave Z off as he heads back to the city. Z's a good friend, and sometimes, when we're both bored or lonely, a little more. We met early on at MIT and have been hanging out ever since. Sometimes I can't believe I went to that school. Dad pushed it after a full scholarship rolled in, and I couldn't argue with his logic. "Something to fall back on," he said. Still, would I have been better off across the river at Berklee? Anyway, none of that matters now.

John reaches in his pocket and pulls out a BMW key along with two other keys. "Here you go."

"What's this?"

"You'll need a car out here, so those are the keys to the 335i, plus the ones to the house and studio. If you'd rather drive one of the other BMWs, just let me know and I'll swap the keys."

"I'm sure this is more than fine."

"Want to take a look?"

As we walk over to the garage to check out my new ride, I can't help but smile. So now I'm living in a studio in the middle of the Harton Woods for free, I'm about to record all of my songs, and I'm driving a BMW. Not in my wildest dreams could have I predicted this. Okay, that's not exactly right. I've been dreaming about something like this all my life, though I must admit, the actual details are a little off.

No surprise, the car is beautiful, black-on-black, sleek and low to the ground, with extra wide tires, a far cry from the junkers I drove growing up in New Mexico. I sit cradled in the driver's seat for a long time, John next to me, as he does the BMW-manual-from-memory thing. Voice-activated commands. The navigation system. The sound system. What a car. I need to take her out for a test run.

"If you want, we can take a ride and I'll show you all the local shops. There's this great ice cream place in the next town over."

We switch seats. Best to let John lead the tour. As we cruise into town, the moonlight reflects off the snow, making the entire place brighter, like Christmas without the window dressings. We slow to a crawl and John encyclopedias the history of local businesses, like he's lived here his whole life, like he knows each owner personally. Maybe he does. Joe Worth owns The General now. Built in the 1890s. Burnt down during the Depression. Sally's cucina has excellent veal saltimbocca. Jack's cinema sometimes plays foreign stuff. John's animated as he describes each place, like he's been waiting a long time to show someone all of his shiny things. It's kind of nice.

Once we're done with the shop tour, he pulls into an unplowed parking lot on the outskirts of town and does spinouts in the snow as The Civil Wars blast through the speakers. Being from New Mexico, I've never done spinouts before. They turn out to be loads of fun, and I'm instantly convinced everyone should go out of control in a controlled way more often. At one point, I ask to switch places with him so I can do the spinouts myself. Even better. By the way, The Civil Wars harmony is amazing.

After snow-circles, John takes me to the homemade ice cream place, which for some reason is open in the middle of winter. After studying each flavor like he's seeing it for the first time, he tells me I have to try the coffee frappé, which is to die for. In twenty-four hours, this man has consumed more sugar than I have in a month. The frappé is flat-out spectacular.

My take on the local tour? Shop history—once is more than enough. Spinouts and ice cream—every now and then, please.

#

The next day, John and I enter the studio around ten, him with a pot of coffee and yet another sugar fix in hand. Immediately, he goes into work mode, sits down at the console, hits *record*, and asks me to do the Paige Plant concert thing. Guitar strapped on and mics in position, it's like I'm at the Somerville coffeehouse, where I sometimes play, or my favorite street corner in Harvard Square, though in those places I rarely have the audience's undivided attention—or good equipment. I take a sip of coffee with a water chaser. Do it again. For some reason, I have this urge to go up to my room, get all of my paintings, and set them up around me. Strumming randomly, I wait for the urge to pass before launching into my first song.

An hour and fourteen songs later, after I've given the best show of my life, after I've validated why John offered me such a sweet deal in the first place, I finish the love song. Always save that one for last. I slip my guitar, my headphones off, and wait.

John leaves the control room, comes into the studio, hands in pockets, head down, and says, "You have an incredible amount of raw talent."

"Thank you."

"Let's take Solly for a walk and get some air. We can debrief in the woods."

Hundreds of acres of conservation land surround John's place. Solly, who seems to know exactly where he's going, picks a trail. We follow him in silence. Smoke, from burning oak in John's wood stove, colors the crisp air. Fresh snow still balances on evergreen branches. Occasionally, I'll brush a branch with my glove to free it back into shape. The woods remind me of the desert in New Mexico close to my parents' home. Not the trees or the snow, but the sense of space, of being part of something larger. Sometimes I would walk there for hours with my best girlfriends and, filled with hope, talk about boys and fame and money.

"I believe you have the potential for multigenerational appeal," John says.

"I hope."

"Here's the thing, though. As they currently stand, your songs might get you a little bit of recognition, but they'll be forgotten in a year."

What did he just say? Did he listen to the same songs I played? Who the fuck does he think he is anyway? Just an old guy who never made it. I mean, all he needs to do is record my stuff as is; push a few buttons and adjust a few knobs. That's the deal. You know, everybody else loves my material, so what is he talking about?

"You think?" I ask.

"Why do you want to be famous?"

"The spotlight," I say. "The recognition. The stuff you can buy with money."

"And the songs?"

"The songs will get me there."

"And service?"

"You mean like charity work? I'll do the Paige Plant Foundation when the time comes."

Up ahead, say fifty yards or so, a deer crosses the path. Solly freezes, then gives chase for a bit until the deer is out of sight. It's almost as if he knows he's lost a step with age, but he can't help but chase out of habit. Sometimes I wonder if age just locks in the habits, so that autopilot takes over and steers you toward the end. And if that's true, when does it start?

"How old is Solly?"

"Ten."

"Ah." Okay, push John a bit, see what's behind the curtain, see if he really has what it takes to help me make it. I mean, this is a tough business, and at my age, I'm running out of time. I need a shark who's on the same page, my page, who's laser-focused on now, who's strong enough, vicious enough. "Got something against fame?"

"If you focus on writing great songs, fame may or may not follow."

"I can't accept that. I want both."

"I know. And that's fine, but the only way to get multigenerational fame is to not focus on it at all. Instead, try to tap into the place underneath emotion and write from there."

"Oh."

"What?"

"The big wide calm."

"What do you mean?"

"For years, I've been wandering around with this phrase, the big wide calm, never exactly sure what it meant. I even wondered if you'd touched it yourself when I first met you. Maybe it has something to do with the place underneath emotion."

"Hmmm. Sounds like you've known the name of your album for a long time."

#

I pop out of bed at five in the morning. I don't think I've been up this early, well, ever, but work is calling. Honestly, I can't think about anything else. I've been here for a day, and I've already nailed the name of my album. How cool is that? Best to write it down. Best to write everything down. You know, it will be worth something someday. I ransack an unpacked box and find a journal my dad gave me a long time ago. It's empty except for what he wrote on the first page. "Paige, you can save the world with your songs. Love, Dad." I smile and go all warm and fuzzy like in one of those Hallmark made-for-TV movies. Mom would say life is a bunch of Hallmark cards. But I would say it's a rock documentary where a world-renowned recording artist rises from humble beginnings and changes the world with her music. Yeah, yeah, that's the story. I flip to a fresh page and write down *The Big Wide Calm* over and over. I could fill the whole notebook with just the title. But I don't. Instead, I open my laptop and copy the lyrics for each of my songs to the journal. Ink is better than font for lyrics. Always has been, always will be. Don't know why I didn't do this before.

Fred goes off. Nine. I named my cheap Chinese alarm clock last year to help me like it more. Plus, he's a good conversation piece on first dates. "Every morning Fred goes off like clockwork." I should do a photo album of all the expressions I've gotten after that line. Anyway, time to shower and get ready for my ten-o'clock session with my psycho killer muse.

After the shower, I study my reflection in the vanity mirror. Shoulder-length thick brown hair. Check. Olive skin. Check. Big brown eyes that, when used properly, can get a person to do almost anything I want. Check. Straight, petite nose. Check. Knowing smile that never gives away exactly what I know, with good teeth, except for the crooked chipped front one. Gotta fix that when I get money. It's a face destined for album covers, posters, billboards, stadium monitors. It's the face of the Grammy-winning album, *The Big Wide Calm*.

I slip into jeans, a heavy sweatshirt, and soft, furry-on-the-inside boots, you know the ones that Tom Brady endorses. That man. Anyway, my room is over the studio, so I bounce down the stairs a few minutes before ten. John is waiting for me on the piano bench, coffee in one hand, a cannoli in the other. The sugar thing is getting old. I need to get this guy on organic everything, or he might die before we finish.

"We need to chat about food," I say.

"Why?"

"I'm an organic girl. I mostly eat vegetables and small portions of organic meat and fish. And you?"

"Takeout. Chinese. Italian. Indian. Pretty much every restaurant has takeout these days. And a couple of glasses of wine every day."

"The wine is cool. How about we stock up on healthy stuff?"

"I can't cook."

"You mean you haven't read fifty books on cooking?"

"No."

"It's not that hard. We'll figure it out together."

"Can I still have donuts every day?"

"You're going to die."

"There are worse things."

So, while it's true that John might have all human knowledge stored in his head, and he might be my psycho killer muse, it's also true that he would starve without fast food. What happened to this guy? What could be worse than dying early? I mean, how can he know so much and so little at the same time? And just to put a fine point on it, has the guy ever had his cholesterol checked? Okay, enough already. Time to get going.

"What should we work on today?" I ask.

"I've been thinking. How exactly would you describe 'the big wide calm'?"

"That's the billion-dollar question."

"Sometimes I figure things out when I take a long drive. It's calm in the car."

"That's what you think I should do now?"

"I don't know. You need to figure out what puts you in touch with the big wide calm before you write an album about it."

"But I already have the songs."

"They may change."

As much as I hate to admit that John's right, he does have a point. Ever since he mentioned the multigenerational thing, I've been reeling in the nightmare that my stuff isn't good enough. Or maybe it's that I'm not good enough. Nah, I'm good enough. But I don't want to be a flash in the pan. Staying power is the name of the game. All of the great songwriters—Dylan, Cohen, Lennon, McCartney, Aimee Mann, Ani DiFranco—were able to touch something and channel it into their songs. Must be their version of TBWC. With the exception of my love song, I haven't really done that. Actually, I haven't done much of anything yet. What's going on? I rarely fill with doubt.

"I may have to write new songs for TBWC. Do you think I should?"

"Do whatever you think is most courageous."

"Such a waste."

"Nothing's really a waste at your age. It's all helping you go exactly where you need to go."

"How about at your age?"

"That's a longer conversation."

"I'm not sure what to do about the songs."

"Why don't you go for a drive and see what pops up? That car is capable of wonder."

The black on black of the 335i suits me, immediately puts me at ease. At first, I voice-activate some music. Some folksy woman with a pretty voice is singing about how some man completes her. I get this queasy feeling in my stomach until I voice the radio off. I head up 495, then up Route 3 into New Hampshire. The car is so smooth that at first I don't realize I'm pushing ninety. I slow down, but just a bit. John threw me for a loop with one word—multigenerational. How do you create lasting art? I was so much further along a few days ago. Is that what a psycho killer muse does? Knocks you down to building-block level, then holds up a giant tower right in front of you and says, "You can build this." And does it all with gentleness.

A couple hours later, I reach Squam Lake, which I somehow sense is less commercial than Lake Winnipesaukee, though I really have no idea. I get out of the black beauty, zip up my sweatshirt, and sit on the hood, where the engine warms my rear. The lake is solid ice, covered with snow, except for a few parts that have been plowed into temporary roads. After a time, some guy follows one ice road and drives his Ford F150 across the lake, dead doe draped across the back of the truck bed. Jerk. A beautiful female is not just a piece of meat. The guy reaches a small island without incident. Once on land, he cruises up to a house, opens the garage, and pulls inside like the whole drive-on-water thing, the kill, was no big deal. How does he get home when there's no ice?

I slip off the car to make snowballs. Big ones. Softball size. After I line up ten or so, I throw them all in rapid succession in the general direction of truck-guy-island. They distance-out after twenty feet max. No matter. The act still felt good.

Done and back on the hood, I drift back to the love song I wrote after my boyfriend at the time, P, dumped me for a Barbie Blonde he met at Newbury Comics. You know, I refer to all of my male friends just by the first letter of their names. At some point, this may become confusing, but probably not until I go through the alphabet a second time. Anyway, at first I was clueless as to what was going on with P, then one day I happened to pull up to his apartment building just as he was slipping in, laughing and flirting with the Barbie Blonde.

Having acquired a taste for confrontation somewhere along the way, I pulled out my key to his place—which was doubling as the pendant of my necklace—and a short time later followed them inside. I tiptoed up the stairs and slipped into the apartment unnoticed, which, believe me, despite my considerable skills, wasn't that hard to do. In front of the bedroom door, I eyed P and Barbie Blonde naked in bed. P was on top of her, inside of her, and her legs were straight and doubled back over her, so her feet were almost touching the pillow. Definitely not a Barbie pose. I still had the key necklace in my hand so, instead of saying anything, I decided to throw it at P. In the only act of athletic greatness of my entire life, I hurled the key right at him and it burrowed right into his asshole. P what-the-fucked, flipped over and, as I was giving him the finger, said, "Paige, it's not what you—"

The car engine has cooled, and it's freezing on Squam Lake. I slip off the hood, jump back in the car, and start the long ride back to Harton. There's a peacefulness on the way that's come from somewhere. Maybe from knowing I'll never be a Barbie Blonde or a P. Maybe from knowing I'm going to write all new songs for my multigenerational masterpiece. Maybe from knowing one doorway, one tiny pinprick of a knothole into the big wide calm is pain. There have to be others.

\#

"Can I hear your songs?" I ask.

John goes off into how-shall-I-answer-this space. We're back in the studio. Same start time as yesterday. He's on the same piano bench drinking the same coffee from the same mug, though today he appears to be eating an apple instead of some sugary thing. I'm sitting across from him on a folding. You know, folding chairs are almost as important to us musicians as all of the recording stuff. The wood stove has the place up to like eighty, even though there's a light snow falling outside. Solly slowly pushes up from his spot at John's feet. He wags his tail a few times as he makes his way toward his doggie door and out into the snow to find his pack.

Finally, after securing a suitable answer, John says, "I don't play my songs anymore."

"Why?"

"My time has passed."

"They're not on the Internet?"

"Not everything is on the Internet."

I nod, but how is that possible? Are the songs really that obscure that no one has found them and put them online? I need to talk with Z. Maybe he knows more about John's songs. How many are there? What did he write about? What's the real story about why he stopped? Anyway, I figure it's best not to push it at this point—John must have his reasons—so I change the topic back to me and my music. That's why we're here. Best to stay focused on the prize.

"You were right about driving. I figured something out," I say.

"What's that?"

"One way into the big wide calm is through pain."

"Ah."

"What?"

"Nothing. Shorthand for 'I think you're right,' that's all."

"You know that one?"

"Yes."

"Care to tell me how?"

"This isn't about me."

Well, he's right about that. Still, I wonder what happened to him. Charnel grounds? Pain-as-a-way-in? I feel sorry for the guy. Except for Solly, he seems to have no one. But that has to be his choice. I'm sure there are a lot of age-appropriate women who would find him desirable. I wonder if I'm the first young, female . . . ah, just ask. "Have you ever invited anyone else to live and record here?"

"No . . . I've helped other musicians record now and then, but never what I offered you. You're special."

"I am? Why?"

"I don't know. You just are."

There's symmetry, a softening on John's face, lazy eye and all, for the first time since I've met him. He really does think I'm special, which is good because I think the same thing. Best to get a little synergy going between us, and that's as good a place as any to start. Don't need a detailed why yet. Okay, now that we've got that out of the way. "What should we do today?"

"I've got to go into town," John says. "Why don't you write in your journal and see what comes up? I'll put a few pieces of applewood and oak in the stove, and if you want, you can use my reading chair and write by the fire for the day. I'll be back tonight. We can talk more then."

"No music?"

"Not yet. You're still clearing out the clutter."

And with that, John's off. I've had more sustained silence here in a couple days than I've probably ever had. When did my need for silence, for space, get squashed? Was it at home? At school? At work? We have access to so much stuff. Too much, really. Is that what he's doing with all his books? Trying to distill way too much down to just enough? Trying to find that one ultimate love song in the clutter of wannabes?

I take John's advice and curl up with my journal in front of the wood stove. The applewood and oak burn sweet, sad, and for some reason, conjure

P. I replay the entire relationship for hours, only pausing on occasion to pet Solly, who, right after John left, joined me by the stove. Finally, after spinning on P in Technicolor detail, and looping a few times on the key scene, I go into the months after the breakup. Haven't done that before. How would I distill that time? I mean, it was so painful. Three months of hell. Best to forget. I didn't think any guy would ever leave me like that. What is it about Barbie Blondes? I smoked, drank, ate more. . . . Anyway, lots of people do that. No big deal. But what did I feel? How did I learn? I pick up my pen and write *I no longer believe in you.* That's for sure. I went from loving the guy to hating the guy in an instant, but even when I hated him, I kept hoping for some magical way to undo it. What an idiot. What else? *I no longer trust you.* Okay, Paige, while this line is true, you're not exactly doing the lasting art thing, are you? Dig down deeper.

You know, I had this recurring dream during those months. P and I were sitting on his sofa watching a DVD of my all-time favorite concert film, *The Song Remains the Same.* Our legs were crossed, and we were eating popcorn. For a moment everything was okay—calm, relaxed, with probing hands and lips. The butter on my fingertips, P's taste on my tongue, Jimmy Page's guitar solo on "Dazed and Confused" all made me sure I'd woken from the Barbie Blonde nightmare. Then I'd wake, suddenly, sheets in a tangle, sweating. They say pilots flying without instrumentation over the ocean sometimes can't tell the water from the sky. My dream was kind of like that. Inside it, the tightness, the weight, the shivers left my body, like I was floating in wide-open sky. Then I'd wake and discover I'd crashed in the middle of the ocean, and was sinking fast, with no land in sight.

Solly sits up and hands me his paw. I get out of my chair, find his rawhide bone, and give it to him. Love for a pet . . . it's so much easier. When I sit back down, words start to flow like they were always there and I finally cleared enough space to see them. Maybe John is right about clutter. A few minutes after I do the faucet—no, the firehose thing—I reread "The Story of P."

I no longer trust you
I no longer believe in you
I no longer respect you
I no longer hate you

And when I realized that
Hate was the last thing that
Connected us
I realized that I no longer loved you

For when someone kills love
Suddenly, violently, without regret
As you did
There is no choice
But to go into the pain
Into the great shiver
Through the tiny pinprick
Of a knothole
Into the big wide calm
Here, all my fear is gone
And I know one thing for sure
I will never fear love's death again
Because it's one doorway to this place

From here, I wish you nothing but peace
I hope that your truths
Set you free
As mine have me

Where did that come from? I read it again. Yep, that's how I felt during those
months, though I would never have been able to put it to words back then. A

key into a dark hole ended up being a door opener, a way in, the inspiration for my first poem.

I close the journal, run upstairs to my room, and tuck the journal under my pillow to age. Best to let words age in whatever place you call home. You know, poems are like lyrics, but not the same. Poems are more immediate, more direct, freer. There doesn't have to be a structure or a cadence to them, which makes the bad ones easier to write and the good ones much more difficult. "The Story of P" is a good one; it's my first step on the road to *The Big Wide Calm.*

I bounce down the stairs into the studio. There, I scan John's music library. There must be ten thousand CDs, all arranged alphabetically. I run my fingers along the A's. Alicia Keys. The Allman Brothers. Animal Collective. Audioslave. He has good taste. I settle on an old album by Arcade Fire, load it into the CD player, and push the volume way up. I dance like a banshee.

#

John pushes open the studio doors. Cold air, wind, and snow billow in for a second to check out the place, then think better of it and retreat to the woods where they can be with their own kind. John has many bags from Whole Foods that he's precariously balancing in his hands and arms. He puts the bags down on the floor and, much to my surprise, joins me as I dance. Didn't think he was the type.

Guess what? He's good. He has no dance skills whatsoever, but it doesn't matter. He lets go, moves to Arcade Fire like he's five years old and dancing for the first time. It's contagious, and I find myself opening, matching him.

After the first song, he rushes over to the mixing console, clicks and pushes a few things. He glances over and smiles.

"My dance playlist," he says.

How can someone whose face is in a steady state of sadness have a dance list? No matter, the first song starts. I don't recognize it, but it's great. We dance through the entire set, maybe twenty songs. I don't know a single one, which somehow improves the experience. When we finish, John finds his piano bench, which I'm beginning to think has some deeper meaning for him, and I find the floor. It feels like it's a hundred degrees as sweat rolls off my face, but that doesn't matter. I'm happy. And John looks happy for the first time since I've met him.

"That was fun," I say. "I'm starving."

"I went to Whole Foods."

"I see."

"How was your afternoon?"

"I wrote something. Want to hear it?"

"Sure."

I run up to my bedroom and pull the journal out from under my pillow. The leather seems a little darker, like it's aged maybe ten years instead of an hour, though I'm not at all surprised by the time-lapse thing. Back in the studio, I read the poem to John. He asks me to read it again. As soon as I finish, I start to chatter about moving on to write my next song, but he jolts both hands out in front of him, palms facing me, and says, "Stop."

"What?"

"You can't read something like that, then idly chat about random topics like you never read it in the first place. Read it again, and then let's sit with it for a bit."

I do just that. You know, he's right—the words carry much more power when given space afterwards. Like sympathetic strings on a sitar, my poem has silent, sympathetic frequencies that require space after spoken. Maximum emotional impact space. I've just discovered a secret world. So honest. Small doses only, please. After about a minute, I can't stand it anymore and say, "So?"

"You need me to tell you what you already know?"

"Yes, please."

"It comes from the place that all of your songs should come from," he says.

"I know."

"You're radiant."

"You've also got quite the look on your face. What else?"

John stands up and walks over to the window. He's still sweating and his face is beet red. It's the best he's looked since I met him. If he were ten years younger, I might even turn him into a J. A couple of times he starts to say something, but stalls. Get it out, man. Finally, he blows on the window until it fogs over, writes "TBWC" on the fog, and says, "You know, you can also get here by dancing."

Suddenly, I'm overcome by this urge to eat, drink, and have sex. I need a new letter, like, this minute, but with all prospects at least forty miles away, I go over to the Whole Foods bags and rummage a bit through containers of prepared goods. Two out of three will have to do for now. Grilled Thai chicken with peanut dipping sauce. Portobello mushrooms marinated, baked, and served with rémoulade. Shrimp satay grilled and served with lemon aioli. At the bottom of the bag, I pull out plastic forks, knives, napkins, and plates.

"Let's eat."

"We can go up to the house if you prefer."

"Nah. Too hungry. Let's stay here." I prepare myself a plate and pull out a container of freshly squeezed orange juice, but instead of returning to my spot on the floor and stuffing my face, I walk over to John and hand both to him.

"You didn't have to."

"No biggie."

A few moments later, I return with my own plate and juice.

"Move over."

John makes space for me on the piano bench. We sit down and eat mostly in small talk. He's an Aquarius; I'm an Aries. Winter is his favorite season; I love spring. He also played a Martin guitar when he performed. That sort of stuff. At one point he smiles, reaches over and gently wipes something off my face. A dab of peanut sauce. You know, I've had a lot of good food since coming to Harton, but Whole Foods' takeout may be the best of the lot. Anyway, two days in and I have an album name, a poem. At this rate I'll be out of here in a month. What's next?

#

Fire engine sirens! Is the studio on fire? Fred says 3:00 a.m. I jump out of bed and watch a red engine race up the main driveway toward the house. A moment later, I'm pulling a sweatshirt over my head as I sprint up the driveway. What the . . . ?

The front door is open. I rush in. In the kitchen, fire extinguisher foam covers the eight-burner Wolf stove. What a waste. The place smells like burnt meat and ammonia. Just awful. John and the men are laughing about something. John puts his hand on a fireman's shoulder and ushers him a step toward the front door before he notices me.

"Paige?"

"What happened?"

"False alarm. I couldn't sleep, so I decided to try my hand at a few new recipes from a cookbook I bought today. Didn't go so well, but these guys helped me out."

"Oh."

John continues ushering, talking, laughing. I hear him say something about keeping the whole incident off the record. The two firemen, probably a little older than me, look like an F and a C. Where is all this hunger coming from? A few moments later, John and I are standing in the foyer watching the truck drive off into darkness.

"I'm sorry I woke you," he says.

"Can you promise me something?"

"What's that?"

"Don't try cooking again without me."

"I always learn new things on my own."

"That's your problem."

John looks at me like I've just told him he has bubonic plague. Or at least like I've said something totally random. I mean, I know the guy is a genius and eats knowledge, but I already told him we would figure out the cooking thing together. Did he want to practice by himself before he practiced with me? Is he that tightly wound that he has to know how to do something well before he does it with anyone else? How lame is that?

"I'll walk you back to the studio," John says.

"No need."

"I insist."

"You know, you don't need to take care of me."

"Sorry, I didn't mean—"

"Just take care of yourself, John. From now on, let's cook together."

STILLNESS

The next morning I hear John fumbling around in the studio just as Fred pisses me off. 8:16. Jeez, John, did you sleep at all last night? I roll out of bed and slip into jeans and a T-shirt. Time to kick John out and tell him to come back in a few hours. In the bathroom, I throw some water on my face. I look like crap. Not exactly grand entrance material. On the way down the stairs, before I can see John, I say, "John, what are you doing here so early?"

Much to my surprise, there's a young guy dressed in jeans and an *Achtung Baby* T-shirt standing in front of the mixing console, playing around with the buttons, knobs, and sliders. He has long, sandy-blond hair and is half-decent looking, though I would consider any male in the world half-decent at this point. He looks like an R.

"Who are you?" he asks.

"I was about to ask you the same thing. Paige Plant."

"You're kidding!"

"Yeah, my dad named me . . ."

"Bono Yorke."

"No!"

"My mom loves U2."

"What are you doing here?"

"John offered me a one-year apprenticeship yesterday. You?"

"The same a few days ago. Let me guess, he told you you're special and that you could make multigenerational music?"

"Exactly."

27

Fuck me. At this point I'm fighting this incredible urge to run up to the house and do a one-hundred-decibel scream at John. Here, I was just getting used to the idea that he might actually care about me, that he might really be trying to help, and I find out that's he's given the same pitch to someone else. At least it's not a Barbie Blonde. That would have been too much. Still, I'm thinking I'm out of here by noon. This was too good to be true.

Just as I'm about to do the twenty questions thing with Bono, John walks in with Solly at his side.

"Ah, I see the two of you have met."

"Yes," we say in unison.

John is carrying a tray with three mugs, a pot of coffee, and a white bakery box. He places the tray on the piano bench, puts the piano top down, then moves the tray on top of it. Bono and I join him at the piano and form a perfect isosceles triangle. Solly stands at attention at John's side, waiting for his morning dose of sugar. Any minute, I expect John to launch into "(What so Funny 'bout) Peace, Love, and Understanding."

"So, John, we just discovered we're both special," I say. I tried to say it without any real color in my voice, but it's clear that I spray-painted John red from the expression on his face, which is some weird cross between pleasure and pain.

"Sorry. Let me explain. Coffee? I also have chocolate éclairs if you're interested."

I take coffee. Bono takes John up on an éclair. Of course he does. Bono kind of looks like a young John, and for a moment, I wonder if he's his illegitimate son. Or maybe what I'm seeing is that whole clueless-wise thread that so many men, regardless of age, have in common. You know, the one that allows them the wisdom to build something as grand as the World Trade Center and the violence to kill thousands while knocking it down. Why is that? I don't think it's true for women. Certainly, I don't have it. Wouldn't the world be better off with women running it? I mean, the top-fifty-songwriter-net-worth list is dominated by men, and look where that's gotten us.

"Paige, Bono auditioned a few weeks ago, but I didn't make the final decision until yesterday. I thought the two of you might complement each other."

"Why?"

"Just a hunch."

"I'm more of a solo artist."

"Me too," Bono says.

"Why don't you try to write something together today and see what happens? If there's nothing there, we'll all know it soon enough."

#

"How do you paint a song?" Bono asks.

We're standing in my bedroom looking at my fourteen paintings. I figured I'd better show them to Bono before we started working together so he could get a feel for my stuff. I guess I could just play him a few songs, but for some reason, showing him the paintings seems better. How do I paint a song? Good question. I wish I could tell him there's some structure to it, but there isn't. Sometimes I do the entire painting with a dominant color. Picasso I'm not, but I do dig his whole different-colors-for-different-periods thing. Sometimes a color might represent a particular emotion. Red, say, for love or anger. Blue for sadness. Yellow for joy. But sometimes the colors don't mean anything, and I just channel whatever's coming up at the time. On a rare occasion, I use all of my colors. That's the way it was when I did the oil for P, when I was still in love with him, before he fucked me over with Barbie Blonde. A rainbow-esque oil with Paige and P front and center in portrait mode, naked from the shoulders up, staring out at the world. He's sweeping my wet hair off my forehead with his hand. We both have that I-just-got-laid look on our faces. Or maybe it's that what-we-have-is-rare look, the we're-going-to-beat-the-odds look. Around our heads are some of the lyrics to the song, each in a bold color. *Your whisper tonight / with the help of sunlight tomorrow / will open me in ways longed for and unsaid.* Or *Here I forget names*

and places and times and things / Here I forget what is possible and impossible.
Ah, how sweet.

"I like the oil the best," Bono says. "Who's the guy?"

"Old flame. Burnt out now."

"Ah. Will you do oils or watercolors for your new songs?"

"Oils."

It's true. Last night, after the fire, I couldn't fall back to sleep right away. While staring up at the all-too-perfect wood ceiling, I zeroed in on the paintings for the *The Big Wide Calm*. They'll all be oils. For a long time, I thought the oil was about romantic love, but I've come to believe it's more about going all in. TBWC will contain nothing but all-in songs, so oil. Okay, there it is.

"Do you want to hear my stuff? I've got it on my computer back at the main house. Moved in last night," Bono says.

"The fire didn't wake you?"

"Nah. Slept right through."

"Not today. Let's just see if there's anything here. I'm not optimistic, but let's give it a try."

"Maybe another time?"

"Sure."

We go back down into the studio and set up on two foldings facing each other. Bono pulls out his Gibson Dove guitar. Nice. I pull out my Martin. At first we just dazzle up and down the fret board for a bit. As all musicians do, we need to establish who's the better guitar player. You know, kind of that alpha male thing, except whoever came up with that phrase didn't know there were women like me out there. Anyway, it turns out that we're both quite gifted, though one of my rules is that all ties go to Paige. After a bit, we both stop wowing.

"Any idea how we should start?" Bono asks.

"Not really."

I retune the guitar to an alternate tuning—EAEEBE. It's strange, but I like it, even though I've never written anything using it before. I go back to doodling. Maybe if we just sit here long enough and mess around, we can tell John that we tried but nothing popped. Best to be honest with John. This is his show.

"What's that?" Bono asks.

"Nothing." I replay the riff Bono asked about. It's finger-picked with a nice slide up and down the fretboard in the middle of it. It's quite good and I can see why he likes it. Maybe it will be my fifteenth song. If nothing else, Bono seems to have good taste. I should add him to my mailing list. One hundred strong and counting.

"Keep playing it over and over." At first Bono does nothing, but after a few loops, he starts to hum a melody on top, adjusting it slightly on each loop until he locks in one he likes.

I must admit, it's catchy. I've always been drawn to the riffs of a song and to the lyrics, but not as much to the melody. Bono seems to be just the opposite. He starts with melody. I hum a harmony on top, which is frackin' good. I'm thinking we just wrote the chorus in like five minutes. Yeah, we need lyrics, but those will come easy.

"Nice melody."

"Thanks. Nice riff."

For the rest of the day, we work nonstop, only taking an occasional break to stretch or put a log on the fire. I focus on the stuff that I'm good at, and he focuses on the stuff that he's good at. We make suggestions on each other's ideas. At first I don't like it when he changes one of my lyrics or makes a minor modification to a bit of music, but when I do the movie thing and step back a little bit to watch, I have to give it up to him—he has improved on my light bulb. You know, it's always been important for me to do everything on a song myself—my songs are just too precious to let someone else mess them up. With Bono, though, collaboration has been . . . well, okay.

It's almost dusk, and we are pretty much done with the song. John and Solly pop back into the studio to check on us. Solly immediately runs up to me, sits down, and hands me his paw. I kneel down and shake. Sometimes I think Solly is the real brains of this operation and John takes all of his cues from him.

"How did you do?" John asks.

"Pretty well," Bono says. "Want to hear it?"

"Sure." John sits on the piano bench and closes his eyes as we get ready to play.

We perform the song for John. Bono sings the lead and I put the harmonies on top. I carry the guitar load, and he adds a bit here and there. It's amazing how well we sing together after only a day. It finally dawns on me why John was playing The Civil Wars the other day in the car. He wants us to be a duet like them. Nice try, John Bustin, but that's not going to happen. I am world famous multigenerational recording artist Paige Plant. I don't need a second.

When we finish, John sits with his eyes closed for a long time. Is he sleeping? It's like that piano bench has some strange hold over him, like it's his doorway into, well, something old. Like regular napping. I've got to ask him about the bench one of these days.

Finally, John opens his eyes and smiles. "What did you learn by writing together?"

This is not the earth-shattering-great-song line I expected from John. I glance over at Bono. He's in the same place as I am. No matter. Best to go with the flow when it comes to John, even though the duet thing isn't going to happen. So what did I learn? I have no idea. He should be in one of those old bad Japanese samurai movies where they are always asking obscure questions that may or may not be deep.

Anyway, I toss his faux deep question around for a bit, then say, "It's all about the song."

"Once the ideas were flowing, it didn't matter if the idea was mine or hers," Bono says.

I have this urge to gag, but I hold it back and feed my landlord-producer-Zen-master a bone instead. "Collaboration can really make a song much better."

As we're talking, John is watching both of us and nodding, like we're getting graded real time on our first test. Finally, he says, "You're both right. Writing multigenerational songs is about trust. Trust that a creative wave will come and you have enough skill to ride it, which, with a little honing, you both will. And trust to surround yourself with good people who can help you make your song better."

Okay, so while I get his point, I have no interest in working with Bono as part of a duet. I mean, yes, we're great, but I'm greatest on my own. I'm fine with John helping me, but as far as I'm concerned, my one-song novelty act with Bono Yorke is over.

"Are you suggesting that we should become a duet? Because—"

"No. Not at all. I'm suggesting you each have a great album in you and that you can help each other make it better."

I nod. Good. That was easier than I thought it was going to be. Every time I think I know where he's going, he doesn't.

"And one more thing. At the end of the year, after you've both done everything you can to make your multigenerational album, I'm going to pick a winner. If you win, you'll have the opportunity to sign a recording contract with the new label I just created, SollyHarton Records."

"You want us to go all in and help each other, and at the same time, you want us to compete?"

"Yes."

"Why?"

"The songs will be better."

"But won't there be a tendency to sabotage each other's work?" Bono asks.

Exactly. I must admit, after only knowing Bono for a short time, there are many places where we're on the same wavelength. I kind of like having him around, even if I am going to kick his ass in this competition. I wonder why I haven't started calling him B yet?

"Not if you follow the rules for the competition," John says.

"Which are?" I ask.

"You commit to share the initial version of each song you write with the other person as soon as the first pass is complete. You commit to making each song as good as it can possibly be, regardless of who wrote it. You commit to not accepting help from anyone who doesn't live at the compound. You commit to producing one song per month for the next twelve months. Oh, and one more thing, you commit to not having sex with each other. I'll draw up the written contracts and have them ready for your signatures tomorrow."

I look over at Bono and give him my no-sex-is-not-a-problem look. He does the same. This bothers me a little—in that I believe all men want to sleep with me—but just a little.

"What happens if someone breaks a rule?" I ask.

"You're immediately disqualified."

"How will you know if we're following the rules?"

"The contract requires both of you to take a vow of honesty and for you to let me know if you break it."

#

I sign the contract John has placed on the piano. Nothing elaborate. One page with the rules he detailed the day before. I shake his hand, shake Bono's hand, and say something trite about getting to work. Bono's hand is sweaty.

First thing I do is go for a walk in the woods with Solly. I need a strategy to win this thing. Twelve songs. A contract to promote the music and tour. It's a perfect setup. I have to win. Failure is not an . . . oh please, enough with the clichés. I do wonder if there are hidden cameras all over the studio, the house, the woods. Maybe this is just one of those reality TV shows that you don't know you're on until the end.

So there are a few ways I can go about this. The first is to play by the rules. I guess it makes sense to start there, though I'll only stay there as long as it works. I'll focus on the first song. It has to be consistent with the theme for the album. Thirty days should be plenty of time to write and record. There's no way Bono can come up with an album title as strong as mine. Actually, there's no way he can write songs as good as mine, but all I need to worry about now is song one. Eventually, I'll write the song, "The Big Wide Calm," but not until I've got a few new songs under my bra.

The Harton Woods are striking in winter. The crisp air, the castle-like trees in all shapes and sizes, an occasional animal track in the snow, the stillness. Including college, I lived in Boston/Cambridge for seven years. When you're around city people, students, noise, work, it's easy to forget the power of the country. In New Mexico, it was the desert. Here, it's the woods. But really they're the same thing. Balm for creative souls, for wounded souls, for all souls. Maybe that's why John lives here.

After walking for a good two hours, I return to the studio. John and Bono are working on some inferior bit on the piano. I nod on my way up to my room. It looks like Bono's strategy is to play to John's help gene. Not bad, but not my style. At least for now, I'm going to let the songs speak for themselves.

I sit cross-legged on the bed and open my journal to a new page. *Stillness.* How to write about stillness and not make it boring? Maybe stillness is a way into the big wide calm. Who knows, maybe they're the same thing. At some point, I'm going to have to figure out exactly what this big wide calm thing is all about. Anyway, I stare at the blank page and wait. That's how it always starts. *There is nothing like the stillness / When it's time for me to heal.* Not bad. While I'm mostly a guitar player, I do mess around a bit on the piano. "Stillness" is a piano song, with soaring strings, or maybe just a cello, backing it up. Maybe one of those big symphony drums where the song builds to its peak. That's the thing about a well-crafted song—it always builds. Layer on more parts, increase the volume, increase the emotional intensity of the song, whatever. Sometimes I'll bring it back down at the end, but only after the peak. Another line bubbles up—*A gift / A light of rediscovery.*

Above the bed, there's a ceiling fan spinning, which is annoying me. Who would turn on a fan in the middle of the winter? Was someone up in my room while I was away? I need to set some rules of my own with those guys.

No matter. Back to the song. I reread the first verse. *There is nothing like the stillness / When it's time for me to heal / A gift / A light of rediscovery.* A simple piano part underneath would work, just a few triads on the quarter or eighth note to provide a little structure around the melody.

Is the piano free? I don't hear Bono or John downstairs in the studio. Good. I don't want either of them to hear my idea. Too early. I bounce down the stairs. No one is around. At the piano, I recreate the part just as I heard it in my head; loop until I zero in on a melody that works with the piano part. What a melody. It's sweet, intimate, unlike anything I've ever written before. See? I've already learned what I needed from Bono. Don't need him anymore. I open the journal and reread what I've written. Still like it a lot and add: *There is only a fan spinning / In the room where I sit / It's like a castle in the air / As it circles endlessly.* That's the other thing about writing a song. Use everything around you. Annoying fans. Your room. Whatever. Nothing is fixed. It can all be rearranged into something boffo, especially when you don't think about it too much.

I force a few more lines, but after fourteen songs, I've learned that forcing a song is, well, a waste. I scratch out the forced lines and call it a day. You know, I'm off to a good start, and I'm thankful. From what I heard of Bono's song, I'm going to win round one. Was there ever any doubt?

#

"Would you like to go out to dinner tonight?" John asks.

A short time later, the three of us are in John's BMW, this one an X5. The man lives by himself and has four BMWs. Yes, I am using one and, open and shut, he's given one to Bono, but I mean, does he really need four? Does he even have a clue that there's a climate crisis? Anyway, we make our way to this restaurant in the next town over called Gibbet Hill. It's like this giant barn that's been redone into a restaurant. It's cool. In the center is maybe a twenty-foot-wide stone fireplace with an enormous hearth loaded with three-foot logs. It skyscrapers all the way up to what must be a thirty-foot ceiling in the center of the restaurant and resembles a giant penis. God, I need a letter.

We settle down at a table next to floor-to-ceiling windows that overlook a snow-covered field artfully lit by spotlights. John and Bono are on one side of the table; I'm on the other. The dark fields, circled in light, are eerie. I half-expect freakish creatures to dart in and out of the shadows, moving so fast that they reveal nothing.

I scan the menu, thankful for a few organic, local choices. I order a half-portion of organic hanger steak and some greens. John orders a thirty-two-ounce porterhouse. Bono does the same. Please, guys! I fully expect them to hold hands soon and start talking about the Red Sox. When the waitress returns, she brings a pot of homemade potato chips. No wonder John likes this place. The two of them almost down all the chips in just a few minutes. I try one, and I mean, they're pretty amazing, but a whole pot? I scan the place, looking for another random goddess that I might ask to join us to balance these two out, but scrap the idea after a half scan. You know, I can handle both of them. Actually, I can handle all of them.

We small talk until the food arrives, which happens American-fast. The steaks are perfectly done, and my greens are seared just the way I like them.

"How's the songwriting going?" John asks.

"Well," I say.

"How about you, Bono?"

"I've got the basic idea down, as you know, John. The chorus is done, and I've written a verse. Still need a few more verses and probably a bridge. It's going to be a pretty full song, so we'll need to figure out how to get a backing band in to record in a week or two. It's a great song about love, which I think has real commercial potential."

Of course you do, Bono. I mean, I can forgive him for the ambition bit. All rising stars have that. But the guy is so arrogant. Yeah, he has some chops, but he hasn't even finished the damn thing, hasn't even asked for my help yet, per the contract, and has already declared it a great song. How frackin' feeble. My strategy at this point is simple: it's best to divulge as little as possible. That's a good strategy, in general—divulge nothing, never let yourself be vulnerable, strive to help all Barbie Blondes dye their hair brown. Okay, the last part is random, I know, but there are too many Barbie Blondes in the world.

"I'm glad things are moving along," John says. "Bono, if I asked you to describe Paige in one word, what would it be?"

Bono contemplates yet another faux deep question from John, calculating his answer like it's worth a million dollars, which maybe it is. He looks over at me, smiles, and says, "Ambitious."

"And Paige?"

Okay, so there are a couple of ways I can play this. One is to say Bono is ambitious. Echoes are the safest answers. But Bono needs to be called on his stuff. I mean, his whole little speech about his million-selling-commercial love song was just too much to let go without at least one direct whack. I look over and smile at him before answering, "Arrogant."

Whack! Whack!

"You're calling *me* arrogant?" Bono says.

"You think *I'm* arrogant?"

"Think?"

John puts both hands out in front of him, palms up, and says, "Stop."

Apparently, this is his go-to move. Don't get me wrong, it's not a bad move. It demands attention, but he's used it twice in a few days. Come on, John, get a new move for variety, if for nothing else. Pound your fists, or if you really want to go big, stand on the chair and say something like, "Now that I've got your attention . . ." Anyway, "Stop" does the job this time, especially with Bono, who seems like he's going to fold in on himself. What a pleasant thought.

"One of the reasons I brought you together is that you are both ambitious *and* arrogant. Don't misunderstand; you need both of those parts to make it in this business. The problem is that you don't need them to write great songs. It's just the opposite. You need to be open, vulnerable, and truthful. You need to know and love all of your parts."

Slowly, I cut my steak, take a bite, wash it down with some wine. I never thought about my parts before, but now that I have, I'm perfectly willing to love them all. "You think we're both arrogant?"

"Yes."

"What's the difference between being arrogant and confident?" I ask.

"Ego."

"What does that mean?"

John taps his index fingers on the stem of his wine glass for a long time.

I sip my wine like I'm in the middle of some weird wine glass duel. Do not speak next, Paige Plant. John's choice, by the way, an Altamura Cabernet, is outstanding. I don't know anything about wine, but I'm thankful he can pick out the winners from the dogs. Anyway, this is exactly the non-answer answer that John prides himself on giving. At some point, his random mystical words are going to get old, but not yet. What the heck does ego have to do with songwriting, anyway?

"That's all I'm going to say about ego tonight. Instead, let's order some dessert. They have a great chocolate cake here, which with a scoop of vanilla ice cream is to die for." John goes all distant again as he works on what's left of his steak.

Wait for it. Wait for it. Here it comes.

"I will say one more thing. I'd like you both to think about times in your lives when you've forgiven someone for something. You may find some fertile ground there for your work, both together and apart."

Bono and I nod. I really have no idea what John wants us to do, but I'm not going to be the one to look stupid in front of Bono. At this point, I'm thinking John has a random comment generator wired into the back of his brain that uses some proprietary algorithm to generate requests that sound wise. See, all my time at MIT was good for something.

Later, back in my room, still wired from the day, and the chocolate, I open up my journal and read my two verses on stillness. A good rule of thumb before you write a new bit is to reread what you did last a few times.

The repetition helps bubble up ideas from someplace deep down, someplace light, someplace new.

From that place, all different sized bubbles float up. It's like Ms. Lyric has already written every possible line, and my sole job is to watch them float up for a while, then pop them at just the right time onto the page, perfectly arranged. For the next hour, I do just that, until I'm sure I have something, until the bubble generator runs out of soapy water. Careful to navigate the scratch-outs and arrows, I reread for the first time my night's work. *Every now and then I visit this place / To stop circling / To forgive myself / This time to let go of / Ambition / Arrogance / Here the fog lifts over intimacy / I can see myself / All that I love / I can see a road as home / Contentment as change / I see you / I am learning to accept what comes / Even to embrace it / I will stumble again / That much seems inevitable / I may lose sight / You may lose sight of me, as well / That is why I want you to see me now / Remember.*

Like that, the lyrics to my song one are done. Where did that last verse come from? Every now and then words come without even a speck of real-world inspiration. I love those the most. I still have a lot of work to do on the music, but I'm good with the lyrics. Oh yeah, one more thing about writing lyrics. You always need a "you" in the song. I have no idea who the "you" is in this particular song, but I know enough to know I needed one. Actually, I could use one in real life, too. Preferably someone who likes dark-skinned, strong-willed brunettes who happen to be musical geniuses on their way to great fame. I mean, if the guy doesn't believe I'm a musical genius, why bother. Right?

Anyway, back to the song. Sometimes I think my songs are like emotional carrots dangling out in front of me. They come from some place that dares me to follow. Which, of course, I do, even when I'm not so sure I'm ready.

#

The next morning I'm up at the crack of dawn. I build a fire in the wood stove, French press a pot of coffee, sit in front of the piano with my journal propped up and opened to the lyrics for "Stillness." After a few sips of coffee, I start to sing the first verse over and over, say twenty times, until I've got it down. Once you have lyrics and a basic idea of the melody and music, repetition takes over. People think great songs pop out as finished bits on the first pass, but that's not even close to being true. Yeah, the idea can be there. Yeah, yeah, it's a diamond in the rough. But without repetition, without incredibly hard, tedious work that would drive most crazy if they had to sit through it, you've got nothing. Anyway, I work through the verses and the chorus. For me, this is the hardest part, the courageous part, the part where you turn the sketch into a painting, to put it in visual terms. After a few hours, I play the song all the way through for the first time. Good. More to do, but good. Time for more coffee. Caffeine is the only essential nourishment when you're in writing mode.

At the stove, I boil some water. There's not really a kitchen per se in the studio, just a baby stove, a small refrigerator, and a sink. Kind of like the ones I had in my studio apartment in Boston, or the ones you might see in an extended-stay hotel. As I wait for the water in the kettle to boil, "Stillness" is playing over and over in my mind. I'm adding the band. Strings for sure. A drummer. A bass. There's even a spot on the chorus where I can add an acoustic guitar bit, which is a requirement for every song for this album. I plunge the coffee and carry the carafe back to the piano. I start from the top again.

"Is that your song?" Bono asks.

Fuck. I wasn't ready to share it yet. Oh well, best to get this over with. The song is so strong, I doubt there's much he could add. "Yeah."

"It's beautiful."

"Thank you."

"Do you want some help?"

"Why not? It's in the contract."

Bono sits next to me on the piano bench, but I give him a look. Piano benches are sacred ground, and only one musician at a time is allowed to sit. Well, except for Dad. And John. When I was a kid, Dad and I played "Chopsticks" all the time—it was our thing. I tap my finger lightly on the B-flat key, remember-smile. Why doesn't Bono know the bench rule?

A registered-look later, he stands back up and leans against the piano. "Probably better if I stand."

"Probably."

I play the song all the way through. On occasion, he tries out a harmony, trying to get a feel for what works. Some of his ideas are good; some are awful. Paying homage to the god of repetition, which Bono also seems to worship, I loop through the song five times, stopping at the end of each loop for a caffeine injection. Finally, at the end, it's time to see if John's little experiment is going to bear any fruit.

"What do you think?"

"On the verse melody, I could add a bit of harmony on a few lines."

He sings what he's proposing. It's good. We do the lines together with the piano. They're good. We do the whole verse. Also good. Okay, I guess I'm going to ask him to sing backup on "Stillness." I hope he has the decency to return the favor.

"I have one other idea."

"Shoot."

"You know on the chorus, where you build up? What if you changed a few of the notes like this?" He sings my chorus melody with his modifications.

So now he's gone too far. It's my song, not his. My face warms as I launch into the only classical piece that I know by Mozart. He was also a genius. I'm okay with Bono's harmony bit, but the chorus melody? Yeah, we wrote a song together the other day and there was some give and take, but we started that one from scratch. This is different; it's a violation.

After I've Mozarted Bono long enough, I ask, "You want to change my melody?"

"Just a few notes. I think it works better."

"Sing it again a few times." As I'm listening to Bono, my breathing slows, and I'm eventually able to focus on his idea instead of its arrogant, giant-ego creator. Okay, maybe that's a little strong, especially because his bit, truth up, is better. Not only is it better, but I have that feeling I sometimes get when I'm writing, you know, the one where the warmth in your chest signals the song is baked. I take a deep breath and say, "Not bad. I can work with that."

"Thanks."

"Can you show me yours now?"

"Sure."

We switch spots on the altar. Bono plays his song. It's okay. More up-tempo than mine. Definitely more commercial, though I don't even know what that means anymore in the age of iTunes and Internet radio. Mine is better, though not by as much as I thought. And on top of that, I can see a few bits that will make his even better. Too bad.

Bono finishes the song and holds the last chord down longer than needed, apparently waiting for me to say something.

"I like it. The melody is catchy and commercial."

"Thank you."

"Of course, I have a few ideas."

"Of course."

I detail places where the lyrics are too sappy. I mean, how many songs are out there that say "I will love you forever"? Is that even possible with anyone other than family? I feel like I'm Lennon and Bono is McCartney and my job is to knock some sense into him and keep him from writing "Silly Love Songs" over and over. Okay, unfair dig, Paige. You're dissing one of the greatest songwriters in history. Still. After I de-sappify the lyrics, I add a harmony that's more atonal, edgy, which, well, makes the song.

"Wow! Would never have come up with that harmony on my own. The lyrics, too," Bono says.

"I guess John is onto something."

Almost on cue, John walks into the studio with Solly. That's the other thing about John, psycho killer muse, Zen master—his timing is impeccable. And he never wears a watch. I scan the studio for hidden cameras again.

"Good morning. How are you folks doing today?"

"Well," Bono says, "we're helping each other with our songs."

"Can I hear them?"

We play both songs for John. Bono is the opening act. I'm the headliner. John doesn't say anything along the way. When I finish, I spin around on the piano seat. Bono sits down next to me, which I allow, given we're both about to get John's can't-be-anything-other-than-cryptic verdict. John is standing, and I realize it's the first time I've been with him in the studio when he didn't spend the majority of his time on the piano bench.

"I can see you both helped each other out. I'm glad. Each song is much better as a result."

"How can you tell?" I ask.

"Paige, on your song, Bono helped you with the harmonies and also with the melody on the chorus. Bono, on your song, Paige helped you with those atonal harmonies and also made your lyrics a little less sappy."

"You got all of that from one listen?" I ask.

"I've been doing this for a long time."

"Are we ready to record?" I ask.

"You are."

DAD

There's nothing better than a hot shower in the winter. It's cocooning in the best possible way. So I'm washing my hair slowly, massaging-in the pomegranate shampoo, playing my song over and over again in my mind, when hunger hits me. I need to do something about my current predicament. I mean, I get the contract stuff, but I'm out in the woods in the middle of nowhere with two men—one I can't hook up with and the other is much too old. I need to call Z and have him make regular house calls. Or get a Rabbit vibrator. Or check out the townies. Maybe all of the above. Out of the shower and back in my room, I take a manual detour on my bed. Best not to let big hunger linger too long. It demands attention. Doesn't take much, and before I know it, I'm dressed and ready for a day of recording.

As I'm about to go down to the studio, my phone buzzes. Dad. Hate when he calls right after a moment. He wants to visit next week, wants to check out my new arrangement, wants to meet John. End call. I love Dad. He's always been my one sure thing. He's the one who guided me down this path—passed on his love of music, bought me my guitars, taught me to play, changed my name. And until John, supplemented my income. Still, I am twenty-five and, while I love spending time with him, I need to do the fame-and-fortune thing on my own. Don't need his protection anymore. Best to manage John, Bono, and my career myself.

I do my Audrey Hepburn grand entrance bit. What can I say? I love the woman. Much to my surprise, the studio is filled with musicians. A drummer. A guitar player. A bass player. A string quartet. John. Bono. They all pause and glance up. For a moment, I'm sure I gave them a moan-laced cheap thrill from my bed a few minutes ago. You know, it's kind of funny I didn't hear them, but I've always had a singular focus on the important stuff. Anyway, I do the meet-and-greet thing until John tells everyone it's time to start recording. He wants to do the whole song in a single take. No recording of single parts and building the song in pieces. Full takes with the full arrangement. How cool. I've never done that before. Can't wait.

For the rest of the day, we rehearse. Not that I've done it a lot in the past, but my general rule on performing my songs with others is to not be too controlling. I mean, they're the experts on their chosen instrument, right? Still, it's my song, and I do know what I like and dislike. Bono and I play what we did together earlier. It's even better with age. The bass player syncs up quickly. Same with the drummer. But the strings are another story. They come up with this part that is, well, mushy-sappy at best. I hate it. I want something much more atonal, edgy, quirky. After a few heated exchanges, we work something out that still isn't right, but may be the best I can do with these folks. If this continues, I'll need to swap them out. Before I know it, the day is shot. The song is coming together, but we're not there yet. Everyone says their goodbyes. John and I remain behind.

"What did you think of today?" John asks.

"Getting there. What did you think?"

"Remember, they're all artists."

"What does that mean?"

"Just like Bono, find where they can complement your work and ask them to commit to performing with just as much emotion as you have."

So this throws me for a loop. I thought I'd done a stellar job with the musicians. And for the most part, they gave me exactly what I was looking for. Even more in some cases. "I didn't do that?"

"On the ones you agreed with, yes."

"Oh."

"Goodnight, Paige."

"Goodnight, John."

That night I dream that I'm headlining three sold-out shows at the Garden. It's the most important night of my life. Everything has to be perfect. I'm hard on everyone, but particularly hard on the string section. Just when I'm about to lay into them the second (or is it the third?) time for not putting enough emotion into the song, they morph into children and ask me to take them to John's favorite ice cream place for coffee frappés after the show is finished.

By the end of the week, we've got "Stillness" down, and we record it in a single take. I'm not overstating it when I say it's a masterpiece. I've gotta give it up to John—he knows how to do the full-production thing. I can't wait to play it for Dad.

#

Z calls. You know, I've never been so happy to hear from him. He invites me to Boston for the night. Perfect timing on many levels, but especially one. There are three kinds of women in the world when it comes to sex. The first kind works sex into a well-balanced life; sex is clearly one piece of the puzzle. The second kind cares more about companionship. For her, loyalty, trust, and kindness outweigh desire and lust, though she enjoys a good romp when she has it. The third kind is a spend-all-day-in-bed kind of woman. That's me.

Until a short time ago, I thought P was the male equivalent to my kind, my one true lust. Ha! Ever since senior year at MIT, when he stole my hat one day while we were walking down Massachusetts Avenue, I was all caught up. I entered a multiyear can't-get-enough sexual whirlwind. I mean, he wasn't my first or anything like that, but I had never come close to anyone who could make me feel that way before. Senior year, there were times when we would skip class and stay in bed for twenty-four hours straight trying, well, everything. It was as if our bodies had their own language and took over in each other's presence. There were times when we were so perfectly entwined that I thought I might stay there forever. What was I thinking?

I guess, in the end, everyone does their own thing. I mean, it's the American way. If two people walk together on the same path for a short time, well, that's all I now expect. Anything more is delusional. There are days now when I don't hate P, when I'm thankful for our time together, when I can accept that any amount of time people walk together in love, in lust, is a gift. But they're rare. Oh well, ancient history.

As I pull up to Z's apartment, I sex-tingle all over. Here's a little tidbit: women sex-tingle when they know they're about to get properly laid. First time this has happened with Z. Pure lust, I guess. You know, since a key in the hole unlocked my greater-than-Zep future, Z has been willing and able. The times we've gone for it were mostly to help me get stuff or boredom out of my head, at least for a bit. Z's been attracted to me from the start, which I kind of knew but ignored. He's not bad looking or anything, and he's not bad in bed overall. It's just not the same spark. He's waiting for me on his stoop. He's average height, thin, with red hair and lots of freckles. He looks more like a farmer than an aspiring physicist, though when he smiles and gives me his you-are-the-most-amazing-woman-in-the-world look, it's hard not to throw him a bone.

I walk up to him and give him a big hunger-filled hug followed by a let's-go smile and a this-is-just-the-start kiss. That's all it takes and we're off. We pinball up the stairs to his apartment, off the railing, the wall, each other, all the time locked together like a cell in the process of splitting in two. I pin him up against his door and reach down between his legs. I guess he needs this as much as I do. With his spare hand, he reaches behind and pushes open the door. He spins me inside, shuts the door. We do the never-gets-old undress dance and leave a trail of clothes to the bed. You would think someone would have improved on this part of the ritual after all these years, but honestly, there's nothing better than desire, anticipation, and clothes rose petaling.

In bed, Z smiles his beg-for-it smile.

Okay, there's pretty much nothing in the world that I'm willing to beg for, but here's the thing—Z's most distinguishing feature is his tongue. Really. I mean, it's almost enough to create a spark on its own. If he had waited a little longer, I probably would have begged without prompting. Anyway, time's a-wasting.

"There's *nothing*, and I do mean *nothing*, that I want more right now than for you to go down on me."

Z goes to work. Here's the thing about a long tongue: it licks and penetrates equally well. For my money, if you have to choose between a large penis and a long tongue, go tongue, young woman, go tongue. Don't get me wrong, large and long are fine, too, but if you have to choose . . . Z knows my view too well, probably because I blurted it out in a moment of weakness during our first time, which is why he can now get away with the begging bit. It's okay. Best to let him think he has some control. He works in perfect rhythm. Builds slowly. Outside. Inside. Outside. Ah frack, I'm done thinking about it.

After round one, we spend the whole night in bed. Don't eat. Don't sleep. Just endless variations. Why not? We're both twenty-five. We trade hey-do-you-know-this-ones on different positions. We play the thirty-minute game I invented just to keep it interesting with him, where he does whatever I want for thirty minutes and I do whatever he wants for thirty minutes. Guess what, I'm the creative one, though he has a few tricks too. Yeah, yeah, overall there's not the same feeling as with P, but man does Z work at it.

In the morning, on the way out the door, I say, "Next week."

#

As Dad's red rental Jeep Cherokee pulls up to the compound, John, Bono, Solly, and I line up in front of the studio, doing our best *Sound of Music* impersonation. A moment later, Dad jumps out of the car with a big smile on his face. I run up to him and give him a big hug; I've missed him. He's incredibly handsome at fifty. Silver hair, dark skin, tall, with large brown eyes framed by Italian movie star black-rimmed glasses and a smile just like mine.

Dad extends his hand to John, "Alex Pali."

"John. Welcome."

"You're almost off the grid here."

"Almost."

Bono and Solly introduce themselves, Bono with a handshake and Solly with a jump-up-and-greet. Dad loves dogs; our family has had them all my life. He plays with Solly for a bit before we all make our way into the studio.

Dad sits on the piano bench, taps one finger on his thigh, surveys the place. He's a music teacher at the local high school in New Mexico, and while he loves music, he's never been in a high-end recording studio like this. He's clearly impressed with the equipment, with the scale of the place, with the potential, though every time he makes eye contact with John, his face blanks.

Anyway, enough of the big intro. My song is already queued up and ready to go. It's time to see what Dad thinks. Even though he's liked all of my previous songs, this one is different. More important. Which I guess makes sense, given that it's the first song on my masterpiece.

John pushes play, and "Stillness" pours through the speakers. First the piano, then bass after four, then the first verse after eight. I study Dad for early signs. After the first verse, a huge grin spreads across his face. About halfway through the second verse, right after the drums and a cello have joined in, he closes his eyes. When the chorus comes, the strings soar, and the guitar fills in the space. Dad opens his eyes and smiles—he was waiting for the acoustic guitar. After the song finishes, he takes off his glasses and rubs the top of his nose a few times.

"It's fantastic, honey. I knew you had it in you."

"Thanks, Dad. John and Bono helped a lot."

"But it's your song?"

"Yes."

"Can you play it again?"

I play the song a total of seven times. At the end of each pass, Dad comes up with a new way to say it's fantastic. "Work of art." "Beautiful arrangement." "Love the lyrics." Stuff like that.

After the song has settled, John and Bono do the tell-us-about-your-life routine with Dad. Married his college sweetheart. Played in hard rock bands until he was thirty. Loves New Mexico more than any other place. Good. Maybe Dad's warming up. Right before John and Bono head back to the main house, John invites Dad to dinner.

As soon as they leave, Dad sits down at the piano and slowly pushes the F sharp key over and over. I sit down and join him. We do our four hands "Chopsticks" number for a time.

When we stop, Dad says, "Bono seems like a nice boy."

"Man, he is."

"Good musician?"

"Yeah."

"Potentially more?"

"Probably not, given the contract."

"Oh, right."

"And?"

"And I don't trust John."

Okay, I must admit this is not an entirely unexpected development, given Dad's reaction to John so far. I mean, any time Dad's leveled that blank expression at a guy in the past, said guy was gone within a few weeks, regardless of potential. Back then, Dad was just trying to protect me; that's what he did. But I don't need his protection anymore, and besides, John's a good man. Quirky, yeah, yeah, but a good man.

"Really? He's been nothing but incredibly helpful so far."

"I checked him out on the Internet."

"And?"

"And nothing. There isn't a single mention of him anywhere. How can that be?"

This news crush-silences me for a bit until I can lift the weight off. I turn to Dad an ask, "Nothing?"

#

For dinner, John has enough sense not to cook. Instead, he has a caterer do all of the heavy lifting. Not the kind where the cooking is done outside of the home and brought in. That wouldn't be good enough for John. Instead, he contracts a chef and contracts with him to prepare a multicourse gourmet meal right in John's kitchen. I mean, it's not like John to try to make a good impression, but that seems to be exactly what he's doing.

And it's not just the food. All of the books have been put back on the bookshelves or moved to another room. He actually has a living room/dining room space, one giant room that's filled with beautiful modern furniture, elaborate Persian or Indian rugs, and a dining room table large enough to serve twenty. Fresh-cut flowers color up the table. Classical music plays in the background. Mahler, I think.

John sits at one end, Dad at the other. Of course they do. Bono and I sit on opposite sides of table, halfway between John and Dad. With a table this large, we may have to shout to be heard, which would add more unneeded drama. Dad is dressed in his dark brown suit—my favorite—which he insisted on bringing to Harton after I mentioned John's dress habits. John is dressed in his normal attire—his charcoal suit and a red silk tie. He must have, like, twenty identical copies of this getup. I still haven't figured out why the guy wears a suit every day while living in the woods, but tonight at least it's appropriate. Was this how he dressed for his gigs?

The chef pours wine, which at first I think is Lady Gaga's label, but John corrects me, tells me the second G is a J. Italian. Very good. Add "own winery" to list of goals. Next the chef serves an avocado, bacon, and shrimp appetizer that blows everyone away.

Dad glances over at me and gives me his let's-see-what-this-guy-is-made-of look. I buckle up.

"Nice place you've got here, John."

"Thank you."

"Must have cost you a pretty penny."

John smiles.

"If you don't mind my asking, how did you make your money?"

"High tech," John says. "I founded a company that designed and built a chip that's used in a lot of smartphones. Sold it a few years back."

"Ah. That was lucky."

"I don't believe in luck."

Dad takes a moment to adjust his tie until it aligns perfectly with his collar, though it wasn't far off to begin with. Once the what-an-arrogant-asshole wave passes, Dad asks, "Anyone to share all this with?"

"I never married."

Dad cuts into his appetizer and takes a bite. "Delicious."

His strategy is working, and truth up, I'm glad. He's learning more about John's history than I've been able to pick up on my own, and I'm sure some of this will help me manage him after Dad leaves.

John smiles again and takes his first bite. He glances over at the chef and nods. Bono has already finished his appetizer, apparently so he can fully concentrate on the conversation. Ha! He's more hooked than I am. The chef brings over a raw bone-in steak on a plate and places it in front of John, who snaps his fingers. A moment later, Solly is sitting at attention at John's side. John tosses Solly the steak and he immediately runs outside with it, searching for the perfect bed of snow.

"Your dog eats well. He's a full member of the family," Dad says.

"Yes."

"Do you have children?"

"Two. A boy and a girl. A little older than Paige and Bono."

"Do you see them?"

"No."

The chef clears the appetizers and brings out a colorful salad with kale and beet microgreens mixed with arugula, Parmesan, and pine nuts.

John looks over at me and says, "Organic."

"Wow! And at this time of year," I say.

"I have a friend in town with a greenhouse. I connected him with the chef in your honor."

I am honored. Or at least surprised. Maybe there's hope for John yet. Anyway, back to the big reveal. John has two children, which means he did have at least one love. And she must have left with the kids for some reason. Nice work, Dad. Keep going.

Instead, he dead-ends. For the rest of dinner—organic steaks, mushrooms, carrots, broccoli rabe, an ice cream dessert—Dad doesn't have any luck probing deeper into John's past. John expertly deflects any attempt by changing the topic or giving a non-answer answer. While I'm pretty good at that myself when I want to be, he's better. Add it to the list of things I can learn from him.

Dad and I say goodnight and make our way back to the studio. John has survived my Dad's visit, and for some reason, I'm proud of him. What's that about? In the studio, Dad borrows one of my pillows and sets up on the sofa. John offered him one of his many bedrooms, but Dad decided to rough it and spend the night closer to me. Before he falls asleep, he lifts one of John's guitars off the floor stand. I grab my Martin and we jam a little. He is a skilled player, especially when he plays lead. We play for a long time, improvising off of each other. Even though we haven't done this since Christmas, we don't miss a step. Sometimes that musical place without words, without thought, connects two musicians more than anything else. Maybe that's why music is everywhere. We finally stop when our little made-up song has run its course. Improvising is like that—you explore all of the variations off the main idea, until finally the idea peters out, dies a natural death.

"That was fun, Dad."

"It was, honey."

"I'm glad you got a chance to visit."

"Me too."

"What did you think of John tonight?"

Dad paused. "He's hiding something. I'm worried. I think you should leave here with me in the morning."

Okay, there it is. That's the thing about Dad—he says exactly what he means. Which in the past has mostly translated into always letting me do what I want. Sometimes he's been even more supportive of me doing something than I've been myself. But not this time, not with John. Yeah, John seems to have a past. But what person who's lived sixty years doesn't? I mean, John's been nothing but a complete gentleman so far. Okay, I'm out of sync with Dad. How to manage?

John gave me this article to read the other day in which the author said you should always "validate" someone's feeling before telling them a big no. I've skipped that bit for, well, my entire life, but I'll give it a try with Dad now. "Dad, thank you for your concern. I understand what you're saying, and I appreciate everything you've done for me, but for reasons I'm not sure I can fully explain, I trust John. I need to ride things out here and see where it goes."

"I think you're making a mistake."

"Maybe, but it's mine to make."

Dad goes quiet.

You know, maybe the validation thing works. I waver for a bit. How can I say no to this man? I come within a nanosecond of reversing myself, but hold firm until the good-girl wave passes. I mean, good-girl waves have corralled us women for much too long. I have to follow my destiny, and the only thing I'm 100 percent certain of is that John's a big part of it.

"Are you sure, honey?"

"Yes, Dad."

#

Early the next morning, I walk Dad to his Jeep. He slips me a hundred I don't need, but I accept it anyway. Ever since I left for school, it's been part of our goodbye dance. Dad asks if he can visit often. Of course he can. I give him a big hug and wave him off.

For some reason, I want to thank John. It's only seven, but I figure he'll be up, so I wander toward the main house. I slip inside, stand in the foyer, don't hear a thing. It's still hard to believe only one person lives in this place. The house is set up as a series of gigantic pods. The living room/dining room/kitchen pod. The east wing pod, with four full bedrooms—that's where Bono lives. The west wing pod, with John's master suite, an office/library, and, believe it or not, a full-size indoor pool that must cost a fortune to heat in the winter.

I'm about to head back to the studio and catch an extra hour when I hear something faint from the west wing. I should really leave—John's private life is none of my business—but instead I enter a long wood-paneled hallway. First thing I see is Solly sitting at the end of the hallway by the entrance to the master suite. Maybe that's what I heard. Solly whimpering to get into the suite. But why would John keep him out? I mean, John's already told me that Solly has a doggy bed in the master, so what's the deal? I move closer. Someone is crying—no, sobbing—inside the suite. Is that John? Can't be. At the door, I raise my hand to knock, but stop just short of the door. The sobbing isn't like anything I've ever heard before. It's deep, guttural, with a scream of "No!" or "How could I?" every now and then. Gut-wrenching. In the screams, I recognize a trace of John's voice. The confidence is gone. The strength is gone. The faux wisdom is gone. All that remains is loss. Not even in my worst moments with P did I sob that much, or scream like that, and I really loved the ass. It's like the man has taken on all of the pain in the world and needs a release valve when it's too much, when not even he can channel it, when the sheer weight is asymptotic.

As he sobs, a few thoughts bubble up, though for once they have nothing to do with writing a song, winning a competition, becoming famous. First—I'm the only person who has ever heard this before. Second—he needs me to be his witness. Third—I have to help this man.

THE GIFT

I enter the studio bright and early to work more on song number two. A few weeks have passed since the sobbing-bedroom incident. I've said nothing to John about that morning—best to wait for the right opportunity. And John has been his normal Zen-master self since then. It's like it never happened and, well, maybe it didn't. I have been extra supportive, though, cooking a few meals and showing John a thing or two in the kitchen. The three of us have taken Solly for regular walks in the woods each day. We share takeout meals together often. One big happy musical family. We're all getting along so well that I'm just waiting for the first big blowup. After that, I guess I'll know where I really stand.

Anyway, song two has unfolded nicely. I haven't shared it with anyone yet, but today I'm going to bring Bono into the loop. Song two is more up-tempo than "Stillness," which is good because it's best to have variety on TBWC. It's called "The Gift," and it's about strength. *I want to walk next to you and be utterly wild / I want to know how it feels to be that strong.* Or *I want the strength to let you go wherever you need to go.* That's the main gist. Is it better than the first song? No. I'm writing a masterpiece, so every song on the album has to be just as good as every other.

Bono joins me in the studio. Though this song is guitar driven, I still sit on the magic piano bench and play it on my guitar. It's like there's some strange vibrational energy from the bench that makes the music better. Like Muscle Shoals. Bono listens to "The Gift" a few times. Tells me he loves the line *I want to cover you in safety even when I am most afraid.* Does his harmony thing. Only recommends a small change to the melody. Cool. Johnism—

when writing your own stuff, it's best to surround yourself with people who complement your skills. Paigeism—best to learn from people until you are just as good as they are, then dump them. I'm not quite there with Bono, but soon.

"Switch time. What have you got this month?" I ask.

"I'm not ready yet."

"You've got nothing?"

"No."

"We only have a week left. We're supposed to start recording tomorrow."

"I know. Believe me, I've tried. I'm just out of ideas."

Okay, so this is a shocker. I mean we're only at month two and Bono is already stuck? I could see it somewhere down the road, but this is way too early. What should I do? If I do nothing, he'll be disqualified, and I'll win the thing as long as I keep writing. Which I will. But if I help him, he might eventually win. Isn't it best to eliminate your competition? Isn't that what they teach in the business schools? In all of the schools? But he is helping me improve the songs. And I must admit that the competition push is motivating. And it's kind of nice having him around, even if we can't sleep together, even if I've vamped out most of his useful stuff already. Oh, what the heck.

"Do you want some help?"

"You would do that?"

"Sure."

"But if you do nothing, you'll win."

"True, but I kind of like having you around."

"Oh."

"So?"

Bono smiles, you know, the kind where someone holds back a little. He pulls out his guitar and plays a few rough ideas he's been working on. I can see why he didn't develop them any further—they're second-rate. We'll need to start from scratch. We do the improvise thing. Luckily, I like working to a deadline; the combination of caffeine and adrenaline notches me up, and ideas start to flow. Not great ideas, but at least they're something. After a bit, I happen across a riff that clicks for Bono. We go back and forth until we have the basic idea down with piecemeal lyrics. It's okay, though it does sound more like a Paige Plant song than a Bono Yorke song.

"Thanks for doing this," Bono says.

"Anything for a friend."

"We're friends?"

"Yeah."

For the remainder of the day and well into the night, we work on Bono's song. Just about every hour on the hour, he thanks me for helping him, which is appreciated, but too much. At two a.m., I finally call it quits and head up to my room. Bono has a decent song to record in the morning. Not great, but not bad. He'll be around for another month.

#

Recording day. I shut Fred off before he has an opportunity to annoy me. I slip out of bed, jump in the shower, let the rain fall. I've only done this recording thing once before, but I already know the first day is the best. Talented musicians get together to interpret your stuff. What a rush. True, I have to push them to make their bit original, but hey, that's my job. You know, there's a tendency with studio musicians to play something that sounds like all of the other stuff out there. Not sure why, but left unchecked, you end up with the big wide boring. But after last month's little pep talk from John, I'm well equipped to check them today. I mean, "The Gift" lends itself to more intricate parts, which motivate the real players, so it should be easy. Think psychedelic sixties meets Nirvana meets Tame Impala.

I get dressed and bounce down the steps, but there are no musicians. What the . . . ? John and Bono are sitting in two out of three foldings in the center of the studio. I join them. John hands me a much-needed cup of black. Bono crosses his arms over his chest.

"Where is everyone?" I ask.

"Bono told me what you did on his song," John says.

"Anything for a friend."

"Actually, I'm going to withdraw from the competition, Paige. That song is really much more yours than mine, and I didn't feel right about claiming it."

"We did it together."

"You did all the heavy lifting. I just went along for the ride."

I glance over at John. Steel and stone. C'mon, c'mon, master my master. Cut Bono some slack. Yes, this is your show, but enough already. I mean, it's just one of twelve songs, and he can do two next month. I'm the competition, and if I'm okay with it, you should be too.

"Bono is moving out today," John says.

"You won't give him another chance?"

"There are no second chances in this business," John says.

"It's okay, Paige. I didn't have what it takes. I'll keep working at it and eventually get out there."

Bono's face is all stone, too, like he forced the words because the gracious-in-failure god in the sky said that's what he should say. Who is that god anyway, and how can I rewrite his rules? Okay, so I'm not too happy with psycho-killer-muse-Zen-master John. No wonder the guy is alone. No second chances? How can anybody live without the possibility of forgiveness? Wasn't he pushing me on forgiveness just a short time ago? What, it doesn't apply to him? I'm about ready to tell John he's an asshole when I catch this don't-do-it-for-me look from Bono. It's almost like Bono has accepted that the light was too bright for him and has slithered back into the shadows. I feel sorry for him. Why would anyone want to do this if they didn't love the light?

I walk Bono back up to main house so we can get a little alone time. As we walk, there's a cadence to how our boots crunch the gravel. Syncopated. Like Reggae. "Are you sure this is what you want?"

"Yes."

"But why?"

"I'm not strong enough."

"We could help each other."

"Thank you, but I need to help myself first."

At the house, I give him a big hug. We do the obligatory I'm-going-to-miss-you, this-will-make-you-stronger, I-know-you're-going-to-make-it-down-the-road bits. I even shed a tear or two, which are real. Then—poof! He's gone.

Moments later, back in the recording studio, it's time to get back to work and record my song, time to see what the other musicians can add. Looks like I'll need another singer for harmony now that Bono is out. Who knows, maybe I'll do the harmonies myself. Yeah, yeah. One good thing about all of this is, prefetching that John doesn't replace Bono, I'm going to get a lot more one-on-one time.

We record "The Gift" and it turns out fantastic. I mean, really, it couldn't be any better. I'm getting the hang of this working-with-creative-musicians thing, and I've managed to squeeze every last ounce of creative juice out of them and pour it into my song. John is great during the whole session. Lets me do what I want for the most part, which is always a plus, except right after I've taken a false step. Then he does his one-line course correction thing—the drums weren't quite in the pocket on that take, make your vocals a little more raspy next time, the Hammond B3 organ might work well on the bridge—and presto change-o, I'm back in the driver's seat moving the song forward. Two songs in the bag. What's next?

After the musicians leave, John asks me up to the house for dinner. Give him a couple of hours, he says—he has a surprise for me. Wants to tell me a story. Good. Maybe we'll get to the bottom of his morning sobbing incident.

#

Back in my room, I collapse on the bed for a quick nap before dinner. In the corner of the room, my easel is set up with a blank canvas. I haven't painted at all since I've been here. Not sure why. I need to get something down before

I move on to song three. Otherwise, the painting won't capture enough of the song. Time lag stuff. I always do it this way. One-two. Write the song; paint the painting. I set Fred for eight and drift off.

I dream of Bono. We're in Dublin on a pilgrimage to visit his namesake. We walk for a long time out of the city on this winding ocean road toward real-Bono's house. Bono is convinced that if he just gets to see real-Bono, just gets to shake his hand, everything will be okay. Real-Bono will call John and fix it, tell him to give Bono a second chance. Only thing is, when we get to real-Bono's place, there's this thick wooden gate that protects the house, keeps pretty much everything out of view. Lots of previous pilgrims have scratched things into the gate. *Bono rocks. Jack and Joey were here. Please marry me, Bono.* My Bono picks up a sharp rock from next to the gate and engraves *Save Me.*

At eight, I head up to the house, slip in through the front door. John is in the kitchen, in full chef getup, cooking something. The man doesn't do small well. Garlic. Parmesan. Pretty amazing. And unexpected. Solly is sitting at his side, waiting for an occasional scrap. That dog is incredibly smart on the important things; I bet he has a few Solliettes tucked away in the woods.

"You're cooking?"

"Not only cooking. Cooking healthy."

"See, you are trainable. What are you making?"

"Grass-fed organic rib eyes and garlicky greens for the main entrée. A Caesar salad with homemade dressing to start. A fruit dessert—with no added sugar. Want some wine?"

John pours me a glass and I take a sip. It's fantastic, as always. At some point, I'm going to have to learn a little about how he picks his stuff. But just a little. A short time later, we sit down at the dining room table, beautifully set. There's an extravagant tropical flower arrangement in the center and long-stem candles. Very festive, like Christmas but without the red. He has me curious. He's doesn't normally pay attention to these kinds of details. Neither do I, though it's kind of nice. I feel like I should be in a dress with white pearls and pumps, but I don't own any.

THE BIG WIDE CALM

"I've decided I'd like to make you dinner once per week as long as you stay. Sometimes we'll celebrate, like tonight. Sometimes we'll talk shop. Sometimes both. Sound okay?" John asks.

"Sure. Why not?"

"Now that it's just the two of us, I can concentrate on helping you more."

"You're not going to replace Bono?"

"No. The whole contest idea was a little contrived anyway."

"I see." He's made the right call here. I mean, it's hard enough making one multigenerational masterpiece, never mind two, and I'm certainly motivated enough without a competitor, and anyway, I've already lifted what I need to know from Bono, and, and, and.

"Different topic. Did you ever hear the first take of 'Imagine'?" John asks.

"No."

"Check it out." John reaches into his pocket and pulls out a small remote control, which he points toward the living room. A moment later, John Lennon's "Imagine" starts to play.

The basic piano part is the same, as are the lyrics, but the arrangement is much different. Fuller, but not nearly as good. I'm shocked. The first version of the song would have never made it all the way to number three of the *Rolling Stone* Top 500 list. Brilliance can emerge from something that's just good? The song finishes and we sit in silence for a bit.

"What do you think?" John asks.

"I'm blown away. It's not nearly as good."

"Exactly. All of the basic elements are there, but they went too far on take one."

"Sometimes it's better to strip something back and go simple," I say.

"That's how the emotion gets through."

We eat our steaks, which, by the way, are fantastic. So are the garlicky greens. And John does a good job of filling my wine glass whenever it gets close to empty. I hold my liquor well, so the constant flow is boffo with me. I've even won a few barroom bets with guys who thought they could out-shot me. Not a chance. After the second bottle, I channel Dad and do the probe thing a bit.

"Did you ever strip down one of your songs?" I ask.

"Yes, but only after I'd been writing for a long time."

"Why did it take so long?"

"I didn't have anyone to teach me."

I nod. Okay, as John's only student, maybe there's a little opening here. John's wine glass is empty. I reach across the table, grab the bottle, fill his glass. Maybe he doesn't hold his liquor as well as I do.

"Do you have any I can hear?"

"None."

"What happened to them?"

"I erased all of the masters one day."

"How come?"

"Another time."

John jumps up from the table and goes over to the refrigerator. Jeez, John, that was abrupt even for you. He pulls out a beautiful fruit tart. I can't believe he made it himself. He sets it on the black granite counter, which makes the tart look even more beautiful. Blueberries. Strawberries. Kiwis. Blackberries. All arranged in this perfect spiral. He fires up his cappuccino maker, you know, one of those four-spout things like you see in all the coffeehouses. A short time later, he returns with the tart and two perfectly frothed cappuccinos. Both are fantastic. Of course they are.

We finish the night with small talk about sports. Apparently, the man loves the Celtics, watches every game, has all the statistics of every player in his head. Most of the names and numbers sieve right through except for Larry Bird, who even I can remember was quite good. How much room exactly is there in this John's head? I mean, really? Synthesize all human knowledge, I get. But what's the point of knowing the field goal percentage of every Celtic for the last fifty years?

On the way back to my room, I'm borderline schoolgirl giddy. I made a little progress; John committed to telling me the song story.

#

For a week, I stare at a blank canvas. No matter what I do, I can't paint "Stillness." It's not like there isn't anything to work with given the lyrics, but for the first time in my life, I'm blocked. I mean, it's like I hit a wall of truth and I'm concussed. For most of the week, I keep drifting to Bono. How's he doing? Where did he go? Did he jump back on the horse yet? That's what I would have done. The answers are all blurs, like they're trying to deny the questions exist at all.

Anyway, I'm starting fresh today. I'm back from a long walk in the woods with Solly and John, and I'm ready to give the painting a shot. I do the snapshot thing in my mind. The head of a woman—me, I guess—expressing arrogance. That one should be easy. Another one of ambition. Also easy. A girl on a bed looking up at a fan spinning. Another girl hitchhiking with a guitar strapped over her shoulder. These images, all smaller, surround the main image, the one of a completely open, vulnerable woman showing herself to the world. That one will be hard to paint. It's all in the eyes, the lips.

I go to work. I pick a dominant color for each image. The smaller ones get all of the reds, greens, blues, and yellows. These pictures are abstract. The viewer sees enough to understand what's going on, but they definitely aren't from the school of realism. The centerpiece sketch, though, is nothing but real. My specialty is faces. Have always loved them for some reason. Some women I know like men a certain way—tall, thin, muscular, whatever. With me, though, those things have never really mattered. It's always been about a man's face. Or a woman's. If the face holds some form of wonder, the rest follows.

Two days later, when I'm done and in desperate need of sleep, the central woman of "Stillness" is the most realistic picture I've ever painted. It almost looks like a photo from one of those old cameras: sweet, sad, my own version of *Les Demoiselles d'Avignon*. From a distance, at just the right angle and light, it looks, well, like me. I guess I'm ready for song three.

WHEN JOHN FELL FROM GRACE

I'm three weeks into song three. It's going well, and I'll be ready to record in the next day or so. Another up-tempo song, this time about trust being even more important than love. Or the other way around. I haven't decided yet. Anyway, over the last month, John and I have settled into a routine. I'm up early every morning, and I meet him promptly at nine in the studio. We have coffee together and a quick bite to eat. John is trying to eat better. On some days, he'll do fruit or we'll make eggs or oatmeal. On others, though, he does his sugar thing. Still, he is making progress—and has increased his probability of making it to seventy to just above fifty percent. Each day, after a little nourishment, we take Solly for a walk in the woods. I've come to treasure these walks more than any of my other time with John. He's somehow more open in the woods, more at ease. So am I. After we walk, we spend the rest of the day apart. I write or paint. He does whatever he does. In the afternoon, I go for a swim. His pool is big, warm, refreshing, and, well, it's important for me to stay in shape if I'm going to be a rock star. Once a week, he cooks for me. Amazing how quickly the man learns new skills. Oh, and Z and I hook up often to keep me from going crazy. He visits. I visit. Whatever.

Today, John and I are out on the trail. It's a beautiful morning. Mid-thirties. Sunny. The trees are still covered with a thin layer of ice from an overnight storm. Deer pass regularly, often outnumbering us five to two. After weeks of talking with John about, well, everything—music, Buddhism, politics, food, the climate, fame—the time has come for the big one. I mean, I've put enough chips in the bank with him, so I'm pretty sure I can go there.

Deep breath. Again. I'm kind of antsy. It's the only time I recall being this way since I moved in; actually, it's the only time I recall being this way in years. Start with the songs and build to the sobbing incident. He already told me he would tell me about his songs, so no big deal. I'm just following up. He'll like the thoroughness, the persistence, the closure. These are admirable traits in a musician, a goddess, a friend. Okay, here it is.

"Why did you destroy your songs?"

John slows for a second and glances my way with a too-quick smile. His eyes cloud over and his hand flutters to his neck. I nod. This is a just-a-gesture moment. I know him well enough now to see that. We're walking alongside a small stream, down a hill. The sound of flowing water is soothing.

"I love the fact that streams are always changing. The water is passing through; it never stops, not even in the winter," John says.

"I love the sound."

John goes to the near side of the stream, and with a few zigzag jumps onto midstream stones, he reaches the other side. From there, he shapes his hands over his mouth into a loudspeaker and says, "I wrote a lot of the songs about the woman I loved."

"The mother of your kids?"

"Yes."

"How long were you together?"

"A long time."

"She left you?"

"Yes."

"And your kids?"

"They all left the same day."

I follow John across the stream. Slowly. He reaches out and snatches my hand as I leap off the last rock. I have no idea how a sixty-year-old man can be so athletic. Anyway, that's enough of the big one for now. Best to pause and walk in silence for a bit. He seems to do best with small-talk chunks followed by larger, silence chunks. It's almost like he's been alone for so long that his vocal cords get tired after they reach their word quota. Hard to imagine that he once performed a full song set in front of a live audience.

I pick up some snow and make a snowball, throw it at a nearby tree, go over to the tree, outline a small circle around the mark the snowball left with more snow. Target practice. First to get to five balls in the circle wins. John catches on, eventually wins 5–4 despite my early 1–0 lead. One of these days. Just as we finish, Solly, who skipped the rock part when crossing the stream, jumps up on me to play, wet paws and all. We hug for a bit before he tires and drops back to all fours. Wet fur and all, I've come to love that dog like he's my own. I'm going to miss him when I leave.

"Want to keep going?" I ask.

"Down the path?"

"So to speak."

"Yes. It's right that you know." John pauses for a long time, like he's reconsidering his last line. Finally, he says, "I wasn't a great partner. I was making a ton of money at the time. My company was doing really well. I thought I was invincible. I was always gone, and when I was home, I was working."

"That's why she left?"

"No."

John's voice shivered the last no. We're getting to the good stuff, the hard part. I need to let him go at his own pace, or not go at all, though I just want him to spit it out. I mean, what could it be? Whatever he has to say, it will be fine. He's done so much for me already, there's very little that could freak me out at this point.

"You know, whatever you tell me is okay."

John sprints ahead on the trail, turns around, and waits for Solly to catch him. When he does, he kneels down and scratches behind Solly's ears. When I reach the two of them, he says, "Okay, here it is. We lived in California at the time, close to Silicon Valley, up in the mountains. Most of the people in our community were also in high tech. One night Grace and I went to a party, and

I was introduced to this brilliant engineer, an MIT grad like you, who had an idea for a chip that held the potential to completely revolutionize computing. Pretty much holographic everything like you see in a lot of movies these days."

"Wow, that's cool." Okay, so I can see where this is going. No big deal. I can handle that. Though I would like him to spend more time with his kids. But he hasn't gotten to that part yet.

"Yeah, it is cool. Anyway, as you might have surmised, I started a relationship with her. We would meet at all different places, but one place we liked in particular was a scenic overlook with a great view of the valley. We went there often. Even though I was in my early forties at the time, parking in that place made me feel sixteen again. About a year after we started, Grace found out about us. She also found out about our secret location, and apparently came there often to watch us from the nearby woods."

"She didn't confront you?"

"Not right away."

So this is a little strange. You know, if I were in Grace's shoes, which I guess I kind of was with P, I wouldn't want to watch a thing like that at all, never mind more than once. Why would any intelligent woman ever put herself through that kind of pain? I mean, confront and dump, right?

"Why do you think she endured the two of you more than once?"

John resumes walking, picks up a broken branch on the trail, and tosses it out of the way. Then another. And another. Fourth branch in hand, he says, "I'm not sure, but I've come to believe she had to see it more than once to believe it was true. When you see something that you believe is impossible, your brain takes a while before it accepts the image."

"So she finally confronted you?"

"Not exactly. Apparently, one day at around dusk, she snuck up in her car behind my car, which was in its usual parking spot. I'm not sure how long she was there watching, but I guess something snapped in her and she floored the gas pedal. Her SUV rammed my Audi until my car went over the cliff into the gully."

"Were you hurt?"

"I wasn't in the car."

"What? Who was in the car?"

John goes quiet.

What does he mean he wasn't in the car? I can't believe Grace tried to kill him. I mean, a key in the asshole, yeah, yeah, but ramming a car off a cliff? No, no, no. Don't get me wrong, he deserved to be called on it and dumped, but he didn't deserve the plunge-to-your-death sentence.

"That night my son and daughter had asked to borrow my car. They're close in age, and they often went on double dates. Apparently, they'd recently found the spot that I thought was so secluded. They were in the car with their dates when Grace struck the back of the car. All four of them died."

I rise out of my body, look down. J was a P when he was younger. He indirectly caused the death of his two kids. And two other innocent people. How did he live with himself after something like that? How could anyone live with themselves after something like that? So that's why he walled himself off in the woods, gave up technology, gave up music, and has been grieving all of these years.

I float back down into my body. I can't stop shaking. I don't know what else to say, so I whisper, "I'm so sorry."

John looks off in the distance at the giant rock formation that's partly covered with a sheet of ice. It has inched halfway down the formation and birthed the most beautiful wall of icicles—long, short, wide, thin, broken.

"So am I. Grace apparently got out of her car after she rammed mine. No one knows for sure what happened next, but I've come to believe that she recognized one or both of our children and tried to climb down in the gulley to save them. On the way, she must have slipped. When the police found her, she was face down, a few feet away from my car, already dead."

"I'm so sorry, John."

"Thank you." He pauses. "So, to finally answer your question, about a month after the accident, I destroyed all of the songs I'd ever written, most of which were about her, a few about the kids. Fifty-six of them in all."

"I understand. . . . I probably would have done the same." Now I get it. John's life's work was really his songs about Grace, not his company, not anything else. When she and the kids were gone, he was done. He'd lost his muse. He'd lost everything. He had to start over. Or he had to accept that he never would. What did he call that thing—a charnel ground? He's been sitting in his own emotional charnel ground for twenty years. "That's when you moved here?"

"Yes."

"No ties to the past?"

"None. I paid a lot of money to erase everything, which was easier before the Internet was so prevalent. Changed my name. The whole package. Even got some ex-witness protection guys to help me."

At this point, it doesn't make sense to hold back my spying bit anymore. I mean, it's just a continuation of the story, right? I scan the Harton Woods. There's a cluster of rocks just ahead, wedged and stacked in a way that seems to defy gravity, to threaten. It's probably been that way for a long time.

I turn toward John and I whisper, "And the sobbing in the morning in your bedroom?"

John stops walking and looks at me with flinty eyes, which blank a second later. "You know about the sobbing?"

"I snuck into your hallway one morning and listened to you right at your bedroom door."

"Oh."

"I didn't mean to spy on you. It just kind of happened."

"It's okay, Paige. I've cried like that at least once a week since the accident. You were bound to hear it sometime. You'd think I would have stopped after so many years, but I haven't. I probably never will."

"You've been grieving for twenty years?"

"Wouldn't you?"

"And Bono and I are like your kids?"

"I don't know. I guess."

"But you pushed him out. Why do that if we were somehow helping you?"

"He didn't deliver."

Okay, so J really is pretty messed up when it comes to relationships. I mean, I get the pseudo-kid thing, and if that somehow helped him, I would have signed up for a year. You know, it's a small price to pay given what he's doing for me. I bet Bono would have, too. But he broke up the pseudo-twins because of a rule? It's almost like he doesn't want to get better. And what about her . . . ?

"What happened to the brilliant scientist?"

"We broke it off. Too much weight."

Well, that appears to be the first thing in this whole worse-than-your-worst-TV-melodrama incident that was the right decision. I mean, the guy was in his forties with a beautiful wife (well, okay, I don't know for sure that she was beautiful, but probably) and two kids, and somehow he assumed his actions had no consequences. I do get the no-consequence thing at twenty, or even at twenty-five. Yeah, yeah, I've done my fair share. But at forty?

Okay, wait, I said I wasn't going to judge the man. He's certainly been carrying a lot of guilt with him ever since. Hasn't he done his time? And he recently asked me to think about the times in my life when I've forgiven someone. Maybe I should do the right thing here and tell him I forgive him. Even though he's not so good at forgiveness himself. But he didn't do anything to me, so I really don't have anything to forgive him for. But I want to. But I don't. Instead I take his hand and say, "Let's go back home."

#

Back in my room, I sit cross-legged on my bed with my guitar draped over me and my journal in front of me. I've got to get this on paper. I mean, if there isn't a song in a story like that, then I have no business calling myself a songwriter. Moments earlier, I left John at his front door and gave him a big hug. I told him he'd suffered enough, though I could tell he didn't believe me. Anyway, now I have this incredible urge to write something down. Right below my heart, I warm, dilate, and my arms tingle. When this happens, I drop everything, find my guitar, my journal. When you've been doing this for a while, you learn to bulldoze a runway, red carpet and all, for the songwriting gods when they want to speak. They're coming. After a few minutes with my pen at attention, the first thing that I scribble is:

> When John fell from Grace, the music stopped
> Like a _____ like a _____ like a well worn ___
> When John fell from Grace, the music stopped
> And the boy, the girl, in all of us died

Okay, that's got potential. I play a few chords on my guitar. Play around with a simple melody, folky, childlike, in G. It holds up for a few passes, sounds great, just with me doing my favorite folk singer thing. Here's something most people don't know about a great song: whether it's played with just an acoustic guitar or a full arrangement doesn't matter. It's great either way. After I'm famous, maybe I'll publish *Paige's Rules for Songwriting*.

Anyway, back to "John Falling from Grace." This is one of those times when I can write the entire thing in one night. Actually, I have to if we're going to start recording in the morning. I go down to the studio, boil some water, press a pot of coffee. Looks like it's going to be my first all-nighter since that physics final when I was a sophomore. That's the class I met Z in. Of course, I aced the test. Even though I have no memory of the material, what will always stick with me is laughing with Z after the exam.

Back in my room, I drink from the cup and replay what I've written so far. It's still good. I need to fill in a few of the blanks and get the chorus down. Best to nail the hook in the song first, and nine out of ten times you want the hook in the chorus. Jeez, another rule. After a bit, I settle on the final chorus:

When John fell from Grace
The songs stopped
White noise filled the waves, the halls, the flock
When John fell from Grace
The songs stopped
And the boy, the girl, in all of us died

Okay, now that the chorus is solid, I'll focus on the verses. Where to take the song? It has to be about redemption, about the search for peace when all is lost, about hope—no, not hope—truth. It has to be about John, about every John. With that as my guide, I get to work on verse one.

John is alone on a path now in the woods
Like all that came before him who draped the world in shoulds
That's the price he pays
For carrying so much weight
That's the price he pays

He's searching for something
Maybe hope, peace, maybe lost love
Or an amulet, an arc, a white dove
That's the price he pays for what he's done
That's the price he pays for all of us

Okay, that's got potential, but I need it to rhyme a little more. I pop off the bed and get my rhyming dictionary. Every songwriter has a rhyming dictionary. It's just as important as my guitar. There's even software out these days that helps with this sort of thing, but I prefer my thick, worn hardcover. With its help, I cross out *for all of us* and replace it with *to return to the sun*, replace the second *That's the price he pays* with *That's the price of fate*. Much better.

Over the next few hours, I write a couple more verses and a bridge to the song. Bridge: *Hey baby, I'm coming back to you / And you're going to be amazed at what I found / It's a giant ruse of mirrors, of lies, of sounds.*

Finally, I put them all together and play "When John Fell from Grace" for the first time. It's really good. I hope he can handle it. Anything for your art, right? It's late. Or early. If I'm lucky, I'll get an hour or two before the musicians arrive. In honor of John, I take the original song three I wrote, you know, the one about trust being more important than love, and delete it. I've never done that with anything I've created before, and strangely, it feels good.

#

Warm and fuzzy weeks follow the big reveal. It's like John isn't sure I'm going to stay around and is pulling out all of the stops. I play along, but he doesn't have to worry. It's kind of nice seeing this part of him; he can be incredibly kind when he wants to be. On recording day for "When John Fell from Grace," which he seemed to accept, he sent down fresh flowers to the studio with a note that said, *You'll do great today. J.*

On another day, we took a trip to Kendall Square and saw a new movie by some famous director John likes, which was both deep and honest. After the movie, we went to the East Coast Grill for dinner, where we had a who-can-eat-the-hottest-food duel. Of course, I won. He's known from the start that I miss the city, but this was the first time we'd ventured into Cambridge together. Actually, he told me on the way that it's the first time he's been in the city in a decade. Talk about warm and fuzzy.

And on many days, we dance. Not to rock and roll like we did that one time in the beginning. No, ballroom dancing. He's pretty good, and he teaches me all of the basic dances. The tango. The fox-trot. The waltz. The cha-cha. Swing. It's surprising how a lot of popular music these days works well with these dances. I had no idea. What's no surprise is how much I like the swing. Truth-up, the big reveal has pulled us closer instead of splitting us apart.

Today, John wants to show me Portsmouth, New Hampshire. I've never been. Neither has he. But according to his research, they have a beautiful downtown shopping area, you know, the kind with tons of old New England brick buildings renovated into boutique shops. During the ninety-minute drive from Harton to Portsmouth, we don't speak at all. Instead, we listen to the new Vampire Weekend album, which, as a matter of fact, is great. Here's the thing about listening to music in a car with someone else—just listen to the frackin' music. Don't try to talk over it. It's not background noise; it's art. Respect it. Cherish it. Understand it. Over the years, I can't tell you how many times I've had to ask my friends to shut it when we're in the car. Anyway, I'm glad John gets this, and the ride is about nothing but the music. When done well, the experience of listening to a great album in the car with another person can be super intimate.

Portsmouth is everything John said it would be. It's a sunny, relatively warm day, and the streets are filled with people walking and shopping. I gravitate to the shoe store, which has some stuff I've haven't seen anywhere else. Yeah, yeah, like most other women on the planet, I do like shoes, but I hate the stereotype, so I limit my purchases. Believe it or not, John gravitates to this kitchen shop that sells maybe twenty different kinds of olive oil. He buys enough to last him, well, forever. I've created a monster.

On the way out of kitchen paradise, John tells me he'll buy me anything I want as a reward for doing so well with my songs. Cool, I guess. But he's done enough, and I don't need anything. Still, when we're window-shopping in front of a real estate agency, you know, one with pictures of local houses on display, I'm tempted to ask for the two-million-dollar waterfront estate that's prominently pictured. But I don't. Knowing John, he would probably say yes. And what would I do with an estate anyway? I'm going to be on the road like fifty weeks per year as soon as *The Big Wide Calm* comes out, and after that, I'll have enough money to buy my own palace. Queen Paige. It has a nice ring to it.

After we loop a few times, we decide to eat lunch at this waterfront fish place, called Surf's. One entire wall is glass, so John asks for a window table overlooking the bay. A moment later, we settle down for some much-needed food.

"I hear the fried calamari appetizer with hot peppers is delicious," John says.

"You hear?"

"Oh, right. I researched."

"Better."

We order the calamari, some iced tea, and we both get lost in our menus. Spending time with John these last three weeks has changed my view of men. All of us girls want the older version of the guy in the younger guy's body. You know, we've claimed the emotional high ground, and we're looking down on all the P's of the world. Roll the big rock up the hill over and over until you get it right! Like Sisyphus. Actually, the image of P rolling a rock up the hill forever is, well, almost orgasmic, but enough of that guy already. Back to my point: if we just learn to accept a man where he is at any given time, find the songs in that version of him—good and bad—then we would do much better as the dominant gender. But we don't. We try to change them, mold them in our image. Too much work. And it never pans out, so why do all the heavy lifting?

The waitress arrives with the calamari and tea. We both order the same thing, sesame seared tuna. Kind of boring, but what you gonna do? At least we're out of Harton. As advertised, the calamari is to die for.

"Thank you," I say.

"For what?"

"You've been very kind, especially these last few weeks."

"Oh, that."

"I'm really okay with your past, you know."

"I wasn't sure."

"I am. This is exactly where I want to be."

Some invisible weight lifts off John's shoulders, and he smiles in a way that makes him look ten years younger. I guess when you stay in, even after the this-is-worse-than-anything-you've-ever-heard reveal, the other person feels fully seen. I see John. It's like I'm learning to read for the first time. See Paige run. See Paige love. I glance down at the table. Did I just say that? It's not romantic, for sure, but do I love him? I fiddle with my fork for a bit like it's a divining rod. Yes. How did that happen? Doesn't really matter, I guess. Should I tell him now? Ever? Maybe he'll misinterpret it and my boffo gig will come to an end. Better to say nothing and enjoy the ride. I return to John, who has this penetrating look on his face like he's heard every one of my thoughts for the last few minutes.

"I need to tell you something, Paige," he says.

"Another cliffhanger?"

He laughs. "Wow, a perfectly placed dig, but not exactly."

"What then?"

"Don't take this the wrong way, but I love you."

I freeze. Okay, he really was listening to my thoughts. Is that yet another one of his Zen-master skills? What to do? I sip my iced tea. I take a bite of my tuna, which, just like the calamari, is to die for. Is there a Surf's near Harton? I stare at a tugboat in the bay doing some heavy pulling. How do those things work?

John is studying my face, trying to get a read. I guess he sees enough to say, "I don't mean romantic love, Paige. I'm much too old for you. But I do love you."

What a relief. The gig will continue. And now that he brought it up, I can tell him I love him, too. I guess this love thing has been building for a while—really, since day one. When someone is such a big influence on your life, has your back as you struggle through creating your masterpiece, how can you not feel something for him? Okay, there it is. Deep breath. Just say it, Paige.

"I love you, too, John."

John smiles. He reaches across the table and cups his hand over mine, like my Dad does all the time. "I'm glad, Paige. It's been a long time since I've said that to anyone."

"I guess I felt something right from the start."

"Me too. It wasn't a spark like I had with Grace, but it was just as powerful."

"Yeah, yeah, I get that."

"The universe connected us before we even met."

"You believe in that stuff?"

"Yes."

That's an interesting point. In my quantum physics class at MIT, the professor went Santa Fe mystical on us one day, and for maybe thirty minutes, he painted a picture of how we're all connected at the quantum level. Cool idea, but I nixed it at the time. I mean, look at the world we live in. If we really were connected, then people would just stop all of this madness. But they won't. Never will. With that said, I do have to admit that John's bit about our connection is true. Maybe some people do connect at the quantum level, but, you know, it's rare.

Anyway, we finish our meals and talk about music. John noticed an ice cream shop on the way to Surf's, so we skip dessert and literally make a beeline there. In no time, we're sharing a bowl of Almond Joy ice cream that's flat-out perfect. Not too sweet, with just enough crushed Almond Joy bars mixed in.

On the way back to Harton, we listen to another album, this time by James Vincent McMorrow. The guy has one of the most beautiful voices I've ever heard. Lumps visit my throat often, regardless of what he's singing about. So John loves me. And I love him. Who would have thought?

SHAMANS OF MOVEMENT AND LIGHT

The next week I do something I've never done before—I decide to paint the song before I've written it. It's a love painting, but not about John. Or Z. And certainly not about P. It's about John-Z, like the "you" in the painting is magically created from the best pieces of both of them. FrankenJohnZ, whose sole purpose is to give our hero what she needs. Ha. Wasn't I saying the other day that all of us women should accept men exactly where they're at? Anyway, the guy is young, tall, handsome, always wears a suit, is emotionally sensitive, writes songs, can go all night, has tongue. Well, okay, that last bit won't be in the painting or the song, but it's impossible not to mention it often.

I open my sketchbook and wait for a few images to pop. Nothing comes. Why is that? Strange. The painting gods don't like FrankenJohnZ. Maybe it's too hard doing both of them together. Now there's a thought. Break it down, Paige. Start with John. What did he look like at twenty-five? I do a quick sketch of his sixty-year-old face, which turns out to be pretty flattering. I should give it to him. Anyway, I tear that page out and use it as my guide for twenty-five-year-old John. Add hair. Remove wrinkles. A little thinner in the face. Lo and behold, twenty-five-year-old John is really good-looking. Okay, enough of him.

Next an image of a girl in bed with a guy, hands behind her head, daydreaming up at the ceiling. The guy is nestled up against her with his head on her chest. You know, the stereotype you see of a guy and girl in bed, only with the roles reversed. Why do we live in a world where so many men want their women to submit? I mean, I get the surrender bit. That's about trust and being taken care of. But I definitely do not submit.

Back to John. An image of a shaman and a woman standing and facing each other in a Harton-like forest practically draws itself on a new page like, well, a shaman has taken over my drawing hand. In the sketch, the shaman has comets of light attached to his hands and is shaping paths, different yellow brick roads out of the woods, except not yellow and not brick. The woman is smiling, at peace, like she knows she'll pick the right road. The man is expressionless, like he knows that fear is a choice or is so numb that, for him, it's over—fear has already won.

Back to Z. A guy and a girl are walking, hand in hand, along a path. From above, an angel, I guess, is holding a pair of wings in her hands and is about to send them to the guy and the girl. Wings of hope. This one is a little sappy in concept, but I'll edge it up when I do it in oil.

That's enough. I'll start painting tomorrow morning. Time for a swim. Right before I leave, I scribble on the edge of my sketch pad, *We shape our way out of here, like shamans of movement and light.*

#

I go down the long hallway in the west wing past John's room, toward the pool. Strangely, as I approach the master suite, the door is wide open. Every other day I've pretty much followed the same routine. Work for most of the day, then go for a late afternoon swim. John's door has never been open before. Maybe I'll finally get a look inside. When I reach the door, I slow to a stop. John is standing a few feet back from the doorway looking down at an unopened foreign letter, you know, made from super thin paper with a red and blue perimeter. They still make those? John's friend needs an email account. Anyway, I say, "Hi, John."

"Oh, hi, Paige. Swim time?"

"Yeah. Been sketching all day."

"Anything you want to share?"

"Not yet. Soon." I try to look past John, get a glimpse of his room, but all I can see is the alcove that has a closed curtain at the end of it. "See you later."

I enter the pool room, which is eighty degrees and humid. You would think that after growing up in New Mexico, I would hate humidity, find it suffocating. But I don't. There's something comforting about it, especially in this room. Maybe it's not the humidity that I love, but the contrast it dials up when I dive into the cold water. Yeah, yeah.

The pool is, well, huge. Like twenty-five yards long with four full lanes. I have no idea why John built such a big indoor pool, but I must admit I'm glad he did. I slip out of my clothes until only my black one-piece remains. I look good—quite mattressable to, well, the vast majority of the male universe. I pull the goggles out of my backpack and slip them on. One of these days, I'm going to wear them when I'm with Z just for the heck of it. Why not? Anyway, I dive in. The water is perfect. The chlorine smells the way something you really don't like smells after you've gotten used to it. Every ten or so laps on my way to seventy-two, I tend to switch strokes. The three B's—backstroke, butterfly, and breaststroke. I own them. I have no idea where I learned all of them, but I did somewhere early on. Probably my dad in one of his Paige-should-experience-everything moments. Here's the thing about swimming that I love—I hardly have any thoughts after lap ten, which I just reached.

When I finish, I pull my goggles off and look up. Second surprise of the day. John is sitting in a chair at the edge of the pool, smiling at me. It's quite the image. He's in his normal gray-suit-and-red-tie uniform, sweating, rapidly tapping his feet on the concrete. For a moment, I think he's tap drumming "Whole Lotta Love," but he's not.

"Been here long?" I ask.

"Since about lap twenty, I figure."

"Ahh."

"I didn't know you were such a good swimmer," John says.

"I love this pool."

"It's peaceful here."

"It is."

"I swam once."

"You don't swim anymore?" I ask.

"No."

"When did you stop?"

"When I built the house."

#

The next day, I finish the painting in the morning. It's spectacular. Maybe the best I've ever done. But I say that about all of my paintings and songs when they're done. Really, it's hard to know which is the best until they've been out there for a bit and the world has weighed in. Sometimes I need external yeah-yeahs to make sure I'm on track.

I'm on a roll, so I jump right into the song. I sit on the floor in my room with my guitar and stare at the painting for inspiration. A visual aid for the songwriter. Wow. Maybe I will write a book about my songwriting-painting process. But not yet. Can't write a book before the masterpiece. This song needs to be strong, up-tempo, start with the chorus based on my line from the other day. *We shape our way out of here like shamans of movement and light.* I've never written a song that starts with the chorus before.

For the rest of the day, I run my process pretty much like I've done on my earlier songs. I'm getting it down. Grace or my muse or a goddess helps me with the initial idea. Fragments pop from everywhere around me. Some old. Some new. No matter what, I stay open to all of them. I cut, paste, rearrange, and sometimes, when I'm really in it, I ride a wave to something magical. A multigenerational album is a collection in which each song has at least one wave embedded in it. Creative waves are like sperm—without them nothing worthwhile comes. At the end, just like the painting, "Shamans of Movement and Light" turns out to be my best song ever.

Chorus: We shape our way out of here like shamans of movement and light
Conjure whispers and elegies, guides toward a distant inside

Verse: We pass by a woman waiting, still hope, familiar eyes
She dreams unfilled, unspoken of fearless times

Chorus: We shape our way out of here like shamans of movement and light
Conjure whispers and elegies, guides toward a distant inside

Verse: We pass by a man wounded from a sudden loss
His heart is laid in time afraid to love again

Bridge: I remember when what we feared the most
Was the light, not the darkness
I remember when old spirits came
Handing down wings of hope
I remember when I knew I loved you
Shedding weight at the cusp of faith
I remember when we learned to stand with seven generations
Past, present, and unborn
Who helped steer us through fire and ash

Chorus: As we shape our way out of here like shamans of movement
and light
Conjure whispers and elegies, guides toward a distant inside

Verse: We pass by a man and woman who know love honors change
They keep pushing, pulling, leaning on each other

Chorus: We shape our way out of here like shamans of movement and light
Conjure whispers and elegies, guides toward a distant inside
Guides toward a distant inside
Guides toward a distant inside

#

About once a week, we take Solly for a super long walk at a local wildlife reserve. Today, the place is dotted with people walking their dogs or riding their horses on well-worn trails carved through hundreds of acres of woods. Solly, more a puppy around friends, darts from tree to tree, scent to scent, and plays with his morning dog mates.

On a circular trail around a pond, about halfway into the walk, Solly cannonballs into the water for a swim. Sometime later he pops out, does the wet dog just out of water thing and shakes off a few times, then bunkers down on the dirt beach. Despite mega-coaxing, John isn't able to move him off his spot. For maybe five minutes, John tugs on his collar. No luck. He sweet-talks a bit. "Let's go, big guy. I'll make you a steak when we get home." Not even the promise of steak does the job. As a last resort, John jogs away. Solly watches him for a moment, still in protest for an unknown cause. I have no idea who is going to win this one.

John waves to me to catch up. I do, even though I don't want to take sides. Right before we both go out of sight around a bend, I slow and glance back over my shoulder. Surprise, surprise. Solly is racing toward me at full speed, wagging his tail quickly as if it's his sole source of locomotion. Nice work, Master John. Forgive me for doubting you.

In no time, I'm back in the studio working. After a steak break, John and Solly join me to hear what I'm working on. I strap on the acoustic and play them "Shamans." You know, I've come to believe an early listen from John is a good thing.

Around midday, Solly wanders out of the studio through his doggie door, probably in search of a hidden bone. A short time later, still in our conversation about improving "Shamans," we follow his lead and do the hands-waving, super-connected walk-and-talk the short distance up to the main house. There, we piece together an organic salad and press some fresh juice. I made John buy a juicer last week, and of course, he's already become an expert.

"Did you see Solly on the way up?" John asks.

"No. Probably on a smelling vacation somewhere in the woods."

"Probably."

We both laugh, but just a bit. After lunch, we wander back out of the house and scan around. We go all-in and search the perimeter of the property. John shouts "Solly" every so often. I do the same. After combing through the woods for a time, we return to the house.

"Solly's lost for the first time ever," John says. He's looking down at the ground, incessantly fidgeting with stuff in his pockets.

I put my hand on John's shoulder, but just for a second. "We'll find him."

Between the house and the studio, there's a round wooden stage maybe four feet off the ground, fronted by a grass clearing big enough to hold maybe fifty lawn chairs. Sometimes in the summer, John lets the local musicians use it for concerts. He never goes himself, never plays, but at least he's really generous with his stuff. Just when we're about to go back in the house to regroup, on a hunch, I go over to the stage and look into the dark underneath. In the back corner against the far stage wall, golden-brown eyes move a little closer toward me. A soft whimper follows.

"Solly, is that you? What are you doing under the stage? John, Solly is under the stage."

A moment later John is by my side, scanning for an opening big enough to crawl through. How did Solly get in there? I shine my phone light under the stage to pave the way. John crawls under until he reaches Solly.

"Hey, boy. You okay?" John scratches Solly behind his ears for a bit and checks for blood and guts. "Good. Let's get you out of here." He nudges Solly. He pulls on his collar. Solly remains firmly planted. Finally, using his arms as forklifts, John slides them under Solly's belly, lifts up a few inches, and gradually pulls him, a few feet at a time, from the darkness.

A short time later on the grass, Solly rolls on his back and points his paws toward the sun. John scratches his belly for a while. "What were you doing there, Solly? I know your favorite place in the summer is the stage top, but not in the winter, and not underneath."

Solly rolls over, sits up, and hands John his paw. I give Solly a big kiss on the top of his snout. A moment later, we all make our way back to the studio.

#

The dog door flaps. Still foggy, I glance over at Fred and scan the floor for Solly. Why would he leave the main house and come to the studio in the middle of the night? I slip out of bed and into my jeans, careful not to wake Z. I creak down the wooden stairs, turn on my flashlight app, and look around. Nothing. Where's Solly? I could have sworn I heard him come in. I go outside and dart a circle of light from one place to another. Don't need to search long. Off to the side in front of the stage, right in the spot where John pulled him out weeks earlier, Solly blankets the ground, head between his paws. His tail wags once.

"Hey, big guy. What are you doing out here in the middle of the night?" Squatting down next to Solly, I rub his back for a time. I do my best John impersonation and try to coax him back into the studio. Finally, when it's clear Solly isn't going anywhere, I run back into the studio, up the stairs, and into my bedroom. Z is already awake.

"Something's wrong with Solly. Can you come outside with me for a bit?"

Z pulls over a T-shirt and slips into his jeans and sneakers. On the way out, he stops in the kitchen and fills a bowl with some milk from a gallon we keep in the studio refrigerator just for Solly.

Outside, sitting on the ground directly across from Solly, Z sets the bowl down. Solly raises his head, sniffs the milk, then puts his head back down.

"I've never seen him pass up milk before," I say. "Go get John."

I stay with Solly and pet him while I wait. There's this spot right below his ear that he loves having scratched. I spend all my time there. A short time later, Z returns with John. John hovers over Solly, with one arm holding the other at the elbow, and goes deep thought. Then he kneels down next to Solly and waves his hand over Solly's head a few times, like he's trying to heal him with one of his Zen routines.

"We should take him to the vet in the morning," I say.

"I don't think so."

"Why not?"

"It's his time. And he's where he wants to be."

"Why here?"

"Summer." John tears up, just short of crying. I've never seen emotion swell in him so quickly before. "Can you help me pitch the tent and get the sleeping bags?"

"Let's take him to the vet."

"It won't help. It's his time."

For the next hour, there's a flurry of activity around Solly. We pull a bunch of stuff out of storage. John pitches the tent, sets up the sleeping bags, fires up two propane heaters, and places a small oil lantern on the ground. Inside the tent, the two of us flank Solly. Nose dry, Solly hands one paw to each of us, forms a chain.

John and I mostly don't leave Solly's side for the next day. Z heads back to the city for work and school, though he wants to stay. During the day, John brings Solly maybe five bowls of ice cream, the only thing he'll eat. He blesses Solly with some mystical saying about the circle of life and sprays him with something that smells so much like pot that the tent appears to fill with smoke. I sing "Solly Solly" to the music from the little nursery rhyme of a song my Dad wrote for me long ago.

In the middle of the night, at first I'm not sure. I try to stir him awake; John does the same. I check for a heartbeat, for breath. Just like that, he's gone. You know the moment, the split second, when life cleared out of Solly was unlike anything I'd ever experienced before. Calm. Full-life-peaceful. Without a word, a gesture between us, John and I rest our heads on Solly's side, only an inch away from each other. We sob for a long time.

#

John and I are about to build a raft. A funeral pyre. Out of the wood from the stage, which we spent a good part of the morning crowbarring, ripping apart. John did most of the destructive stuff. He needed to; I guess sometimes comfort comes from destruction. Before we did the wrecking-crew thing, John circled the stage for about an hour, studying it like he was a sculptor staring at a piece of marble, like he understood that some objects lose their purpose when the person, or the dog, who loves them most dies.

There's a small pond on John's property, past the stage, about the size of one of those man-made ones you see in city parks. That's where we are now. Right on the edge. Later tonight, after we build this thing, we're going to set the raft on fire and launch it into the water. Good thing the pond is in the middle of a one-hundred-acre estate—no need to worry about the neighbors.

We go to work. We align the wood into a rectangular shape, six feet by nine, which sets the outside edges of the raft. Why are we building something so big? I'm clueless, but I follow John's lead. We mostly work in silence, only occasionally speaking when there's no other choice. Instead of nails, we use thick twine to connect the planks. John appears to be an expert at tying strange knots. He teaches me how to tie a zeppelin knot, which apparently is super strong. Really, that's what it's called. We use it exclusively to knot together the raft.

A few hours later, we're done. What a beautiful raft. Almost too cool to burn, but I get why John wants to do it. I kind of do, too. Yeah, we could have spent the day digging a hole, and we could have buried Solly, but somehow this seems much more fitting. John places some of Solly's favorite things on the raft. His bed. A chewed-up, deflated soccer ball. A few bones. Dog bowls. Solly, who's been on the ground next to us this whole time, looks no different from how he's looked during past late afternoon naps. John picks him up and places him in the center of the raft, on the bed, surrounded by all of his stuff. We pile the raft high with so many branches that it resembles a wooden teepee more than anything else.

Before I know it, it's dusk. We're ready.

John balls up a bunch of the twine and places it inside the teepee. He hands me a box of matches and nods. I light the twine as he pushes the raft into the pond. It floats out maybe twenty feet before coming to a full stop. Within minutes, the teepee is ablaze. The air fills with smoke, like cherry incense, like love. John reaches over and takes my hand. I'm glad he does. I was about to do the same thing. He just lost his only living relative, the only living creature who truly understood him, until me, the only one who truly loved him.

The fire slows, but just a little. What is it about fire that starts the big let-go? I'm not sure I've ever seen anything more beautiful. I mean, why didn't I do something like this after P, when I had so much anger? Pile his stuff high on the street outside of his apartment and burn it. Maybe throw in a few plastic Barbies for good measure. Ah, I'm mostly done with him, done with Barbies. When the P-waves come, like they just did, they're smaller and shorter. This is good.

A short time later, it's over. There's nothing left of the raft except a few charred pieces floating in the pond. Without saying a word, John turns away and leads us back to the main house.

#

Inside the house, John makes cappuccino. It's going to be a long night, so caffeine is a good idea. We settle at our go-to spot, the dining room table. I pull my chair closer to John, rest my hand on his.

"You okay?" I ask.

"I'm going to miss him."

"You loved that dog."

"I did."

"Me too."

We sip our cappuccinos until they're done. John pops up to make two more. He returns with the coffee and a full plate of Italian pastries from this place we go to in Worcester. In silence, we finish everything on the plate. Cannolis. Wedding cookies. Tiramisu. Sugar is okay tonight. And honestly, I have no willpower when it comes to that pastry place. John gets up, heads toward the kitchen to make two more cappuccinos. At this rate, I may never sleep again.

Then, as I'm watching him froth, the strangest thing happens—I sex-tingle.

I mean, the tingle has never even come close around John before. But here it is, and it's unmistakable. I try to shake it. I try to push it down. No luck. Okay, do nothing, Paige Plant. You've been through a lot in the last day. Don't screw up your magical gig, your platonic-love-with-your-male-Zen-master thing, just because of Solly, because of loss, because of the big let-go.

John returns with the cappuccinos, a bottle of Johnnie Walker Blue, and two shot glasses. Fuck, I'm toast. Tell him you're tired and you need to sleep. It's still early; he won't buy that. Tell him you're emotionally exhausted. Maybe. Yeah, yeah, that will work. Before I announce my escape route, John looks at me with those sad eyes, those big brown sad eyes, and you know, I just can't leave him. I mean, I'm the only one he has left. He needs me. Instead, I do the out-of-my-body thing and rise above the dining room table. From there, I watch the first shot disappear. And the second. And the third. After that, I stop counting and pay attention to real-Paige's sex-tingle, which has created this aura around her that's so large it's engulfed me, Paige-in-the-sky, in its full glory. Before I have a chance to pull the walk-away marionette strings, which, you know, I really do plan to pull, real-Paige gets up from her chair, sits on John's lap, and kisses him softly on the lips. I whirlpool back down into my body. Fuck.

"Paige, we really can't."

"I'm willing to give it a shot, John."

"I can't."

"Why? Don't you feel it?"

"I do. Don't get me wrong. You're a beautiful woman, and I do desire you."

"Why then?"

John turns his head away, which stays there until I gently guide him back into eye contact. From there, he says, "I haven't been with anyone since Grace died."

Wow, this is an unexpected turn. You know, I get the no-love-since-Grace bit. How could you love again after that? But no sex? I mean, the man is rich. In the worst case, pay for it, man, pay for it. But right now, you don't have to if you just say yes. Unless it's something else. Like what? His penis pushes up through his pants and says hello. Not that. What then? The sex-tingle drops from ten to seven on the one-to-ten scale. What to do? I could back off and let it go. That's probably the right thing to do. Get off his lap and create a little space. Yep, that's what I'll do.

I kiss him on the forehead and stand up. Better this way. Keep it professional. Keep it platonic. Focus on loving him as a friend, as a mentor, not doing him as a—as a what? Should I say something, or is this an expression only moment? As I'm tossing this around, I suddenly, unexpectedly, reach out and take John's hand. Pull him to his feet. Pull him close. Kiss him again. Even better than the first one. The sex-tingle dials up just past ten. Yeah, of course I've seen *This Is Spinal Tap*.

Before I know it, I'm pushing, pulling him toward his bedroom. Well, I guess that's one way to see what's inside that place. John is no longer resisting. Around a beautiful woman, even a man with integrity is only good to a point. Cross the rubicon, and no matter how strong, how principled, no matter how much he knows he shouldn't, it's mega-dwarfed by the yes-I-should. My second kiss did John in, and, well, the body wants what the body wants. Now there's a cliché I can actually get behind.

We reach John's door, which is locked. That's strange. The man lives by himself in the woods and he locks his bedroom door? Anyway, John reaches behind him and pushes maybe eight numbers on the keypad with one hand, as he hooks me close with the other. Under different circumstances, I might have used my considerable MIT decoding skills to memorize the numbers, but the sex-tingle won't allow it. We go into the small alcove, which beyond the curtain opens into a strikingly large room, the largest bedroom I've ever seen. Cathedral ceilings. A king-size bed. A desk. A load of books on his nightstand. An elaborate red rug with an abstract design covering the polished black concrete floors. A huge flat-screen TV opposite the bed; I had no idea they made them that big. Overall, the man has good bedroom taste. Or someone did it for him. Either way, I'm impressed. The far wall looks out to an enclosed courtyard. The spotlights circle different sections of a beautiful rock garden. Is that the pool on the other side?

A moment later, we're on the bed. We're still fully dressed, which is unusual for me at this point in the dance, but somehow that makes it even better. John gently moves his hands up and down my body, careful to work around my breasts, my vagina. His caresses are slow, deliberate, like he's an expert at pleasuring with his fingers, or at least has read a dozen books on the topic. No matter, it's definitely working for me. I kind of like this it's-all-about-me start that we're off to.

Time to visit the thoughtless bliss place.

Back again. John helps me pull off my shirt, my bra, then continues right where he left off. You know, at this point, part of me is ready to get on with it. But part of me isn't. I mean, it will take a few hours just to come for the first time at this rate, which might be my all-time record. Don't get me wrong, I'm not like a bunch of guys I know, the intense short-timers. But I do tend to timeout at around an hour, with plenty of room for seconds and thirds. Anyway, I trust John, and I'm kind of curious to see where he leads. I've learned a bunch from him on other stuff, so maybe.

John pulls off my jeans, my panties, and continues. Okay, so now I'm completely naked, and, well, John is still completely dressed. Another first. He's staring at me so intently; I guess I'm doing the same. Does the man ever blink? Eye-locked with him as his fingers are improvising all over my body is, well, artistically intimate. It's like he's painting and my body is the canvas, or he's writing the score to an elaborate fugue that we'll be able to listen to for years to come. Maybe we will. Magic Fingers seems to be done with the first movement.

He moves up one side of my thigh, and with two fingers enters me and, like that, we're into movement two. Hmm, maybe this won't take a few hours after all. Just as I'm starting to get into a groove, John slows down and says, "Breathe." Fuck John. Really, fuck him. Against my better judgment, I take a couple of deep breaths until I'm dialed back down a notch or two. He builds up again. Okay, I get it. He's creating waves. Cool trick. How long can he keep this going? Maybe my three-hour swag wasn't that far off.

Time to visit that thoughtless place again.

After a dozen or so waves, John pulls out and ends movement two. Talk about multigenerational skills. I thought this guy wrote folk songs?

He pushes off the bed and shuts off the lights. Movement three starts all mysteriously. Too bad. I am definitely a lights-on kind of girl, especially with his no-blink stare bit thrown in for good measure. John undresses and slips under the covers. I join him there. This is a little strange, given how naked and exposed I was for movements one and two, but I go with it. He hasn't let me down yet.

Under the covers, face-to-face, bodies pressed up against each other, we kiss for a long time. I mean, a really long time. His kisses go soft, hard, deep, shallow, with endless variety. He tastes sweet. Of course he does. I'm pretty sure I've never kissed someone this long before. Always got my fill after a few minutes and moved on to the next bit of good stuff. But with John, well . . .

He rolls over on his back and pulls me on top. Okay, this is pretty standard, but, hey, it's a start. Maybe I'll show him a pose or two in a few. He lifts me up a bit and enters me in one fluid movement. Not bad for a rusty old guy. I do my gauge thing and measure him as a belly-buttoner. Pretty good. Anyway, he builds; he stares. Same as with his tongue. Soft. Hard. Deep. Shallow. Slows when I get ahead of myself. Does the "breathe" thing.

For a long time, like an hour, we go at it. I mean, I'm well into hour two of John, and while it's not the most intense experience, it is by far the most sustained pleasure I've had. I can't think of another hour in my life where I've had so few thoughts.

"You're ready," he says.

"I was a long time ago."

"No you weren't."

"You can decide when?" I ask.

"Yes."

"How?'

"Practice."

"But you haven't . . ."

"It's like riding a bike."

John brings me home. And here's the thing: the wave thing that we did on the way up to this is also true afterwards. I mean, waves of Os, not just one. Another first. Yeah, yeah, like every other woman, I've read the articles about the multi-O thing, but honestly, until John, I thought that was just stuff journalists wrote to sell magazines. And I'm not talking two or three. I bet, if I were counting, it would be more like nine or ten. But I'm not.

Afterwards, almost immediately, I fall asleep in his arms.

#

In the morning when I wake, John is already gone. I don't recall the last time I slept coma-like. If last night ends up ruining our musical partnership, it may have been worth it. But, hey, maybe I can have it all.

I look out the window into the rock garden. It's filled with sand, perfectly placed rocks, and is meticulously landscaped, which takes some doing in leaf- and twig-infested New England. The windows of the poolroom are steamed. A silhouette passes by the first window, then the second, then the third. Could that be John? I thought he didn't.

I dress, wash my face in sink one of the large marble bathroom, finger-brush my hair back. Ah, the morning-after glow. It's especially bright today from establishing a new, a higher standard of what it means to get properly laid. Thank you, pyscho-killer-Zen-master John.

On the way out of John's room, I notice a bin filled with unopened letters on his desk. They all look just like the one he was holding in his hands the other day. Air-travel light. Red, white, and blue. Strange.

I head to the main pod. John is sitting at the dining room table reading *The Globe* in his normal getup. Guess he wasn't swimming. I walk over to him and give him a quick peck. Without saying a word, he gets up to make cappuccino, bacon, eggs, and whole-wheat toast. A short time later, he serves me, then watches me eat for a bit. I could get used to this.

"Who was swimming this morning?" I ask.

"I was. Thought I'd give it a try."

"And?"

"I like it. I think I'll keep going," he says.

"And last night?"

"That was a one-time thing."

"Oh." Okay, so I'm trying not to feel let down, but, I mean, it's hard. Yeah, yeah, I knew the John thing would never be a long-term gig because of age, because of my ambition, because I'm going to be on the road, like, forever in a few months, but why not ride the wave for a bit?

"That was about Solly," John says.

"Quite the send-off."

"It was beautiful."

"So why not ride the wave for a bit?" I say.

"You know why."

"Age and ambition."

"Yes. And that kind of love doesn't start with loss."

TALK

John and I hit pretend rewind and go back to right before my ill-fated decision to sit on his lap. Long walks each day, though they're not the same without Solly. More and more gourmet meals each week. Crazy long blocks of work, twelve hours a day, well into the night, mostly on mixing and mastering the first songs. The art in mixing and mastering—I had no idea. Pan a little more left. Compress a little more with less roll-off. A little drier on the vocal reverb. Teacher John is increasing my music vocabulary every day. Ignoring what happened is awkward for a bit, especially because I'm up for going a few more rounds before hanging it up, but, you know, it's not like there isn't a ton of other stuff to do.

I tell Z all about what happened, well, because that's what we've always done when it comes to romantic stuff. Really, that man knows way too much. He's been extra attentive since I told him, and he's even trying to duplicate the three-hour thing. But, hey, he's twenty-five. Sometimes physics rules out. And honestly, I don't want another John—I'm fine with Z's own brand. One of these days I'm going to find a man who understands it's all about variety, not about winning the I'm-the-best-lover-in-the-frackin'-universe contest. Though John might win if he would only do encores.

Anyway, today I throw myself into the next song, which—surprise, surprise—is not going to be a love song. Best to write about saving the world or something big when all you can think about is three-hour-slow-hand John. John gave me something to read the other day that pretty much said all of the world's indigenous cultures believe we're in a very dark period of our history. Without really knowing it, or maybe not admitting it, a corporationis-king world has emerged based on greed, on winning, on the worst forms of capitalism. Maybe I can write about that. It's certainly big enough, though I guess first I should figure out if I believe it's true. That's the thing about big topics. They're so complicated; there's so much information out there on them that you can turn anything into a cause, an us-versus-them anthem.

Still, there are a lot of people struggling in just about every kind of way. Maybe there's a way to speak to them, to paint them a picture of a better world, give them hope. Or maybe not. If the article is right, we're at a breaking point. No one can save the world. It's more about letting it crash and burn first, more about rebuilding after the big fall than about catching us before we go splat. Wanted: emotional warriors for the big do-over. Jeez, that's so depressing.

I'm sitting in my room, journal open. Nothing is coming. My first real songwriting block since I've been here. I hope this doesn't have anything to do with . . . Okay, I need a change of scenery. Go for a drive. It helped once before. I text John and tell him I'll be gone for the day. In no time, I'm on the Mass Pike. No music. Best to drive in silence when you're stuck. Eventually, I exit south toward Connecticut. There was this guy at MIT, R, who used to rave about a pizza place in New Haven called Frank Pepe's. Never made it there in college because R and I didn't last too long, but today, what the heck.

Two hours later, I turn onto Wooster Street. All of the stores, mostly restaurants, are Italian, just like where I lived in the North End. I feel comfortable around Italians, even though Dad never made a big deal of his cultural heritage. I mean, any culture that embraces food, music, art, and love gets my vote. Anyway, halfway down on the left side, there's this incredibly long line in front of Frank Pepe's. It's midday, a weekday, and the line must be fifty feet long. All this for a place that sells nothing but pizza? I park and get in line.

There's this guy in front of me, all Harley-ed up in black leather riding gear. Super handsome. Probably a D. For a moment, I consider the possibility that, after the fall, men like D will ride around on their bikes and put the world back together one person, one community, at a time. Now there's a pleasant thought.

"How long's the wait?" I ask.

"Probably an hour from here."

"Worth it?"

"Hell yes. I come almost every week."

"You from around here?" I ask.

"Graduate student down the street. Yale."

Well, that's a shocker. I mean, my khaki-polo-shirt-secret-society view of the place is shattered. The guy rides a bike and goes to Yale. I didn't think that was possible. I like him already.

"What are you studying?" I ask.

"Medicine."

"Ah."

"How about you? What do you do?" Probably-D asks.

"Singer-songwriter."

"Anything I would know?"

"First album will be out next year."

"Cool."

Okay, so now I'm convinced that Probably-D is going to lead a gang of motorcycle doctors around the country whose sole mission is to put us all back together once Frankenworld comes apart at the seams. When all the stitching is gone, will there still be concert tours? Yes. There's even more need for great music when things come undone. Look at the sixties.

Anyway, we spend the rest of the hour in line playing with our smartphones. I text Dad.

Hey, Dad, how's it going?

Well, honey. Busy at school. John still treating you okay?

Yes, Dad. He's been great.

I text a few friends, who I primarily stay in touch with through short little blurbs like this.

Hey. How are you?

Hey. Okay. Looking for a job. Need Cash.

Any luck?

Not much.

I could spend my whole day texting if I wasn't so busy becoming famous. At one point I look down the line and everyone, and I do mean everyone, is playing with their phones. You know, we could all be talking to each other instead.

When we finally get to the door, Probably-D asks, "Want some company for lunch?"

"Sure. Best to go to a pizza place with a pizza expert."

We're shown to our table. Frank Pepe's is pretty cool on the inside. Dark green wooden booths with tan tabletops fill two rooms. Each table is numbered. We sit at the last table, number twenty-five. At the back of the restaurant is this large coal-fired oven, which apparently is one of the reasons their pizza is world famous. Pizza peels with, like, twenty-foot handles are used to place the pizzas in the ovens. I've never seen a pizza peel with anywhere near that size handle before.

"Why coal?"

"Something to do with the temperature. The oven's approximately eight hundred degrees."

"Ah. So what's good?"

"All first-timers have to have a regular mozzarella pizza and the white clam."

In no time, the pizzas are delivered on these metal rectangular trays. The waitress brings us plates and utensils, but we eat the pizza right off the tray using only our hands. It's not sliced like normal pizza. Instead, thin, long rectangular slices make holding a piece with one hand pretty much impossible. But two works just fine.

On my first bite of the mozzarella pizza, I'm sold. I mean, I'm sure I've never had a better slice. Perfect crust. Perfect cheese and sauce. And there's this tangy aftertaste that makes you immediately want more. Same with the white clam, though in that case there's nothing to compare it to. The combination of fresh clams, garlic, olive oil, and crust is, well, to die for. I need to get John down here.

"These are great. Best I've ever had," I say.

"Yeah, me too."

"By the way, what's your name?"

"Dave. You?"

"Paige."

"You from around here?"

"Mass. Just down for the day."

"Just for the pizza?"

"A little more." Okay, D-who-I-knew-was-a-D-before-you-told-me, I came down here to get unstuck. And I do want to write a big song about saving the world, or at least rebuilding it, and now I'm sitting across the table from you, the motorcycle doctor gang leader and future leader of the free world, so I should take advantage of this opportunity. That's the thing about writing songs that's so hard—you never know where your next idea is going to come from, so you have to stay open at all times. And staying open can be exhausting. "I'm working on a new song and I'm stuck. Sometimes driving helps, and, well, next thing I knew I was here."

"What's the song about?"

"Something big like saving the world, but small enough that everyone can relate."

"That's ambitious."

"Yeah, I do the ambition thing well. Do you think any one person can save the world?"

Dave goes off someplace for a bit to think, which gives me a chance to study his perfectly chiseled face as I guide another slice of clam into my mouth. Finally, he says, "Not really . . . If you take one piece that I know something about, our medical system, it's so broken now that I'm not sure anyone can fix it. And that's just one system."

"Yeah, I get that. But there has to be something."

"My dad's a doctor in NYC. On 9/11, his hospital was flooded with patients. He helped many people that day, but that's not what he focuses on when he tells his story. He said for something like a week it was the most connected, compassionate time of his life. He connected with his colleagues, his patients, even more with me and the rest of the family."

"Yeah, I've read similar stories."

D opens a bottle of birch beer he ordered with the pizza, which I've never had. He pours me a glass, pours himself one, then says, "So, here's my take, Paige—for whatever reason, we've lost the ability to truly connect unless we're in crisis. It's sad. If you can write a song about connecting, something that puts us all into conversation, into the work of healing, I would buy it."

D and I finish our pizza and birch beer which, by the way, is much better than cousin root beer. We exchange phone numbers, say we'll stay in touch, though we both know that's unlikely. Why do people do that? I mean, what's wrong with having lunch with a guy you just met, doing the interesting-conversation thing, then never seeing him again? Why do we all have this need to say we're going to do something we really aren't? Anyway, I box some pizza up so John can try it when I get home. Apparently, the cheese is just as good cold. Not so much the clam. On the ride home, I keep coming back to D's comments on the power of conversation. He's on to something.

#

A week later, I'm still stuck. The deadline is tomorrow. Wouldn't that be something? You know, I sleep with John, get writer's block, get kicked out of Harton because I miss the deadline. What would I do then? I mean, I can't really do *The Big Wide Calm* without him, can I? No. Failure is not an option. I'm going to write the damn song today, and it's going to be great. The best I've ever written. All I need is a kick-start, and then I can build from there.

I go to work. Down a whole carafe of coffee in like ten minutes. Need to spark this thing. Best to start with the lyrics when writing a big song about saving the world. I mean, the music is super important, too, but the lyrics have to be front and center. A listener needs to say, "Wow, that's really what's going on and that really is the way it should be." Sometimes repetition in a song like this works best. Pick a phrase and carry it through, even in the verses. Yeah, yeah, of course that will happen in the chorus, but if you're trying to get the whole world talking, you'll probably need to say it more than once. You know, you probably have to say it seven times. And there it is—the whole world talking. I pick up my pen and write:

> *Can you see us all talking*
> *About where we've been*
> *Where we need to go?*
> *Like children again*
> *Curious*
> *Like old souls*
> *Willing to let go*
>
> *Can you see the people*
> *Living in harmony*

Fuck, that last lyric is too much like "Imagine." Okay, strike that. But the first verse is okay. Let's switch to the music and see what comes up. I lift up my guitar off the bed, play around, search for a simple melody to go with the verse. Strum simple chords. In D. When people hear this, the words should be front and center, and the music should support it. But not million-times-used-before chords. Something catchy. I cycle through strange chords I learned from Dad when he was going through his short but important Police phase, find a few that are pretty good, string them into a progression. Play it about twenty times to make sure. Okay, there it is. Let's see if I can get another verse before I move on to the chorus. I'll carry forward the can-you-see bit from the first verse.

Can you see us all talking
About the violence
In all shapes and forms
About why what we've created
Isn't working
About how we're in a perfect
Storm

Shortly after I finish the second verse, I hear John pop in downstairs. Good time for a break. Good time to see what he thinks of the first two verses. I pick up my guitar by its neck and escort it down to the studio. The room smells like cologne, like way too much cologne, and not something I recognize. Didn't he ever learn that when it comes to the new-scent thing, less is better?

"Hi, Paige. How's it going?"

"Okay. New cologne?"

"Yes."

"Nice. I'm working on my new song. I think I have the first two verses. Wanna hear?"

I sit down at the magic piano bench and play John the first two verses. He asks me to go through them a few more times. He has this incredibly serious look on his face, different from any look I've ever seen from him, more purposeful. After I finish the seventh round, he's still silent. Fuck. He thinks it's bad. Writing these big songs is too hard. I need to go back to something I'm better at—love songs, break-up songs, whatever—something I have some experience doing. Dad was wrong. It's not really possible to save the world with your music.

"You've caught one, haven't you?" John asks.

"What?"

"A flier. Every now and then, we songwriters catch a flier, a song much bigger, better, than anything we could have imagined."

"That's what you think of this song?"

"Absolutely. But I'm already on to the chorus. The chorus has to be incredible, a big enough payoff after the build from the first two verses."

I haven't thought about this yet, but he's right. That's the thing about John. When he thinks you've done something boffo, he's already on to the next bit, pushing you to go even further. I've got to bring it all together at the chorus. Fuck. I *have* to bring it all together in the chorus and, you know, I've only got a few hours left. "Yeah, I agree."

"Want to play a game?" John asks.

"I'm out of time, John. I need to finish this thing, like, now."

"The game will help."

"Oh," I say.

"Game?"

"If it's fast."

"Pick four words that pop into your head right now. Don't think about it. Whatever comes to mind."

Okay, I know he said don't think about it, but I already am, but I haven't thought of any words yet, which is good, I guess, but I want to, which I guess is bad. Fuck. Stop. Take a deep breath. Clear out the clutter and get on with it, girl. You need to get back to work. "Talk. Free. Love. Connected."

"Okay. Now I'm leaving," John says.

"You're leaving?"

"Yes. Go back upstairs and write your chorus. Let me know when you have something."

"That's the game?"

"Trust me."

I do trust John, even after he dumped me. Well, okay, he didn't dump me, but he didn't do what I wanted, which is kind of the same thing. Anyway, I head back upstairs. Set up crossed-legged on the bed, journal in front of me, guitar on my lap. My favorite writing pose. I replay the verses. I say, "Talk. Free. Love. Connected," a few times. I wait for it, until I'm completely in sync with the song, until I lose track of time and space.

"One with the song" is what John would say. Then magically, in a wave, it comes:

> *Let's talk it over*
> *Build something*
> *Ground up*
> *From love*
> *Let's talk it over*
> *Don't you see?*
> *We're all connected*
> *You and me*

That man. How did he know his little trick would work? That's one of the benefits of being sixty. He's had all those years to try what works and what doesn't, to distill things down to little Zen-master games. Every twenty-five-year-old woman should have a John. Oh, I didn't mean it that way.

#

Recording day. In the studio, I teach the musicians "Talk," which they pick up pretty fast. Simple song, I guess. Then something strange happens. They perk up, tell me it's a cool song, start improvising off the main bit, ask me what I think about this or that. Well, this is a first. You know, even the string players aren't giving me their usual hard time and actually have a decent idea or two. For the first time, I feel like I have my band's respect, like they're following me more than John, like they know they're part of something bigger, of *The Big Wide Calm*.

We record the first take. Listen back. Not bad, but we can do better. I push them a little more. They respond well. Around take three, everything clicks and the song dilates. The moment a song opens, when you know you've got it, is, well, orgasmic. As a songwriter, it's also sad because you know you're done with it, but mostly the good kind of release. "Talk" is in the bag.

After we finish, no one wants to leave. Another first. Everyone is chatty; one guy asks me if I've pulled together a touring band yet. Another wants to know what else I'm working on. The cello player wants to know why I like Led Zeppelin more than The Beatles. I rattle off some stuff about Jimmy Page being a great guitar player, about Robert Plant's voice, about John Bonham's drumming and, you know, all of it's true, but none of it's the real reason. The real reason I like Led Zeppelin more is because my dad does. He passed it along, and for as long as I can remember, I've accepted it as true. But here's the thing—these days I like The Beatles just as much. And The Rolling Stones. And Pearl Jam. And Nirvana. And Mumford & Sons. And just about every other female artist out there. I love them all. And here's another thing—none of the songs I've written sound like Led Zeppelin. Or The Beatles. Or anyone else. They sound like Paige Plant. Fuck. Did I just say that?

We decide to alcohol up. John invites everyone to the main house. As soon as we get there, he breaks out beer, wine, and the top shelf stuff. I had no idea he had so much hard liquor in the house. After the first pour, John starts serving all kinds of finger food. Nachos. Chicken wings. Chips and dip. Vegetables and dip. A cake, a pie. Pints of ice cream from our favorite place. I mean, I know the guy has been into cooking lately, but when did he stock up for a party? How did he know this was coming?

Anyway, it's getting late and everyone is talking and laughing in the living room. John even pops open one of his poetry books and reads a poem about a journey, which everyone goes silent over. But only for a few seconds. Then we're back to talking and drinking. I need to call Z and get him out here pronto.

Instead, I wander off into the west wing, beer in hand toward the pool. Best to go skinny-dipping when you're right in the thick of catching one. Best to float in a giant body of water. Chlorinated water, but, hey, that's just a detail. Even though I rarely get drunk, I feel a little tipsy now. The water will balance me out.

I slowly make my way down the hallway, my hand pushing off the wall occasionally to keep me true. When I get to John's bedroom door, there's a crack in it. How come he didn't lock his door? Okay, Paige, get on with Plan A and float, balance, in the pool. That's why you wandered off. That's what you really need. But, you know, there's this pull like there's this black hole inside and I'm dangerously close to the event horizon. Maybe I should go inside for just a few seconds. If I see his bed, maybe it will help me let go, stop me from playing what-if. Yeah, yeah, that's it. I'll be in and out in a few and on my way to the pool. Though, if there really is a black hole in there, I may never get out.

I go in. I stand in front of the bed for a few seconds. That night. But I can't stay with it long. It's too much. And I feel guilty. I mean, I can't be dishonest like this with John. We've come too far for this kind of breach. I turn to leave. Make sure I haven't disturbed anything. No harm done. Just get out and it's like it never happened.

On my way out, I glance over at the desk, which still has a bin of unopened letters on it. What the heck are they all about? At the desk, I hover for a bit, a short bit. Then I reach into the middle of the bin, pull out one of the letters, fold it in half, and slip it into my pocket.

At the bedroom door, I wipe the door handle clean with the bottom of my T-shirt. Best not to leave any prints. Once I'm out of the room, I skip toward the pool. I have no idea why I'm skipping because I've done this maybe once since I was ten. But, hey, it's been a good day, and it's what I want to do, so I go for it. A few moments later, I'm floating naked in the pool.

THE HALL

I hide the letter between my mattress and box spring. At some point, I'm going to either read it or destroy it. Haven't decided which one yet. You know, I can't believe I snatched it. I was drunk. And if he'd only said yes to continuing our little thing, I wouldn't have gone in there. So in a way, it's his fault. Maybe I should just come clean with him now. Or put it back. Instead, I leave Harton and go on the road with Z for a few days. After "Talk," it seems like a good time for a break.

In the car, at first, we're not sure where to go. NYC? Portland? Quebec City? Montreal? But in the end, the choice comes easy. We head toward Cleveland in the 335i, to the Rock and Roll Hall of Fame. Here's the thing about the Hall. Yeah, yeah, it's great in just about every way, but I'm going there for two reasons—Led Zeppelin and the women. To get us in the mood on the way out, I queue up all nine of the Zep studio albums. We listen to them in order. Probably the last time I did something like this was with my dad when I was in high school, and it feels good to do it again, to start at *Led Zeppelin I* and go all the way to *Coda*. Z doesn't much like Zep, which I forgave him for a long time ago, but he's happy to go along for the listen as we pass by farm after farm on the New York State Thruway. How is it possible to not like this band? I mean, they are rock gods, and, well, a combination like Page-Plant only comes across, like, once every fifty years.

After we finish Zep, which takes us all the way to Erie, we decide to break for some much-needed food. We search for a quick-off/quick-on option and settle for a local fifties diner right off the highway. Inside, we order a couple of cheeseburgers, fries, and two chocolate milkshakes. Not exactly the healthiest choice, but John would like this place, and, well, if you're going to do a fifties diner, you might as well go all in. I scan the place as I wait. Pictures of Elvis. Jukeboxes. A poster of a pretty woman advertising Coca-Cola. I don't know why so many people think the fifties was the best decade. Yeah, yeah, it had Elvis, but what else? I mean, weren't American women enslaved back then? What's good about that? And who was that everyone-is-a-communist guy? Anyway, I'm starving, and when the food comes, elbows on the table for support, I down half the cheeseburger in just a few minutes.

"What?" I ask.

Z grins. "You eat like a guy."

"Hey, your kind is good at something."

"I'm glad we're doing this. I even liked the Zep buildup."

"Really?"

"They're growing on me."

I smile. That's the thing about Z—he's teachable, which counts for something in my book. I mean, he's not really a music guy. And he doesn't really get me that way. But he sure tries hard, and there's something to be said for people who adore you. Anyway, I finish the rest of my cheeseburger, pick on a few fries, take my first swig of milkshake. Not bad, but clearly made with cheap store-bought ice cream. Jeez, I can't believe John's turned me into an ice cream snob.

"For the rest of the way, let's listen to the women," I say.

"The playlist awaits us in the car."

Here's a not-so-pretty one about the Rock and Roll Hall of Fame: of the mega inductees, only a small percentage are women. Like one percent, I bet. Aretha Franklin. Tina Turner. Ruth Brown. Etta James. Janis Joplin. Martha Reeves. Gladys Knight. Grace Slick. The Shirelles. Joni Mitchell. Stevie Nicks and Christine McVie. The Mamas from The Mamas and the Papas. The Staple Singers. Bonnie Raitt. Brenda Lee. Chrissie Hynde. Debbie Harry. Patti Smith. Madonna. The women from ABBA. The Wilson sisters from Heart. Donna Summer. Yes, I have the list memorized. Sometimes I add my name at the end just to see if it fits. Of course it does. Anyway, I guess the lack of women in the Hall is just like it is in every other profession, but it's got to change.

Back in the car, from Aretha to Chrissie to Donna, we listen to Z's playlist. It's inspiring, and maybe halfway through, I have this incredible urge to go for a quickie. A short time later, at a rest stop somewhere in Ohio, we do the back-seat thing, which because it's so small limits our options. But, hey, we make do. It turns out okay for both of us, and in no time, we're back on the road. For a long time, Z has a huge grin on his face.

"What?" I ask.

"I've never been with anyone quite like you."

"What does that mean?"

"You know what you want and you go for it."

"You're just figuring this out now?"

#

I feel like I'm in the Vatican staring at the Sistine Chapel. Except I'm not on my back. And I'm not looking at angels. Though Robert Plant and Jimmy Page were pretty angelic in their time. Well, maybe not angelic, but definitely sexy. Is there a sexier voice in the universe than Robert's? You know, if I lived in the seventies, I would have done everything in my power to be a Zep groupie. I would even do both of them now if I had the chance. Preferably together. It's kind of my ultimate sexual fantasy. Who did you have sex with, Paige Plant? Page-Plant.

Anyway, the exhibit is inspiring. There's a history of Zep, most of which I know already, but it's cool to see it in one place. I do come across this line by Jonesy that I like a lot: "The very thing Zeppelin was about was that there were absolutely no limits. We all had ideas, and we'd use everything we came across, whether it was folk, country music, blues, Indian, Arabic." That's a cool philosophy, and it doesn't just apply to the songs. I was also able to see Jimmy's black dragon suit along with a bunch of his guitars, one of Bonzo's drum kits, and Jonesy's onion jacket. You can't take pictures, but I didn't want to anyway. It's better that way. I mean, what's wrong with a one-of-a-kind experience without photo-enhanced memories?

After Zep, Z suggests we tour the whole place, you know, to get our money's worth. So we do. And while there's a ton of stuff that's worth seeing, from a Beatles exhibit to The Who, I find myself gravitating to the women. I mean, in their own way, each of them was super strong, super talented, though the cost of fame weighed on many of them. Some had to sacrifice having families. Others never found love. Others had addictions. The one thing they all shared is they put the music first. Janis Joplin loved the blues, loved Bessie Smith, Billie Holiday, and Lead Belly. There was so much emotion in her voice. And she had the coolest stuff. There's this really striking reddish God's eye made of all different color yarns on display, and a psychedelic Porsche with so much color I knew it had to be hers. And what about Etta James? Is there a better love song than "At Last"? Has there ever been a singer with more hot-blooded eroticism in her vocals? What a role model! And then there's Chrissie Hynde, who owned her rock band, was a great singer-songwriter, wrote blunt lyrics in weird time signatures. An absolute genius, though the one place I lose it with her is on this quote: "It's never been my intention to change the world or set an example for others to follow. I just wanted to play guitar in a rock and roll band and make music that people could dig." I mean, why bother? Right?

Someday, Ani DiFranco will be here. Someday, Aimee Mann will be here. Someday, I'll be here.

After a full day in the Hall, we spend the night in Cleveland before heading out in the morning for the long drive home. I haven't thought about the letter since I left—well, all right, maybe a little, but not much. One way or another, I need to move on it when I get back.

#

First thing I do when I get back to Harton, back to John's, back to my room, is check underneath the mattress for the letter. Still there. I unpack, rest a bit, send Z off with a quickie to Cambridge. It was a good trip, and he's a good friend with good bennies. Will see him next weekend. Or sooner.

What's John been up to? After a quick shower to wash off the road, I go up to the house and slip in. John's sitting at the dining room table reading something, dressed in his habitual attire. I've been gone only a few days, but I've missed the charcoal suit, the lazy eye, the long conversations. He doesn't notice me at first, or maybe he does but is in the middle of reading some esoteric thing that only three people on the planet understand. Anyway, I'm not used to announcing my arrivals, but this one time I'll make an exception.

"Hey, John."

"Oh, hi, Paige. I didn't hear you come in."

"What did I miss?"

"Not much. How was the Hall?" he asks.

"Great. Ever been?"

"No. But I've read about it."

"I figured. It was all about Zep and women."

"Not enough women in the Hall."

"That's for sure."

"Oh, there is one thing. I had a business call with a music executive on another topic. Turns out he's looking for an opening act for a band he's managing, Dakini Bliss. Mostly a major U.S.-city tour. Thirty cities over a three-month period. He asked if I knew anyone."

"And you told him about me?" I ask.

"I did, but I also told him you were in the middle of recording your album."

"Best to finish the album. I'll be the headliner when it's done."

"That's what I figured," John says. "I did tell him he could come out and meet you. Sound okay?"

"Why not?"

John and I chat about other random stuff. Somehow the conversation, or maybe just seeing him, makes me sure. After we're done, I walk back briskly, almost jogging, to the studio. Once inside, I run the stairs to my room, but instead of putting the lights on, I use my phone as a flashlight and pull the letter out from under the bed. Sitting on the bed, I shine a light on it for a long time.

The handwriting on the envelope definitely belongs to a woman. There is no return address, but the postmark is from Italy about a year ago. So John knows a woman in Italy who writes him all the time and he never reads her letters. If it weren't John, I would find this strange, but I learned to go with the flow on John's stuff a long time ago, and I'm sure he has his reasons. I mean, part of me likes the fact that he isn't answering her. Best to stay focused on me and TBWC. Best not to have any distractions.

For a moment, I consider destroying the letter. That's what Z said he wants me to do. But I don't. Instead I call him.

"Hey. I'm about to open the letter."

"Are you sure?"

"No. That's why I'm calling you."

"You know my take. If you read it, it may ruin everything."

"I know. Just needed to hear it again. I'll call you back in a few."

Here's the thing about the letter: Z is right. I definitely shouldn't have taken it in the first place, and I definitely shouldn't read it now, and I definitely should just destroy it. Jeez, three "shoulds." There should be a law against so many in a row. Anyway, it may ruin everything, but I have to read it. For reasons I can't explain, I need to know who this woman is and why John isn't reading any of her letters. But not here, not in my room.

I run down into the studio to make sure no one is there, even though I already know the answer. It's late, and everything is dark except for a few red, green, and yellow lights on some black boxes that John forgot to turn off. I flick on the overhead and sit down on the piano bench. The envelope stares up at me one last time. I take a deep breath and gently open it, careful not to rip anything. I unfold the letter, which is only one page and scented with a perfume I don't recognize. Not that I would recognize a lot of perfumes, but I definitely don't recognize this one. It's nice, like jasmine and honey. Anyway, I start to read.

Dear John,

I hope you are well. Even though I no longer expect a response, I keep writing. I need to and, who knows, maybe one of these days you'll finally forgive me and answer one of my letters.

I'm well. I'm still living close to my parents here in Bologna. I'm still in the same house and still running the same café. There's a young singer-songwriter who just started playing here on Friday nights. He reminds me of you when you were just starting out. He writes the same style songs. His lyrics, even though they're in Italian, remind me of yours. And he has the same emotional intensity that was your calling card back then. At one point, I was convinced he'd heard our first album, but then I caught myself and remembered that was impossible.

The kids are well. Jack is still working in London at the bank. He's still writing songs and occasionally plays out for fun. Nothing too serious. He's still married to Angie. Their twins are also well. Hard to believe, but they're almost ten now. And Joanie is still in Rome. She's painting and living off of her trust fund. Her pieces are stunning. I wish you could see them. Oh, and she has a new love, Roberto. He seems to be good to her, though anyone would be an improvement over Cale.

How's my piano doing? I trust you are taking good care of her. I miss playing. I miss sitting at the bench with you, working out our parts.

I know I've said this a million times, but I am truly sorry, John. Please, please forgive me. We were good together once. It's almost unbearable not having you in my life after so many years together. I know we can never go back, but why not have at least some sort of friendship? And this ruse that you're dead is so unfair to the kids. They deserve to know the truth.

I know I signed a contract, but isn't there another way?

Love,
Grace

Fuck. Grace is still alive and living in Italy? And the kids? And John hasn't forgiven her, so does that mean he didn't betray her? Why would John lie to me about something like this? He could have told me anything. It would have been okay. And why won't he see his kids? And his grandchildren? You know, I can get that maybe he doesn't want to see her anymore, but what kind of man gives up on his kids to live alone in the woods?

And I knew there was something about this bench.

Okay, what to do? Call back Z? I told him I would. He's expecting it. But I can't tell him. Z's not good at hiding his feelings, which I love about him in almost all cases, but not this one. John will know as soon as he runs into Z next time, and, well, that would be a disaster. Just call Z and you'll figure it out real time. Yeah, yeah, that's what I'll do. I push Z on my phone. With the phone to my ear, I tap the case repeatedly, waiting for Z to pick up.

"Hey."

"What did you decide?" he asks.

"I burnt it."

"That's good, Paige. I knew you would make the right call."

"You were right. Thanks for the advice," I say.

"You're welcome."

"Gotta go. Weekend?"

"Sure."

I don't feel good about lying to Z. You know, it may be the first time I've ever lied to the man. But it was the only way. John can't know that I know. At least not from Z. And once I figure out what I'm going to do, I'll make it up to Z and tell him. He'll understand; he always does.

I spin around on the piano bench, place my hands on the keys, and pound my part of "Chopsticks," striking the keys so hard that for a moment I'm afraid I cracked a bone in my index finger. One of these days, I'm going to have to take Dad to the Rock and Roll Hall of Fame.

UNNAMED SONG ONE

I'm in the studio working on my next song. A week has passed since I read the letter. I haven't said anything to John. Not sure if I ever will. I mean, I did steal the letter, and I guess if he wanted me to know the truth, he would tell me. It's really none of my business, and it doesn't change any of the work we're doing on *The Big Wide Calm*, so why stir things up?

I did stir things with Z though. When he came to visit me this weekend, I asked him to stop and buy four long silk scarves, you know, the kind older, well-dressed women wear all the time. Until last Friday night, it seemed like a waste to put perfectly good arms and legs out of commission even for a bit. But that night tying Z up worked. I even put my swim goggles on for added strangeness. There's an image.

Anyway, this song is slower, a ballad. I haven't figured out any of the lyrics yet, but I woke up in the middle of the night a couple of nights ago with a melody in my head. I popped out of bed, grabbed my guitar, and played it over and over again to make sure I had it. I can't tell you how many times in the past I've gotten an idea in the middle of the night, convinced myself I would remember it in the morning, then was unable to recall a frackin' thing when I woke.

I'm just starting to work on the bridge when John comes in with this guy dressed in a perfectly tailored, I'm guessing handmade, suit just like John's. Do they have them made at the same place? At least his tie is yellow. He's probably in his mid-thirties, with shoulder-length sandy blond hair. He's John's height and well built, though it's hard to tell if that's him or the suit. I can't help but stare at two pockmarked scars on his face, one on each cheek.

"Acid," the man says.

"What? Sorry, I didn't mean to—"

"No worries. Everyone does."

"Paige, this is the man I told you about the other day, Ian Summer."

I walk over and shake Ian's hand. "Paige Plant." Talk about a spark. Not since P. You know, the whole scar thing is a real turn-on. I mean, everyone's got ugly stuff on the inside, and they go to elaborate lengths to cover it up. Case in point—liar-John. Having the ugly stuff on the outside like Ian does is more honest. Especially when it's combined with an otherwise very attractive package. And Ian's in the business. And presumably rich. And young.

"Paige, would you mind playing a few of your songs for Ian?"

"No problem." Actually, no problem at all. Maybe I'll even drag this out. I grab my guitar, sit on the piano bench. John and Ian pull up two foldings within five feet of me. They cross one leg over the other at exactly the same time. Of course they do.

For the next hour or so, I play almost all of my stuff, old and new. As I play, neither one of them says a word, but Ian occasionally smiles or taps his foot. At one point, he leans over and whispers something in John's ear. You know, critical silence between songs is intimidating, even for someone with an infinite amount of confidence. It's probably some weird music business test, which I'm sure I passed with flying colors. After I finish my last song, I rest my hands on the top of my guitar and wait for Ian to pass judgment. I mean, isn't that the primary role of a music business executive?

"I'm speechless," Ian says.

"I noticed."

"You're very talented."

"Oh . . . thank you. John helped a lot with the new songs."

"They're the strongest of the lot."

"I think so too."

I slip my guitar into a stand next to the piano and pull the bench closer to John and Ian. John seems to be a little disturbed that I moved the bench.

Good. With my hands palm-down on the bench for support, I cross one leg over the other. Best to match these guys when talking business.

"John told me you're not available right now."

"I need to finish the album first."

"Too bad."

John gets up and goes over to the refrigerator. Ever since Solly died, he's been drinking a large glass of milk each day. Only whole milk. And only out of the studio refrigerator. He pours himself a glass and sips it on the way back to his chair. Sitting again, milk mustache and all, he says, "Paige, I've been talking with Ian about promoting your record next year."

"You're not going to do it?" I ask.

"Not my area of expertise. Ian will do a much better job for you."

"Paige, if you're available, maybe we could have dinner tonight and talk about how I can help?" Ian says.

"Sure. You in, John?"

"You two go. I've got a meeting in town, and I tend to doze off whenever someone mentions a marketing plan."

#

Ian picks me up promptly at eight in an all-black Ford pickup. Not exactly what I expected, but I kind of like that the man dresses in a three-thousand-dollar suit and drives a truck. He's made a reservation at this high-end Italian restaurant, L'Andana, which is in Burlington and specializes in Tuscan food. You know, lots of meat and pasta.

When we arrive, it's apparent within seconds that Ian has spent a lot of time at this place. The valet parking attendant calls him by his first name. The hostess is waiting for him at the front door with two menus in hand, calls him "Mr. Summer," and shakes his hand. She smiles a so-this-is-his-latest-protégé smile at me, then shows us to an out-of-the-way table at the back of the restaurant. Even though Ian hasn't said a word about wine, within a minute of sitting down, a bottle of Italian red is delivered, uncorked, decanted.

"I hope you like the wine," Ian says.

I smile and take my first sip. I've learned just enough from John to know this is no ordinary wine. A brunello, bold, and the aftertaste is great. I nod. This may be the first time in my life that I'm speechless around a man.

"Shall we order?" Ian asks.

"Sure. What do you recommend?"

"A three-pasta sampler to start. They're all good, so why pick one? And the steak is perfectly done."

We order our food. You know, I like the man's philosophy of samplers. I like the fact that he's well known here. I like his wine selection. I like it that he pretty much ordered my meal for me. Actually, I just like the man.

"So you want to be famous," Ian says.

"Not just famous. I want to be around for the long run. I want to create multigenerational albums that make the *Rolling Stone* Top 500. I want people to acknowledge *The Big Wide Calm* as a masterpiece."

Ian smiles.

"What?"

"We're going to get along just fine, Paige."

The waiter delivers homemade Italian bread to our table. I break off a piece and dip it in olive oil, which is infused with hot peppers, garlic, Parmesan. It's probably the best oiled bread I've ever had, especially when I down it with a sip of red. Before I know it, I've devoured all of it. Did Ian have any at all?

"Shall I order more?" he asks.

"It's so good, but I need to save room."

"Right. Shall I tell you a little bit about how I can help?"

As Ian speaks about tours, media exposure, Facebook, Twitter, and T-shirts, it gives me an opportunity to really study his face. His eyes are a shade of blue I'm sure I've never seen before. A tinge darker than cobalt. Though he's clean-shaven, his beard is heavy. He probably has to shave more than once per day. His scars are symmetrical, three lines on each side, almost like war paint, but without the color, scar tone.

Right when he's in the middle of saying something about something, I ask, "Why didn't you have your scars fixed?"

He stops speaking and smiles. "Oh right, we never got that out of the way."

"What?"

"When I was fifteen, I discovered sex in a big way. I slept with a lot of girls at school over a three-year period. During one stretch, much to my surprise, I slept with a couple of older married women from my neighborhood. One of them turned out to be my father's mistress, who was trying to get back at him for not leaving my mom. When my dad found out, he pinned me down on the floor one day and poured sulfuric acid on my face in the patterns you see here. Said he was burning me for my own good. Said the scars would keep me from ever sleeping with a married woman again. Truth be known, it's worked so far."

"I'm so sorry, Ian."

"Don't be. It turns out that the scars made me stronger. It's like I went into the physical pain from the scars, the emotional pain from basically losing my dad forever, and found all that I now have." Ian picks up his wine glass and spins it between his thumb and index finger, like he expects the whirling wine to show red-filtered images of something. "So I wear the scars as a badge, as remembrance of where I came from. I don't want to have them fixed."

"Did you ever forgive him?"

"For me."

"What does that mean?"

"I forgave him for me, so I don't carry around the hatred. But I have no relationship with him now."

The waiter delivers the first course on these long, narrow rectangular plates with three bowls placed on them. He tells us about each bowl. The first is garganelli with a lamb bolognese sauce and pecorino. The second is conchiglioni, handmade seashells with Maine lobster, Vermont butter, and sea salt. The third is bucatini à la carbonara with house bacon, baby pea greens, and pecorino. The smell—the pecorino, bacon, bolognese melded together—is, well, a turn-on. John's been trying his hand at gourmet cooking these last couple of months, and he's quite good at it, but nothing like this. I sample each pasta. Ian's studying me, waiting for my reaction before he eats, which, strangely, I like.

He smiles and digs in. "So what do you think?"

"The pasta is the best I've ever had."

"No, I mean about working together."

I eat more pasta. Slowly. Best to pause here so it looks like I'm thinking it over. I've already made up my mind, but, honestly, it has nothing to do with his marketing pitch. I mean, anyone who can survive a violent act like that and end up stronger is more than okay in my book. And it was with his dad. I can't imagine my dad doing anything other than helping me, never mind harming me. And then there's the sex-tingle.

"I think there's something worth exploring," I say.

"Good."

"But probably not until I'm done with John."

Ian fidgets with his fork before finishing the last of his pasta. Why the hedge? From the get-go I told him I wouldn't be available until after the album was done, so what's the big deal? And I doubt if attraction like this is going to go away in a few months, so really . . .

"I like the title of your album," Ian says.

"Me too. Though I'm still trying to figure out what it means."

"'Talk' is the best song so far."

"I think so, too." Okay, this is all well and good, but not hedge-worthy. Need to get to the bottom of this. Best to see if he can touch, speak of the feeling. If he can . . . "You seem uncomfortable with waiting until I'm done."

"I am."

"Why?"

Ian smiles, this time in a way that lights his whole face, dwarfs his scars. "Do you feel the spark?"

Well, there it is. Ian's feeling the same stuff I do. Not only that, but he said it out loud. I really like this man. "I do." My face warms, and I'm sure I must be blushing, except I'm olive-skinned and I don't blush, though if I ever was going to, it's probably now. "You know, we could date until I'm finished. We don't have to combine work and dating, do we?"

"People like us don't date."

"Why?"

"Because we love our work. They have to be combined or it won't happen."

Well, there it is again. Sometimes someone says something that I've never thought of before, but as soon as it's out in the ether, I know it's true. The only way I would be with someone steady during the next ten years, more than the way I'm with Z, is if we're working together. There's just so much to do artistically, business-wise, fame-wise. And I'll be on the road constantly, conquering the world. There's only one way to do all of that and have a lover at the same time. "You're right. So, what do you think we should do?"

"Let me help you finish the album."

"John's not a collaborative guy that way."

"I can take care of John." Ian picks up his wine glass, reaches across the table in toast, in lust. "Deal?"

I nod. The waiter delivers our steaks. They're covered with arugula and shaved Parmesan, and they look more like salads than steaks. I'm starving and dig in.

"What's the steak sauce?" I ask.

"A balsamic reduction. So, are you seeing anyone now?"

"Z. He's a friend with benefits."

"Z?"

"I call all of my male friends by the first letter of their name."

"Not John."

"Except him."

"What will you call me?"

"I haven't decided yet." Judging from the look on Ian's face, a poorly disguised frown, this is not the answer he was hoping for. But, I really don't know yet, which is further than I normally go at this point in a relationship. I mean, anyone other than Ian would already be an I.

We eat our steaks mostly in small talk, which gives Ian plenty of time to process my haven't-decided answer. At one point, this well-dressed, beautiful, forty-something woman comes over and gives him a big hug along with a peck on each cheek. Then she gives me a you're-just-passing-through look. I wish her well, too. You know, my hunch is this is a man who people rarely say no to, so there's this unexpected benefit to my original no-to-the-tour answer. Just say no, Paige Plant. Do it often and unexpectedly. I guess this is a little manipulative, but someone has to put the guy in his place. And it's best he knows that in all of my romantic relationships, I'm always the stronger one. Well, except for John, though I'm not sure I would classify that one as romantic.

After well-dressed woman evaporates, and we finish our meal, Ian asks, "How about this? I have a loft in Boston. Let's skip dessert and go back there. We can spend the night, then I'll drive you back out to Harton in the morning, and I'll talk with John about working together."

Okay, best to pause again. The sex-tingle is at full throttle, though I think around Ian I need to rename it. Maybe sex-buzz. Or sex-quake. My heart is beating so fast that I'm afraid I'm going to break out sweating in, like, nanoseconds. I'm trying not to show too much, but honestly, I can't help myself. Without saying a word, I fold my linen napkin, put it back on the table, stand up, and take Ian's hand. Who is this guy?

#

Today is telling day.

Ian and I exit from Route 2, drive through Harton center, and stop at The General for coffee, which is better than usual this morning. Coffee in hand, we make our way to John's. Harton in the spring must be one of the most beautiful places on the planet. Everything is in bloom. Everyone is out on the streets. The sky is a sheet of blue, without a single cloud for protection. Like home in New Mexico, there's no humidity. Pretty much paradise.

Last night with Ian was great, but not what I expected. The sex was fine all by itself—Ian has pretty good skills. But that's not what got to me. What got to me was how much we talked, how much we laughed, how much both of those got mixed together with the physical stuff. You know, I've always been comfortable in bed with my partner, but Ian stepped it up a notch, balanced me, pulled me toward home. Though, given we're both so ambitious, it's unlikely we would ever be there. I guess I've met my match when it comes to conquering the world. Here's one small example: out of the blue and right in the middle of, well, everything, he mentioned one of his favorite songs, "Everybody Wants to Rule the World" by Tears for Fears. This song is from the eighties, and not many people my age or his know it, but it's also one of my favorite songs. What are the chances?

Anyway, I'll tell John first. Yeah, yeah, Ian said he would take care of it, but best to do this one on my own. Later, I'll tell Z. He'll understand. He knew I was only passing through for a bit. He's cool that way. I come and go as I please, and he never judges, never asks me to stay. He's just thankful for the time we have together. I don't think I could ask for anything else in a friend. A lifelong friend. I'm not sure what to expect from John though. I have a bad feeling about it in the base of my stomach, in my shoulders, but I can't pinpoint the reason. Maybe it's because John's a loner. I can't imagine him collaborating with Ian, especially after I tell him Ian and I are now lovers. Or maybe it's because John and I spent our after-Solly night together. I don't know.

We enter the studio. My eyes widen. John is sitting at the piano bench surrounded by three puppies, who look like mini-me versions of Solly. They're the same off-white color, with the same silver streak on their backs, and they're doing their best, without much luck, to climb up John's legs. My shoulders tense even more, which only a few minutes ago I didn't think was humanly possible. How could he replace Solly so soon? Flat out wrong.

"Wow, three," I say.

"One wasn't enough."

"What are their names?" Ian asks.

"Stillness, Shaman, and Talk."

I smile, release my shoulder clamps one turn. Okay, I must admit, those are cool names. I'm honored. And the silver-backed mini-Sollys are cute. Maybe this will soften John a bit to my news. Or maybe not. No matter, best to get big news like this out there right away, best to say it calmly and clearly so there's no room for interpretation, best to—ah, just say it, Paige.

"Did the two of you have a good night?" John asks.

"Yes. I showed Paige L'Andana and my loft."

John cracks a faint smile and nods once.

What does he mean by that? Did John know Ian and I would end up together? No. How could he? Not even Zen-master John can predict who I'll take on as a lover. Anyway, back to just saying it. "I have a bit of news, John. I'd like Ian to collaborate with us on finishing the rest of *The Big Wide Calm*. Sound okay?"

"Do you think it will help?"

"Yes. Especially because he's going to help me promote the album next year."

John pops up off the bench and goes to the refrigerator, entourage in tow. There he pours milk into three small bowls for the pups. A moment later, he's back on the bench, ready to verdict. "I'll never be able to replace Solly, but these little guys are a lot of fun. And this place was made for more than one dog." Still sitting, John reaches over to Ian, extends his hand, and says, "Welcome aboard."

That was much too easy.

#

Later that day, I drive into Boston in the 335i. Best to tell Z face-to-face. When something like this has happened in the past, that's what I've always done. And it's always worked like a charm. Best friends with occasional benefits. That's who we are, though for the first time ever, future benefits are more of a question.

I take Z out for dinner. My treat. We don't do expensive places like L'Andana. Cheap is better. Always has been. After a little back and forth, we decide on Borders Café, which is his favorite Mexican place in the Square. They make their own nachos, their drinks are, well, gigantic, and for about ten bucks, they have the best fajitas in the city. They also serve you fast, which is a plus for a conversation like this one. In no time, we're eating chips, fajitas, and we're on our second round of Negra Modelos. There's something great about dark beer.

I take a swig and begin. "I have some news."

"Shoot."

"I met someone yesterday. Ian. He's a little older and in the business. He's going to help me next year when *The Big Wide Calm* is done. Last night, we became lovers."

Z does the lump in his throat thing, goes pale.

"You okay?"

"So this is one of our back-to-just-friends conversations."

"Yes."

Z's gaze ping-pongs for a bit between the napkin holder and the flat iron skillet holding what's left of his fajitas. Wow, he ate fast. A moment later, he reaches across the table and interlaces his hand with mine.

"You know, Paige, I love you."

"I love you too, Z."

"I always will."

Okay, Z's last line is not leaving me all warm and fuzzy. That's how I normally feel when he uses the most overused lyric in the world, which he's done many times over the years. As I have with him. "But?"

The waitress comes over to check on us. We order another round. Z doesn't normally drink this much beer, but tonight he's holding his own. She's tall, blonde, pretty. Z's attracted to her, as apparently are the vast majority of men in the restaurant. I scan the restaurant one more time just in case my least favorite letter is in the audience. Our order in her head, the waitress scurries off. Z checks her out for a bit, then returns to me.

"Paige. I love you, and I'm *in* love with you. I probably always have been, but I didn't want to say it out loud until now. Some things you can't take back."

"Oh."

"I know it's not the same for you."

The waitress returns with round three. Z guzzles down, like, half the bottle. I do the same, which is strange because I never guzzle a thing, but, hey, I want to match him.

"I need to go away for a while," Z says.

"But you're in school."

"Sorry, I mean I need to leave this relationship for a while."

Did he just say that he needs to leave? How could he? He's always been here for me. Fuck. I mean, we're best friends. Why does he want to leave? You know why, Paige Plant. Because he was holding out hope. Because he thought that maybe one day I would fall in love with him. Because today, for the first time, he sees something different on your face, something new, something about Ian.

"For how long?" I ask.

"I don't know."

"Give me a feel. Weeks? Months? Years?"

"Months."

"Months?" Okay, maybe this whole thing with Ian is a mistake. I mean, I can't imagine not seeing Z for months. I talk to him every day. I tell him everything. We do the benefit thing well. Months? "Why so long? Why is this time different?"

"You're going to make me answer that?"

"I just don't understand."

"Ian is different."

#

With Ian on board, it's time to get back to the follow-up to "Talk." Ian's office is in downtown Boston, right off of the Common, and while he travels a lot, he's been around for most of this week. I've pretty much seen him every day at the studio, though I spend most nights in Boston at his place. Best to limit Ian's visits to the Harton Woods to daytime. There's something about having him stay in my little room that doesn't seem right. During the last few days, we've talked a lot, laughed a lot, gone for long walks, snuck in quickies, but I haven't done a lot of writing. Or painting. We've chatted about both, but not much has come from it.

Anyway, today it's time to get serious about the new song. It's still a ballad, and it seems like writing a love song is even more the way to go now. I have a couple of weeks left before we start recording it, so that should be plenty of time to get something done, even if I've wasted most of this week.

I go down to the studio. On days like today, the true first day of a new song, John gives me space, pretty much like he's done all week. Somehow he knows just when to pop in and just when to stay away. For sure, he knows I have to do this part on my own. You know, that's part of the joy and the burden of being a great songwriter—we create art from nothing by ourselves. Anyway, guitar on my lap, I get comfortable on the magic piano bench and search for a riff, an alternate melody that I like. After a good hour of checking out different fragments, I'm not happy with any of them. Some are boring. Some are derivative. Some are okay, but not up to John-inspired multigenerational standards.

Sometimes a change in instrument is all it takes to spark an idea. I switch to piano. One of the things Dad taught me early on was to improvise on the piano. Even though I'm not a great player, there are times when I'll just sit down and start playing and, like that, an hour has passed. I hit record on my handheld recorder, which John gave me the other day, which, by the way, all songwriters should have to capture creative stuff as soon as it comes up, and

I begin to play. Music flows out. I have no idea where this stuff comes from, but come it does. I'm kind of a poor-woman's version of this guy Dad loves, Keith Jarrett, who improvises all of his stuff. After a bit, I stop. Lots of notes, passages, but nothing worth saving. I hit erase.

Maybe another change of scenery will help. I go for a walk and ask John to meet me. A short time later, we're at the head of our favorite trail with the pups. We make our way into the woods. The forest floor is mottled by sunlight. The pups dart from tree to tree, like Solly did on days when he beat his age. At one point, Shaman flips over in a circle of sunlight and warms his belly.

"I was surprised to hear from you on a writing day," John says.

"Yeah, yeah, me too. Zero progress today."

"Down?"

"Just the opposite. I've been really happy this week. Ian and I are getting on really well."

"Ah."

Well, there it is. John's famous little one-word-tip-of-the-iceberg answer. The man has seen every possible songwriting scenario before and has exactly the right solution at his fingertips for this one, but he won't give it up right away. He's going to make me work for it. It's annoying . . . and almost always helpful. "What does that mean?"

"You only have so much energy."

"And?"

"You have to choose."

"Between what?"

"Falling in love and multigenerational art."

Is that really true? I've only been with Ian a week. Am I falling in love with him so quickly? John is saying pretty much what Z said the other day. I'm getting it in stereo. But why do I have to choose? Why can't I have it all?

"Falling in love uses the same energy as creating art. In a way, you're making music with your lover. There's none leftover for the song," John says.

"I don't accept that."

"I know. You'll probably write decent songs. They just won't be great. They'll rehash old ground or unintentionally copy an artist you admire or . . . fill in the blank."

I'm only one day into this song, but there's something about what John just said that's true. How can that be? While I forced myself to write today, I was more interested in going to Boston to see Ian. It's a beautiful day. And I feel, well, better around him. He's my canvas, my soundscape, but apparently not my muse. John still holds that title. Along with teacher.

"I'm not sure I believe you," I say.

"I know. Ride it out for a while and decide for yourself. Maybe you'll prove me wrong."

The pups get tired about halfway through our walk, so we cut it short. We carry them back to the house. I hold Shaman like a baby, front paws over my shoulder. Every now and then he licks my ear. He smells good; the fresh air has infused his fur. Even though all three dogs are John's, I feel like Shaman is mine, like if I had to choose, he would be the one. But it will be years before I can have my own dog. The road will keep me from my own Shaman.

Over the next week, I write the song. It's still unnamed. Ian is involved every step of the way. He helps me choose between different musical bits, I run lyrics by him, and he even helps with the melody. He's not a musician himself, but he has a good commercial ear. He's all about what will sell albums and, more importantly these days, concert tickets, which is where the real money waits. I continue to see him every day and night, and by time the song is finished, I'm convinced I've proven John wrong. Strange thing is I haven't shared the song with him yet. I mean, it's almost like he dared me, and, well, I didn't want to come back to him until I beat the dare.

Anyway, today is the big unveil. John has assembled all of the normal musicians. Just like on the other songs, we'll spend a few days learning it, and then we'll record it in a few takes. I run the guys through the chorus first. *In the underlight you're familiar, warm / as our silhouettes move across the room / In the underlight I see you best / faithful to no single form, completely free.* They nod, smile, pick it up quickly, though there isn't the same chatter or energy like there was after "Talk." Except from Ian, who already seems to be trying out marketing ideas with the musicians. This one could be the single. Women will love it. It's about love *and* freedom. The man can teach me so much about the business. Or I can just let him do it, which is probably better.

John is mostly silent throughout, which is fine. You know, he's still processing, still distilling it down to a few sum-up words that will help me move the album forward. One of the finest of his many skills.

Seeing the two of them side-by-side, each one so different, brings back the bit about how a woman can't get everything she wants in life from one person. I love John. He's my teacher, my friend, my muse. I owe him so much, even if he is a big liar. And apparently I'm falling for Ian. He's my lover, my future business partner, maybe the father of my children. Is it really possible to know something like that after such a short time? I don't know, but he's off to quite the start.

Toward the end of rehearsal day, the band tightens up and the song comes together. I'm happy with it. It's not as good as "Talk," but it's a solid album track. And it is multigenerational, despite all of John's warnings. It's late. I tell the band that's enough for the day. I ran the entire day myself, which is becoming easier and easier to do. After the musicians leave, John, Ian, and I hang out to debrief. John opens a bottle of wine and pours three glasses. Some Italian type I've never heard of before. Valpolicella.

"So what did you think, John?" I ask.

"You made progress today."

"You're there," Ian says.

I glance over at Ian, who's sitting across from me next to John, and smile at him. I sip my wine. He does the same. He gets the message and will be silent for the rest of the conversation. While I love the fact that he's already my biggest fan, I don't need praise now. John needs to tell me what he really thinks of the song, what, if anything, will make it better. It's time to push, not rest in rainbow-tinted land.

"What else, John?" I ask.

"We should go into salvage mode tomorrow."

"Salvage mode?"

"Sometimes what emerges doesn't cut the muster for a multigenerational song. When that happens, it's worth spending a few days to see if you can salvage it."

"Does that work?"

"Sometimes."

Okay, two things. First, is John talking salvage because it's what he predicted would happen and because he has to be right? Wouldn't be the first time a man had to be right in this world. Or is psycho-killer-Zen-master-liar John actually telling the truth? I'm not sure, though there's no evidence he's ever lied to me about songwriting. Second, it's time to bring Ian back into the conversation. He looks like he's going to explode if he doesn't say something soon. And I did bring him on board for exactly these kinds of conversations. Best to balance the creative and business sides of things if mega-fame is the goal. "Ian, what do you think?"

"I understand what John is saying, but I disagree. I think we could take that song on the road tomorrow and it would help you sell your record."

"That may be true," John says.

"But?" I ask.

"In its current form, it doesn't belong on this album. It's just not strong enough."

"How would we salvage it?"

"We'd ask the musicians to improvise. Maybe a jazzy version. Or one that's more atonal. Or even a country version. And I'd ask you to do two or three versions of the melody that we can meld together with the different versions. Then we'll see where we are."

"What happens if it doesn't work?" I ask.

"We'll add a month to the process. You'll write a thirteenth song."

"Having B songs is a good marketing strategy," Ian says.

"Okay. Let me think about it."

We finish our wine and say goodnight. It's too late to drive back to Boston with Ian, so I guess he's going to spend his first night in Harton Woods. We go up to my room. It's clear Ian hasn't been in a room like this, well, for years, but he's good about it. He undresses, neatly folds his clothes, and slips into bed. I'm still getting used to the neat streak, but, hey, it's a small price to pay.

He smiles his fool-around smile, but I'm still on John's point.

"What did you think about John's idea?"

"The song works for me as-is. I don't think you need to change a thing."

"It probably doesn't hurt to try."

"It takes more time, which adds up. You have so much talent, Paige. You could be out there now."

"I'm not ready yet."

"I don't know about that. You could take the five new songs plus the best of the first fourteen and that could be *The Big Wide Calm*. If you did that, you could open on the Dakini Bliss tour."

"I need to stay the course."

"Think about it." Ian gives me his fool-around smile again. The man is so persistent.

#

In the morning, I salvage. You know, there's no harm in trying, and I'm okay with a few extra days. For the full day, we try out different ideas. A jazzy version. A country version. An atonal version. The musicians like it, since they're shaping the song even more than usual. I also play around with the melody, which at first I'm hesitant to do because it came to me in a dream, and I've always operated by the never-change-an-idea-that-comes-to-you-in-a-dream rule. Truth-up, some of the variations are better than the original. We also make new versions by adding, subtracting parts. The pared-down version. The lush, fully layered version. At one point, we play around with different reverbs, compressors, EQ, panning, doublers—the stuff you normally spend more time on when mixing. Here's an important one: trying to salvage a song with these things probably means the song isn't very good in the first place.

John repeatedly and effortlessly nose-dives from fifty thousand feet to ten and back again during the day. In one moment, he's commenting on the melody, and in the next, he's debating the merits of panning the guitar to two or three o'clock. Watching him work at so many levels is inspiring—he's all-in, and he knows so much about songwriting. Those are two of three things you need to make multigenerational art. The third is talent, which I'm okay on. Oh, and maybe there's a fourth—luck. That's also been going my way lately.

At the end of the day, "Unnamed Song" is much better, but I agree with John, it just isn't good enough. My first throwaway from *The Big Wide Calm*.

Even Ian agrees now. In the morning, he was quiet. I mean, he made it pretty clear last night what he thought, and for the first few hours, he seemed to be waiting for me to come to my senses. He wasn't in a full-blown pout, but, well, almost. In the afternoon, he perked up and started weighing in. He clearly liked some of them, the jazzy one in particular, better than others and lobbied for those versions. By the time I made my final decision at the end of the day, he was already back on his B-song point from the previous day. You know, I always liked albums where the not-good-enough-to-make-it songs end up available to the public. Some good will come from cutting "Unnamed Song."

"Thank you, John," I say.

"For what?"

"I learned a great deal today. Sometimes making multigenerational art means throwing out one of the babies. But first you have to do everything you can to save her."

John smiles.

"And doing everything requires a lot of knowledge."

"Or at least a knowledge of what you know and where you need help."

"That too."

"It's a good song," John says.

"Just not a great one."

"That's true."

Truth from liar-John. Oh well, enough about John, Grace, and the letter. Will I ever tell Ian about the letter? Probably not.

Ian and I say our goodbyes to John and head back to Boston for the night. In the car, we cycle through the first five songs from TBWC a few times. "Unnamed Song" definitely doesn't stand up to the others, and I'm even more sure I made the right decision. There's a calmness that comes from letting the song go, from knowing that I did everything I could to salvage her, from releasing it to the B-side netherworld. You know, deciding what to jettison may turn out to be the hardest part of becoming famous.

PENANCE

Early pool day. I've got stuff do later in the day with Ian, so I need to get my swim in now. I'm still religious about the swim thing and am pretty buff as a result. I make my way out of the studio toward the pool, wearing just my black Speedo and flip-flops. The weather has been fantastic lately. Sunny. Mid-eighties. New Mexico-esque. For a moment, I consider jumping in the 335i and heading to the town beach, which fronts this Walden-like pond, but I don't. I've become accustomed to chlorinated water, to the twenty-five-yard pool-blue lap, to the compound.

Anyway, I reach the main house. Ian's truck is parked in front. Strange. He had an engagement last night in Boston, so we spent our first night away from each other since L'Andana. I mean, I expected him out later in the day, but not this early. No matter, I'll slip in and surprise him. He's never seen me in my Speedo before, and I'm sure he'll like the view. Maybe he can join me for a swim—no bathing suit required.

In the foyer, just as I'm about to announce myself, I overhear John say, "Let her down easy."

"I will. I do care about her," Ian says.

"I do, too. More coffee?"

What the—? At this point my flip-flops freeze me in place. Mega-weight is going to crush me down, pancake me so nothing taller than an inch remains. Where are the pups? Please don't give me away before I can move again. Who exactly is he letting down easy? Me? Someone else?

"Here you go. Another double espresso. The test was for her own good. And she made the right decision. She put multigenerational art first, above fame," John says.

"Still, I feel bad about the whole thing. I wish I didn't agree to help you in the first place."

"Years from now, she'll thank you."

"I doubt that."

"Just tell her you're going on the Dakini Bliss tour and you won't be around. Tell her it's best to end things before they get too serious."

You've got to be kidding me! The whole bit with Ian was a setup? A giant test to see if I would make the right choice? I can't believe John would do that to me. And Ian? I thought we had something. I mean, I was thinking he might eventually be The Guy, or at least my steady on the road for the next ten years. How stupid is that?

One of the pups barks. Fuck. Exposed. Then another joins in. Finally Shaman. I knew he'd be last. I can still slip out and John and Ian will probably never know, or I can confront them. Not much of a choice, I mean, I would never run. Best to go in guns blazing and give them a piece. A moment later, I join them in the kitchen.

"Guys."

"Paige?" Ian says.

"In the flesh . . . On my way to the deep end."

"Nice suit," Ian says.

"Too bad you'll never see me this naked again."

"What?"

"I heard you guys. A test—really? You planned the whole thing? You needed to know what I would do? Look out, world—Ian and John, two of the world's greatest assholes, are at work. Oh, and on choosing multigenerational art over fame, let me make it real simple for the two of you. From this point forward, neither of you will have anything to do with my career. I don't need you. Never did. Do you even understand how fucked up what you did is? Stupid question."

"Paige, I can explain," John says.

"Fuck you. I'm out of here!"

"Paige." Ian stands up and takes a step toward me.

"Don't. Oh, and one more thing, John—I know Grace and your kids are still alive, you fuckin' psycho."

I storm out of the place, run back to the studio, grab some clothes, and jump in the 335i. I head toward Cambridge, toward Z.

#

Z isn't at his apartment. I text him. No answer. I know he said he needed a few months away, but this can't wait. I'm in pain; I need him. And I'm sure he'll be okay with the news now that Ian is out of the picture. At least, I think he will. Anyway, I head over to his lab.

Sure enough, he's in the lab tinkering with something that looks like a mini-version of the particle collider at CERN. I don't hesitate, walk right up to him, give him a big hug. At first he hedges, holds his arms a few inches from my body, but soon after he gives in, returns my hug. Everything is going to be okay.

"I have news," I say.

"I gathered."

"The thing with Ian was a test."

"Of what?"

"Me. John wanted to see if I would pick making the album over going for fame too soon."

"Really?" Z asks.

"Yeah. I picked the album."

"I'm sorry, Paige."

"Want to get some food? I need to vent."

"Give me ten."

Z goes back to playing with his collision gear while I wait for him in a nearby office. I feel better already. There's something to be said for a man who you tell everything to, who's always there for you no matter what, who has an extraordinarily long—strike that last bit. You know, it's less complicated with Z when we don't do the benefits thing. And, really, we only do that when I'm lonely and horny, so maybe it's time to rise above the big I and respect the rest of what we have. Especially since he confessed his love during the last round. It's not fair to keep jerking him around. Though I guess he gets something out of it, too. I guess we should talk about it and decide together. Okay, there it is.

Z pops his head in the office. We head out of the lab, out of MIT, and onto Mass Ave. We walk for a bit in silence. Z reaches over and drapes his arm over my shoulder and pulls me off balance a few times as we walk a city block. I smile. I miss the city. Life wasn't so bad before John, before Ian, before the Harton Woods.

"Do you think the benefits part hurts us?" I ask.

"Sometimes."

"Do you think we should stop?"

"Sometimes. There's a lot here without it."

I wrap my arm around Z. I'm sure everyone we pass thinks we're lovers, and it's kind of cool that we're not. I mean, how many best friends get through the one-sided thing and come out closer? Pretty amazing. Pretty honest. I certainly can't say that about liar-John or liar-Ian. I'm done with those two.

"What will you do about John?"

"He's toast. I'll make *The Big Wide Calm* on my own. Can I crash at your place?"

"Always, but—"

"But what?"

"You need John. The album will be better if you stick in there with him," Z says.

"Fuck him."

There are so many restaurants on Mass Ave. of just about every variety. Indian. Italian. Chinese. Afghan. Sri Lankan. Vegetarian. We stop to look at the menu at this vegetarian place that specializes in cleansing smoothies. Z stands behind me, let's me lean back on him, wraps his arms around my waist.

You know, he has a point. The first four songs with John really were better than anything I'd ever done before. Even "Unnamed Song." But how many more of these little head games can I tolerate? I mean, enough is enough, right? "I don't know. The man has so many secrets. For all I know, he really could be pyscho-killer John."

"You don't believe that. Dump Ian for sure, and, yes, I'm biased. But use John until you finish. Dump him then if you still feel the same way."

"Want to go for one last all round before we nix the benefits piece?"

"I thought you needed to vent?"

"That is venting."

#

The next day I head back to the studio. Overnight, Z convinced me to work things out with John. I called ahead and told John I wanted to speak. Surprise, surprise, he said any time, said he'd wait for me in the studio. You know, Z is right; *The Big Wide Calm* will be better with John, and he's mostly been good for the music. Manipulative, but good, which I didn't believe was a possible combination until Z made the point. Anyway, I'm not sure how things will go today, but I'm willing to give John a shot.

Ian's truck is in front of the studio when I pull up. Fuck. I'm not ready to see him, to have that conversation. I take a deep breath. And another. Best to get it over with, I guess. I step into the studio. Where's John? Ian is sitting on the magic piano bench. He does a little half-wave, followed by a little half-smile. He must feel really bad—he doesn't do anything halfway, which is, well, was one of his best traits. I pull up a folding, flip it around so the back faces him, and straddle it.

"I'm surprised to see you here," I say.

"I came to apologize."

"No need, Ian. You were just doing your job. Now it's done, so you can get back to your real love."

"It started off as a job, but I did feel something."

"Right."

"I did. Is there anything I can do that will make you believe me?"

Well, the simple answer to that question is no. But wait. String it out. Delay. Best to hold out a little hope before I slam the door on the fucker. Okay. That should do. Good to go. "The hole you dug is too deep."

"I'm so sorry, Paige."

"So am I. We're done here."

Ian stands up, tries to give me a goodbye hug, to which I shake my head no way. A moment later, he's out the door. Good riddance. As I watch his truck pull away, I riff on the fact the all-or-nothing quirks of romantic love are convoluted at best. I mean, one day I'm falling in love with the guy, planning out our next ten years, renaming the sex-tingle because of him, and the next I'm telling him the hole is China deep and we're done. I guess that's the way relationships go, but it's so bounded, so black and white. What would the world be like if love wasn't so fragile, so humpty-dumpty-ish? Anyway, one knotty conversation down, one to go.

I boil water for coffee. Best to let John come to me. I'm sure he'll figure out Ian is gone and it's his turn soon enough. Ian probably called him, or he was watching the whole thing on surveillance cameras. Probably the latter. I pour the water into the carafe. Fair trade, shade-grown, organic Ethiopian stuff floats to the top—my only bit of joy so far today. At the magic piano bench, I pour myself a cup. A few sips later, I pick up my guitar off the stand next to the piano and start playing. "Ian, Ian, bo-bian, banana fanna fo-fian, Ian. Asshole, asshole, bo-basshole, banana fanna fo-fasshole. Asshole." Almost as if my "assholes" summoned him, John enters the studio. He's brought the pups with him—I'm sure as part of his soften-Paige strategy. Won't work, but I'm happy to see Shaman, who immediately lopes over to me and tries to jump up on my lap. I pull him up. Apparently, he knows who is going to win this round.

John flips the folding around and sits down. "Hi, Paige. How did it go with Ian?"

"Why are you asking me a question you already know the answer to?"

"Why burn bridges? He can help you down the road."

"I can help myself. I'm done with Ian. Let's move on."

John straightens up in his chair, shifts about, repeatedly curls one hand inward.

Good. Just wait. He has no idea what's coming. "I'm debating if we should continue working together, John. I can only do it if you meet my conditions."

"Like what?"

"No more games. No more manipulations. No more secrets. No more Zen-master stuff. Just direct and honest conversation on how to make the best possible multigenerational album. We'll partner side by side on every song. Agreed?"

John taps both feet on the ground very fast. Talk and Stillness think it's a game and wag their tails as they try to bite the tassels on John's alligator loafers. He looks down, and while playing with them says, "Sometimes I let you figure things out on your own, even though I know the answer."

"All or nothing. Take it or leave it."

John goes distant for a bit, tries to cover it with dog small talk. Finally, he says, "Okay."

"Good. I'll put this all in writing and ask you to sign the contract."

"What?"

"You heard me. I want all of this in writing in a contract."

"Why?'

"Because maybe you'll actually honor it if it's in writing. Which brings me to my final topic for this conversation. I want to hear the whole Grace story. No more lies, no BS about cars, sex, and cliffs. If you can't tell me what really happened, the deal is off."

John reaches down to the floor and picks up Talk. His voice goes all childlike as he tells Talk what a good dog he is for a long time. Finally, he says, "I'll tell you the whole Grace story, Paige. When would you like to hear it?"

"Tonight at dinner. Make something earth-shattering, and break out the really expensive wine. It's your penance."

#

I dress up for dinner. Really. I spent the entire afternoon shopping for a fancy dress, pumps, the whole getup. Last time I dressed like this was in high school. That's not true. I've never dressed like this before. Back then it was about a boy, about a future memory, about what all of the other girls were doing. This is about pure unadulterated power.

In front of my mirror, I slip into a black sleeveless dress. It fits perfectly and highlights my arms, which are fit and toned from all of the swimming. I clasp on the fake pearl necklace and earrings I purchased earlier in the day. They look fantastic with the dress. Going classic, when you're all about everything but, works perfectly in a play-against-type way. You know, this dress-up thing may have legs.

I'm not a makeup girl. I had to buy mascara, blush, and lipstick today. Never wear the stuff, at least not yet, but, hey, if you're going for a look, it's best to go all in. John taught me that—well, not about looks. Now I'm going to play it back to him in a big way. When I walk into the main house tonight, before I even say a word, he's going to know he's lost his power, his control. He's been messing with the wrong woman.

After a little extra time to put on my makeup, I'm ready. I slip into my pumps, which, at four inches, are not that easy to walk in. Who invented these things? And more importantly, why? I'm tempted to Google an answer, but I don't. Anyway, after I master them in no time, I make my way to the main house thirty minutes late. Yeah, yeah, being late is also part of schooling John. Instead of walking in, I ring the bell. He should come to me.

A moment later, John opens the door. "Wow. You look beautiful."

Good start. Men around beauty. Put on a little black dress, pumps, some makeup, and they think you're a goddess, which, of course, I am, but still. John is dressed like John is always dressed. Nothing special. The man is so fixed in his ways. Maybe it's too late for him; maybe not even a contract, a little black dress, can whip him into shape.

We make our way to the dining room table, which is beautifully set. Candles. Flowers. Linen napkins perfectly blossom from napkin rings. Did he do that? The wine has already been decanted. Mahler is playing in the background.

"What did you pick for wine?"

"A 2002 Screaming Eagle cabernet. The best I own." John pours me a glass and waits for me to sip it.

"Nice." Actually, it's the best wine I've ever had, but I'm not going to tell him. I have no idea how much it cost, but I could drink a lot of it.

Over the wine, which goes fast, he tells me about dinner. He discovered Mario Batali a few weeks ago and has pulled together the whole meal from one of his books. Dad never cooked when I was growing up. That was Mom's thing—she's the one who taught me to cook, to appreciate, the good stuff. Veal shanks with lemon and caper berries are already simmering in a stew pot and smell fantastic. He's in the process of chopping the fennel for an olive and fennel salad that sounds like it was designed for me. For dessert, he's making a chocolate walnut torte from Capri. Like everything else with John, he built his chef skills from scratch. It gives me hope.

We sit down at the dining room table and start on the salad. The licorice from the fennel and the tanginess from the olive meld in a way I could never have anticipated. I've always loved fennel, but the olives put it over the top. John's been researching Paleo diets, and he's convinced himself that vegetables and protein at every meal will keep him healthy, well, forever. He's off to a good start with the salad.

"So let's hear the Grace story," I say.

"You want to get into it now?"

"Why wait?"

"It's a long story. Let's enjoy the food first, then we'll do it in the living room over coffee and dessert."

Okay, so this is the first test. He needs to get right out of the chute that I'm completely in charge, that there's no room for negotiation, that this is my show.

"Let's do it now. I'm sure we'll still enjoy the food."

"Are you sure?"

This is a gesture-only moment, so I tilt my head a little to the right.

John takes a long breath, then sips his wine. "Okay. Here goes. So, as you know, Grace and the kids are still alive. You probably know more than I do because I'm assuming you read at least one of the letters."

"I'm sorry I stole the letter."

John nods. "The real story starts many years ago, when I was about your age. It's true that I was a songwriter for a long time on my own, but I never had any success until Grace and I started playing and writing together. In our twenties, we did five albums and played all over the country."

"The piano is hers?"

"Yes."

"And that's where you wrote?"

"Yes."

"After the fifth album, we decided to have children. Jack and Joanie were born just a year apart. I got caught up in the whole parenting gig and took a hiatus from songwriting."

"That's when you started your high-tech company?"

"There never was a high-tech company."

"What? But all this?"

"Microsoft and Apple. I have a musician friend who went to work for Microsoft back in the early eighties. He convinced me to invest all of the money we made from touring and the albums in Microsoft stock. Ten thousand invested back then is worth over three million today. Then I did the same thing again when Jobs came back to Apple in the late nineties, only I had a lot more to invest then."

John says he'll be right back. He goes off to tend to the veal and start some side vegetables, carrots and mushrooms, which he knows are two of my favorites. He's definitely working the food angle. You know, the Microsoft and Apple bit makes sense. I never figured out how he could write songs and be a high-tech guru at the same time. But the bit about writing everything with Grace is new. Why did they stop? And how did she betray him? And if they sold albums, why can't I find any trace of them now? And why is he pretending to be dead? And. And. And. And how much money does the guy have? I bet a hundred million.

John returns from the kitchen with the veal and the vegetables, which he first plates for me, then for himself. The veal is juicy and pink in the center, just the way I like it. The carrots are sweet, braised with brown sugar. The mushrooms, doused in butter, seem to be a medley of every possible variety out there. Shitake. Button. Oyster. Black trumpet.

John manages a little smile. "So, back to the story. After Jack and Joanie were born, we had to decide how to support ourselves. The royalty checks from the first albums weren't enough, and we weren't playing out anymore, so one of us had to work. Grace volunteered, and I agreed to stay at home with the kids. We were living in San Francisco at the time, so she went to work in a recording studio, not unlike this one, in the heart of the city. I refused to sell any of the Microsoft stock, so we needed every penny she made. It was enough for us to get by for a few years."

"Better eat your food before it gets cold."

John nibbles on a shank caveman-style for a short time, places it back on his plate. He folds his arms across his chest, fixes his gaze on something in the living room, and continues. "Grace's recording studio hours were all over the map. Sometimes she worked during the day on corporate jingles, but other times she'd stay out almost all night working with a punk band. As a result, I had a lot of time to myself and started reading almost everything I could get a hold of from the local library. That was when the first seeds were planted."

"Zen-master seeds?"

"Yes. I was still relatively young, and I wanted to make my mark. And, increasingly, I became convinced that my mark was outside of music. Even then, the world was so complicated. No one understood what was going on, and as a result, it seemed like no one could fix it. So I committed to. You see, I was just as ambitious as you once, though 'committed' is actually the wrong word. 'Obsessed' is probably better. It got to the point where, even when Grace was home, I buried myself in my books, searching for solutions. Her sole purpose became to relieve me from taking care of the kids so I could study more. Other than sleeping, we spent no time alone together. We stopped talking. We stopped having sex. We stopped seeing friends. I even started resenting the kids. All I wanted to do was read. Needless to say, Grace and I came undone."

"You really thought you could change the world?"

"Don't you?"

"I guess we have that in common." I play with what's left of my veal and vegetables before finishing them. So John drifted away from his true loves—music, Grace, his kids—because he lost it on saving the world. In a way, I get that. I mean, I'm going to do monumental things with my music, and I can't imagine having kids or a spouse while I'm doing all of that stuff. You know, in the end, it's all about timing. John met Grace too soon. Or he decided to save the world too late.

We clear the table, give the scraps and bones to the dogs, who have been waiting patiently at John's side this whole time. As John pulls out the torte and makes two of his expertly crafted cappuccinos, I don't speak. Neither does he. He knows I'm doing the replay-and-absorb thing, trying not to color the story one way or the other. It's hard.

Back at the table with our coffee and sugar, John jumps right in, almost as if the dessert pause was too long. "Grace met a man at the studio. A folk singer who was younger than her. She helped him record his first album and, eventually, they had an affair. I was so consumed with my reading that for months I didn't have a clue what was going on. Then one day, Grace brought home a mix of one of his songs and I knew."

"From the song?"

"Yes. I was only a verse in, and I knew she'd written it with him. You have to understand that, for me, the most intimate thing you can do with your partner is create songs. I probably could have gotten over the affair, but I couldn't handle them songwriting together. Later, I found out that they'd co-written over half the songs on his album. After that, I vowed to never write again, and I deleted all of our old masters. I would have kicked her out if I had the chance, but she beat me to the punch. Playing the song for me was her way of leaving. She couldn't say goodbye directly."

"I'm so sorry, John." I reach across the table and put my hand on top of his for a second, but it's not enough. I get up, take a step toward him, and give him a hug. I can feel him tense up a bit, but I hold on. Strange. He's not wearing his normal cologne; I like this one better. It's more natural, like fresh-cut oak.

You know, I get the bit about songwriting. I mean, there are lots of reasons why I could never write with a guy, with anyone really, but one of them for sure is intimacy. It's just too much risk. To create a love song with your partner, then be betrayed by him? No way. It would wreck me. After a few minutes, I kiss John on the forehead and return to my seat.

John waits until I'm settled, smiles, then continues. "At first, the kids stayed with me, and Grace went on the road with the folk singer to promote the CD. She even sang backup in his road band. But I couldn't take care of the kids alone. I was going deeper and deeper into my obsession, partly in grief, and the kids were too much of a reminder of a happier time. That's when everything changed."

John gets up to open another bottle of wine, but instead of de-corking one, he de-corks two Screaming Eagles. I'm glad we're going to get drunk. Last time this happened, well, things went in an unexpected direction, but, honestly, there's no chance of that tonight. And what's strange is that even though there's no chance of it, I feel closer to John than I ever have before. I see him clearly for the first time. Some of his story is nasty stuff, but all of it is real. I think. I guess this could all be another elaborate story, though I'm sure it's not.

"How much does that stuff cost?" I ask.

"About six thousand a bottle. More?"

"Of course."

"Back to the story. By then, money was starting to pour in from Microsoft. We went from just getting by to being millionaires seemingly overnight, which was good for me, given that all I wanted to do was read. Grace got caught up in the money, or maybe the folk singer pushed her, I don't know, and she cashed out her half. I'm not sure how she did it, but she blew her piece in just over two years. One day she showed up at my door and told me she was broke. That's when I proposed."

"You're kidding me."

"No, no, not that kind. I told her I didn't want the kids anymore, that I wanted to focus on my work. Don't misunderstand, the kids adored me, but I found it increasingly difficult to pick them up from school, make them meals, help them with their homework, guide them. Basically, I wanted to abdicate all my parental responsibilities. So I proposed setting up trust funds for the three of them and funding them with fifty percent of whatever money I made in the market over the next ten years. I only had a couple of conditions. First, the kids needed to believe I was dead. They could never know I abandoned them. Second, I would change my name, erase all ties to the past, and never speak to her again."

"That's why I can't find your albums?"

"Yes. Plus I look a lot different now than I did in my twenties, and most people who are interested in me musically think I was an east coast solo act instead of part of a west coast male-female duo."

"That's why you like The Civil Wars?"

"Yes. We sounded something like them in our time."

It's my turn to pop up from the table. I tell John I'll be right back and make my way to the bathroom. As I'm washing my hands, my reflection in the mirror catches me and won't let go. She has something to say, and it's a big deal. I wait as she builds strength, but in the end all she mouths is, "You're Paige Plant," before smiling, waving, fading back to me. Strange. Oh well. You know, I look good in a little black dress. Will have to wear one to my first awards ceremony. By then, they'll be giving me custom designer dresses for free.

Anyway, did John abandon his children because he was in too deep with his save-the-world thing, or did he jettison them because Grace destroyed him? Probably both. How can I work with, be friends with, or love a man who abandoned his children? I'm not sure if I can continue, if I can finish *The Big Wide Calm* with him. And those kids, who are now older than I am. They both needlessly lost their dad. I mean, who does that? Maybe Dad was right. Maybe I should have stayed tried and true to him. Maybe I should have followed his advice and left when he wanted me to.

Or maybe not. John did open up tonight. He did seem to tell me the truth. And we're so much alike on the big change, save the world front. And TBWC is going to be a masterpiece, so how can I not stay?

Back at the table, John empties the rest of the first bottle into my glass.

"Was it hard to leave your kids?" I ask.

"I wasn't capable of being in any relationship then."

"And now?"

"Too much time has passed. It's better this way. And they don't need a dad anymore."

"But they're your flesh and blood."

"Sometimes chosen family is all you need."

Well, there it is. We've tried on a bunch of different faces during these months. Zen master-student. Lovers. Friends. Colleagues. But that's the first time he's said something that captures all of them. Chosen family. Dad once told me there's nothing more important than family. Back then, he was talking about immediate family, about blood, but, you know, what he said extends. Is John my extended family? Has our blood thickened to brother, sister?

"In the bathroom, I wasn't sure I could do this anymore," I say.

"I know. A man who abandons his children has no right to talk about chosen family."

"Why did you lie to me the first time? It was such an elaborate story."

"It was easier to have you see me that way than as someone who abandoned his children because of an obsession. And in a way, Grace and the kids did die for me back then."

"I understand why you don't want to see Grace, but they're your kids."

"Not anymore."

AIR

I'm having a hard time with John. A week has passed since he told me the real story. Should I forgive him or not? Right after he told me, I did. I understood. I loved him. We would continue. But I lied. Or I changed my mind. Now, I'm clear I haven't forgiven him. It's like the universe is testing me, playing a dirty little trick, asking me to forgive my one unforgivable. I mean, I'm pretty open to most stuff, but abandoning your kids? And for what? Did he really think he could save the world? Still, I need to finish *The Big Wide Calm*, and to do that, I need him. I'm torn up on this one. Best to get to work after the shredder, but not on music. That's too close to him right now. Painting. That's what I'll do, but not a song, whatever comes to mind.

In front of a blank canvas the size of a large flat-screen TV, the largest one I've ever worked with, I start to paint abstract children's faces. Ten pairs of boys and girls. All ages. Five years old. Ten. Teenagers. College students. I paint in oil, with every color on my palette, so the faces hold all the loss, all the joy, everything John missed out on. I don't know what Grace looked like, but on my canvas, her children are beautiful, with long, flowing dark brown hair, dark skin, and big brown eyes. Like they were my own. And they're wounded. Like in that Edvard Munch painting, *The Scream*, only softer, and less scary in the eyes. How could they not be scared? Death robbed them of their dad. Nothing would ever be the same. And, it was all unnecessary if he had just told them the truth.

Though painted-in-oil Jack and Joanie are thankful in a way; John provided for them. At least they had that. So there's a money glow in some of their faces that one day I'll have. But they would have traded it in a minute if only John could have attended their soccer games, their recitals, if only he could have been at Jack's wedding, or helped Joanie work through the loss of her first love. I want to shove the painting in John's face and say, "See what you did! See what you missed!" I'm so lucky. Dad has always been there for me. He never abandoned me, not even in the smallest way. I haven't seen him since his visit, but we text all the time. Maybe I'll go home for a few days. Maybe a whole week.

At the end of the day, the painting is done, which even for me is fast, though it's done little to settle me. I'm going to push the canvas on John, make him hang it in his house, or better yet, in his bedroom. Force a constant reminder, make the lost faces part of his charnel ground. Right? Maybe that will wipe this unsettled feeling clean. Or maybe I need to scream this out—for myself, for his kids, for all kids. Fuck.

Framed painting in hand, righteous indignation full throttled, I head to the main house and go in. Never thought I'd feel this way about anything or anyone. But I do. I mean, I guess we all have our limits. Do not abandon your children. Period. There, I said it. Before finding John, I wave my finger in the foyer a few times at all of the invisible deserters shivering at my gear-up as I repeat the do-not-abandon mantra. John's sitting at the dining room table reading a Noam Chomsky book. Of course he is. Only a week ago, I glimpsed something real, something genuine; now, I'm thinking about burning his books or smashing them with something.

I walk right up to him and ask, "Do you have a hammer?"

"Why?"

"I have a gift for you."

"What is it?"

"Get me a hammer and nails."

John goes out of the dining room. The dogs, minions who don't know any better, tag along—except for Shaman, who stays with me. A moment later, John returns, hammer and nails in hand. I take both from him and, with a nod, signal him to follow me. We make our way to his bedroom where, without a word, he unlocks his door. He's changed the code since our night together. Of course he has. Inside, over his bed, there's an abstract painting on the wall, which is one of those splash paintings that was all the rage years ago. I slip my shoes off, jump up on the bed, and remove the painting. The hook that's in place will do nicely, so I drop the hammer onto the bed and start to slip the nails into my pocket. On the way a few points catch on my palm and prick me. What the—? I wipe two pinheads of blood on my jeans. A minute later, my painting is hanging over John's bed.

"What do you think?" I ask.

"I think we need to talk more."

"I don't. I need to yell, scream, punch you."

"The painting is beautiful," John says.

"The newest member of your charnel ground."

"Come down from there. Let's go back to the dining room."

John tries to help me down off the bed. His charming routine is not going to work this time. Silently, we walk back to the main pod. After he makes two cappuccinos, he joins me at the table.

"I haven't forgiven you," I say.

"I know."

"I thought I did, but I didn't."

John nods, sips his coffee, wipes a little foam off his upper lip. Second time I've seen him milked up. For sure, he'll never be in one of those *Got Milk?* commercials where famous people do the poster-child thing wearing a milk mustache.

"How could you abandon your kids? I mean, you missed out on all the important stuff. And for what?"

John goes into piercing-eye mode. His breath slows almost like he's meditating, and his eyes widen just a bit like he's trying to make sure he sees, absorbs, all of my stuff. It's normally one of my two favorite looks in the world, along with Dad smiling at me for doing something well, but today it triggers a swell from the base of my stomach that spins up out of nowhere like a twister.

"Don't look at me like that!"

"Like what?"

"Like you're trying to understand. Fight back. Get angry. Do something real. Get the fuck out of your head."

"Do you need to stop working with me, Paige? If so, I understand. This is exactly why I didn't want to tell you the real story."

"Fuck you, John! What did you think you would find? They were your kids! Your flesh and blood. What could possibly be worth so much?"

"You."

That's it. He's now given me the biggest BS line in the history of the universe and must pay. I reach into my pocket and pull out the five or six nails. Like bullets, I fire them one at a time at a stack of ridiculous-topic books John has on the table. Empty, I grab Shaman, storm out of the house, jump in the 335i, and once again race out of Harton as fast the black beauty allows.

#

Two hours later I'm in Z's apartment. Like all cheap apartments in Cambridge, Z's is small. The walls are close enough to blanket us, to keep the city out. I'm sitting on the sofa in his living room nursing a beer, have been for the last hour. Shaman is on my lap. Z is sitting next to me, feet up next to mine on the coffee table, one hand scratching behind Shaman's ear. The place smells like dog hair and Z, which tranquilizes.

"I need to get a dog one day," he says.

"You can have Shaman."

"Really?"

"John needs to pay."

"Oh."

I feel even more unsettled here than I did in Harton. I'm in the middle, on the fence, and I don't like it. I can't leave John and I can't stay with him. I mean, all I seem to be able to do is come up with lousy clichés. Fuck. What is this place? I have no idea, but I need to get out of here. It's cracked.

"You can stay with me for as long as you need," Z says.

"Thank you."

"But I think you should go back and finish what you started."

"At least you're consistent."

Z takes Shaman and bounces him on his lap like a baby. For a moment I'm convinced that Shaman is smiling, but, well, he's not. I get up and grab another beer. Before I return to the sofa, I unbutton my jeans, drop them to the floor, and step out of them. The cool air wraps my thighs in freedom.

"Do you have something in mind?" Z asks.

"I'm just more comfortable this way."

"Oh. I'm glad."

"Only around you . . . Why do you think I should go back?"

Z stops bouncing Shaman and hands him back to me. Shaman's fur engulfs, warms my thighs. Z slides his arm around me and I lean on his shoulder. Where's the popcorn and the movie? I mean, if someone snapped a picture now, the world would think we were married and living in the suburbs. Which at least is stable and settled. There's nothing wrong with that, is there?

"John's been searching for you for twenty years," Z says.

"I know, what's that about? It's just a line."

"Have you ever known John to use a line before?"

When it's come to music, John has been nothing but honest. Well, except for the Ian thing. Still, I've come to believe we've both been searching for each other for a long time. "No."

"And don't you want to be the most famous female singer-songwriter in history?"

"Gender has nothing to do with it," I say.

"And didn't you say you felt closer to him when he told you the real story?"

"I did."

"So you love and need the man, but you're afraid because he's flawed, because he made this unforgivable mistake."

I do love John. That's not the question. And for sure, the man pushes the limits of what it means to be flawed. That's also not the question. But what a colossal mistake. I mean, I just don't know if I can forgive him. "Why won't he contact them now?"

"Why is that so important to you?"

"I don't know. It just is," I say.

"You need to decide if you love him, even if he never does."

I spend the night with Z in his cubbyhole bedroom. Just sleep. The sex-tingle is far away, at work with the vast majority of other twenty-five-year-old women. Shaman is balled up at our feet. Occasionally, he gets up, circles around, and plops down in exactly the same spot. I hold Z close throughout the night; he's such a good man. At one point, as Z pitches a tent in, like, no time, I start to sob.

#

Shaman and I enter the studio. Mozart's *Twenty-fifth Symphony* is playing softly in the background. John is waiting for us on the magic piano bench, Talk and Stillness at his feet. Even though it's mid-morning, it's a perfect summer day—ninety already outside, but chilly inside from the air conditioning. Shaman lopes up to his brothers and gives them jump-hugs. It's hard to imagine them as full-grown adults. When I reach the bench, I sit down on the floor cross-legged and pat the oak a few times. A moment later, John joins me. You know, there is some pleasure in seeing a sixty-year-old man, formally dressed, crunch up on the floor. I reach out and take both of his hands. The dogs try to get in on the action, but I gently cast them aside.

"I'm ready," I say.

"For what?"

"To finish the album."

"Ah."

"And to forgive you." I flip John's hand over and run my thumb along his extra long life line, then lock my eyes on his. He needs to see it in my face before he trusts it. Or at least that's what I would need. "I do have a few more questions, though, if that's okay."

"Yes, Paige, that's fine."

"Question One: What did you figure out over the last twenty years? Question Two: Why did you say I'm worth all of this?"

John smiles. He pulls his hands back and pushes up off the floor. Standing, he reaches down for my hand and helps me up. "I want to show you something."

We leave the studio and make our way to the main house, but instead of heading into the main pod, or even the west wing, we head toward the east wing. That's a rarity. We stop in front of a large floor-to-ceiling painting at the end of the east wing hall, one of those that gives the illusion that the hallway is much longer. John uncovers a hidden button in the wall and pushes it. The painting and the wall disappear into the ground and expose a secret hallway. We go in.

The hallway is dark with concrete walls. The air is damp, stale, and cool. So John has a secret room in his house. I mean, I'm zero percent surprised. How could he not have one? At the end of the hallway, he flicks a switch. The room is also concrete, a good size, maybe twenty feet square. There are no windows, no decorations, just a table and chair with a projector and a laptop on it. The projector is pointing at a large screen that completely covers the far wall.

"You have a secret room with only a laptop and a projector?"

"Sit," John says. He turns on the laptop and the projector, then takes out a small remote control. He leans against the side wall, one foot up for support. With a slight turn of his head in either direction, he can see me or the screen.

"For twenty years, more I guess, I've been trying to distill what's wrong with the world down to just a few things. One lesson I learned was that all of the complexity was contributing to the problem, so it was critical to take a step back and look for the big patterns. This room used to be filled to the ceiling with books, documents, newspapers, anything I thought was important. The walls were covered, and I used different color string to connect events on the wall, like in detective movies. But I got rid of all that and distilled everything down to a short presentation."

"Do you come here often?"

"I haven't been since I met you."

"Why?"

"I don't know. Ready?"

I nod.

"You can look anywhere and find a lot of pain, a lot of suffering, and much of the humanitarian work being done these days tries to break the suffering down into more manageable chunks. Malaria. Hunger. Gun control. Pick your favorite cause. The NGOs do lots of good, but you can't fix the problem by only fixing a piece of it. My work has focused on how one might treat the whole system."

"You can see the whole?"

"Yes. It starts with education."

John flips, like, ten slides on the current state of education in the world. Pretty dismal stuff. Thirty-one million primary school dropouts. Two-thirds of the illiterate people in the world are women. Girls are less likely to begin school than boys. At the end of his pitch, he asks, "In developed countries, why do you think we educate our children, and how do we educate them?"

This last bit catches me as I'm mentally exiting the room. He spent twenty years on this? Interesting questions, but c'mon. Was the answer in the slides he just showed me? If so, I missed it. I do the scolded schoolgirl thing, but not for long. You know, life is too short. Isn't the problem that we aren't educating children enough? Don't we need more? Why and how are not really the relevant questions. Certainly not as interesting as why he's convinced I'm part of this.

"We educate them to work at jobs that in ninety-nine percent of cases carry on the status quo. And to do that, schools teach what society wants them to learn."

"What?"

"Think about it. You're a creative person. You paint. You write songs. You want to change the world. Did any of those things come from your education? It was probably quite the opposite. I bet you had a few folks, even at MIT, tell you that you should focus on doing something more practical. Now think about most jobs. A lot of professionals, supposedly well educated, work in cubicles in finance, engineering, even teaching, and pretty much do what they're told all day. In fact, we celebrate obtaining jobs like that, but they're not what most people dream of doing with their lives."

"I guess. But those jobs allow them to be free, to buy houses, to marry, to have children. Those are all good things."

"Do you really think they're free?"

"Yes."

John studies my face, apparently trying to figure out if I believe my last answer.

I do. I mean, look at Dad. He's worked his whole life in the same school system. Has taught thousands of kids about music and often talks about how much he loves it. He's been married to the same woman all these years and has lived in the same house. And raised me to follow my dreams. That is a good life. And this country's education system enabled all of it. What's wrong with that?

"You know, Dad's had a dream life, which was enabled by our education system."

"He realized all of his dreams?" John asks.

"Absolutely."

"Are you sure?"

"Yes."

"Well, it's just that he changed your name. And pushed you to front the next Zeppelin."

I pop up, walk over to the screen, block out some random statistic about children's education. My body, and I guess my face, is covered in bar chart.

Even though the room is cold, even though there's not much heat from the projector, my cheeks warm and prickle in the bright light. "Yeah—what's wrong with that?"

"Nothing necessarily, if that's the name you would have chosen on your own, and if you really wanted to front the next Led Zeppelin. The funny thing is, for the most part, your songs aren't anything like Zeppelin songs, and as far as I know, you've never fronted a rock band."

I lift out of my body and hover above John and presentation-Paige. She has this contorted look on her face like she's trying to play Twister with her cheeks, her nose, her lips, her eyes, until "Fuck you!" releases the contortion and sends her toward the door. I better jump back in.

"I'm sorry, Paige. I didn't mean to—"

"Class over. You spent twenty years on this crap?"

A moment later, I'm on the path back to the studio, but instead of going in, I jump in the 335i and race toward the highway. How did we jump from education to Dad? I mean, I've never once questioned Dad's choice or intentions. Who does John think he is? My whole life has been geared around Paige Plant and fronting the next Zep. Now John Bustin suggests that Dad somehow wronged me? What the . . . ?

Asshole.

I never make it to the highway. Instead, I stop for ice cream at the local shop. There, I down a kiddie-sized pistachio waffle cone that's to die for.

#

For a long time, ever since a Pali-infamous flight from San Diego to Albuquerque, I've been afraid of flying, which is not good if you want to be a rock star. I was with my family, returning from a short vacation to visit the San Diego Zoo, when one of the engines caught fire. Terrified, I thought my life was going to end before it started. I remember squeezing Dad's hand so hard that I was sure I'd broken it. Thirty terror-filled minutes later, we emergency landed on some military airstrip. It was the only time I've ever seen Dad cry from fear.

Today, it's pretty cool that the fear is gone as I level off at thirty-five thousand feet. After my little blowup with John, I phoned home and told Mom and Dad I was coming for a short visit. Best to speak face-to-face when shaky. Maybe that's why I'm not afraid now. You know, bigger stuff on deck. Dad offered to book the ticket for me, but I told him I had it covered. John's stipend has come in handy. About an hour into the flight, when I'm sure my newfound flying confidence has some staying power, I reach for my backpack and pull out my journal. On a fresh page, I write *Air*. My second poem. Scratch outs and rearrangements later, I mouth the poem as I watch a small Texas city pass below.

> *Thirty-five thousand feet above ground in this missile with wings*
> *I wonder why this time the fear has subsided*
> *I spent years avoiding these control-less cabins*
> *And when I did buckle up*
> *I would sweat a drop for every bump*
> *Or chain drink until indifference replaced dread*
>
> *Today the sky is eager and invites me in*
> *Clouds, air, and land intertwine*
> *In an unknowingly knowing dance*
>
> *I go in willing*
> *Give myself up to the joy of this place*
> *I don't visit here often enough*
> *Somehow I know that will change this year*

When the taxi drops me off, Mom is waiting at the front door. My house is like many in Albuquerque—southwestern pueblo style. Three bedrooms. Quarter-acre lot. A schoolteacher's house. Part of a middle-class neighborhood of good friends. Pretty much the exact opposite of Harton Woods. I love this place and always will. After a long hug, Mom and I catch up for a bit.

Work is good. Dad's still a handful. She stayed up late last night making all my favorites—vegetarian lasagna, a pot of sauce filled with veal meatballs, minestrone—which would take me a week to eat, though that's not the point. Food is love, and she's missed me.

Dad's out in the garden tending to his vegetables, and for a moment, Mom and I watch him from the kitchen window. He's bent over a tomato plant and his shorts are a little too loose, exposing a bit of his bottom. We laugh. Dad's had that garden ever since I was a girl, and next to family, his job, and Led Zeppelin, it's his favorite thing in the world. He would take me there every summer to pick the first tomato, and together we would each take a bite. There's nothing like that taste, sweet and tangy, still alive, still invisibly connected to the vine. I go out and give him a big hug.

"How are the tomatoes this year?" I ask.

"The San Marzanos are coming along nicely."

"That's good."

"Glad you came home."

"Me too. Dad, can you come inside when you're done here? I want to talk with you and Mom."

"Sure, honey."

Back in the house, as I'm waiting for Dad and sipping a glass of Mom's lemonade on the living room sofa, I swear I smell a hint of John's cologne. Impossible. You know, I guess John was just watching out for me. I mean, if I'm going to dedicate my whole life to music, it should be on my own terms. No? And he does have a point. My songs don't sound like Led Zeppelin, or any rock band for that matter. If I had to put a label on them, well, as I said once before, I would just call them Paige Plant songs. And on my name, Dad was just trying to set the stage. It is a cool name, though Paige Pali is cool, as well. Dad comes into the house, cleans up a bit, then joins Mom and me in the living room. He sits in his favorite leather chair, the one where he's hosted many audiences over the years.

"Mom, Dad, can I ask you a couple of questions?"

"Sure, honey," they say together.

"Why did you rename me?"

Mom looks at Dad like she knew this was a twenty-years-in-the-making conversation. Dad lightly scratches the arm of his chair a few times and smiles an I-got-this her way.

"Mom and I both agreed to name you Paige, and, as you know, you were Paige Pali for the first five years of your life. Then one day, as you were playing around with my guitar, you sang a ten-second song you made up. Your voice was powerful, clear, unique, even at that age. That's when I got the idea."

"Mom, what did you think?"

"I thought Paige Pali was a perfectly acceptable name, but Dad convinced me over time."

"Paige Pali is a great name. And fronting the next Zep?" I ask.

"That was all me. They were—are—my favorite band. I could think of no greater thing for you to do with your life than front the next Zep," Dad says.

"Mom, what did you think?"

"I liked that one."

Why didn't I ever ask these questions before? No idea. Still, how can I say no to this man, disappoint him? I mean, his intentions were nothing but good, and he's given me so much. And if I do pull it off, you know . . . who wouldn't want that? But the *but* has grown louder since John.

"That's a pretty wonderful goal."

"I think so too. And you're on your way now," Dad says.

Okay, here it is—one of those fork-in-the-road moments. Stay the course in the name of family harmony, out of respect, or tell them the truth? I start to lift out of my body, but for some reason the ascent peters out and I stay put.

"I am. But . . . fronting the next Led Zeppelin isn't really my goal."

"What do you mean? I thought—"

"So far, none of the songs I've written for *The Big Wide Calm* sound like Zep, with maybe one exception."

Silence. Dad gets up, says he'll be right back. He's a smart man. He understands. Best to let him process at his own speed and come back to me when he's ready. You know, I've got to get going on the next song. Maybe I'll write it about him. Never done that before. It would be an honor. Mom makes a whatever-I-want-to-do comment, but Dad's sudden departure has me plane-crash terrified. Where did he go, and what's taking so long? When he returns, I glance at the kitchen wall clock, which betrays me—only a few minutes have passed.

"What have I always told you to do when things get difficult?" Dad asks finally.

"Stay the course."

"Exactly."

"But that's the thing, Dad. Things aren't difficult. They're going really well, but just not in the direction you set for me."

"In John's direction?"

Okay, there it is. Dad didn't like John right from the start, but now he's boiled the whole thing down to picking him or picking John. No wonder men have messed up the world so badly. I shift my body a little until I'm square with Dad, fold my hands on my lap, let strength rush in. "No, Dad. In my direction."

"He has too much influence over you. I don't like it."

"Mom?"

"Your last five songs are fantastic, Paige. Better than all your other work, though I love it all."

"Thank you, Mom."

Mom gets up and walks over to the mantle. She runs her fingers along all of the family photos. One for each of the last ten years or so—Christmas, Thanksgiving, birthdays, vacations. "Sounding like Paige Plant is better than sounding like Zep. Alex, you need to support Paige on this."

Dad stands up and goes over to the mantle. He does the finger-along-the-picture-frame thing that Mom just did. This is how they've always worked out the big stuff. I mean, Mom is flexible on most things. "There are lots of ways to get from A to B," she always says. But every now and then, she course corrects, reels Dad in, puts her foot down. Good timing.

Dad reaches out and takes Mom's hand. "If you want to change your name back to Pali, that's something your mom and I would welcome."

"I like Paige Plant, Dad. That was a good call."

#

A few days have passed since my last visit to the concrete cellblock. After visiting Mom and Dad, I glided back to Harton and, first thing, directed John to finish what he started. I told him about my conversation with Mom and Dad. Told him he was right to raise his concern; told him with anything like that in the future, he shouldn't hesitate to speak up; told him you don't create multigenerational art by being a wimp.

John is flicking through slides, the ones he didn't finish the first time, and talking nonstop. I've never seen him this animated before, not even about my songs. You know, I like it. The concrete cellblock suits him; he almost looks like he's giving a TED talk. Some of John's slides make the quantum physics point. We are all connected; there is no us versus them. Some make the point that doing nothing is a political act because it promotes the status quo. Some make the point that true democracy doesn't exist anywhere in the world and that representative democracy, which is mostly what's in place is, well, not even close to being representative. John's been slowly building his argument, and as he covers each new slide, I find myself agreeing with him often, but also disagreeing with him often. Now we've come to charnel grounds.

"What is it with you and charnel grounds?" I ask.

"Charnel grounds are the glue that holds all of my work together," he says.

"Why? I mean, I understand that charnel grounds are above-ground burial sites, and I understand that they're really scary, but what does that have to do with saving the world? Talk about random."

John smiles, like he already anticipated my question. "I've come to believe that saving the world means collectively letting go of our fear of death, of attachment, of craving, of our aversion to impermanence."

Well, there it is. John is in full Zen-master mode. Was there ever any doubt that twenty years of research, of searching, would all come to this? He could have saved a lot of time if he had just taken on a Buddhist teacher. "And sitting with a bunch of dead body parts can cause that?"

"You're thinking about it literally. Do you remember when I first met you, I told you I was interested in emotional charnel grounds?"

"Yes."

"Let's say collectively, subconsciously, the world wanted to move closer to letting go of the things I just mentioned, and let's say at some level we understand that everyone needs to spend time in a charnel ground to get there. But because that's impossible, maybe what we've done subconsciously instead is create one giant charnel ground around all of us. I'm not talking about a real charnel ground with piles of bleached bones and corpses partially eaten by crows and held together by the sinews—"

"Jeez, John."

"Sorry. I'm talking about emotional charnel grounds. War. Homeless shelters. Famine. Corrupt prison systems. Our political systems. Corporations. Capitalism run amok. Look around you. There are a million examples of desperate, hopeless, terrifying places. And all of these institutions, structures, processes are things we've created. They were our choice, at least in part. Why would we do something like that?"

"You know, probably because men run the world."

John goes distant for a time, like he knows I'm partially right, like he's verifying his theory still holds. Round trip complete, he says, "Maybe. Or maybe we're exactly where we need to be—constructing charnel grounds that will help us enter a new age. It just means that the old one has to fall apart first. That's where you come in."

"Wait. Wait. You think all of the suffering in the world was created on purpose? One giant charnel ground to help move us forward?"

"Yes."

"That's ridiculous. Why would we do that?"

"Because we're human. We make big changes starting from great pain."

Okay, I need to riff on this last point. I can buy part of what John is saying. I mean, it doesn't take a rocket scientist to understand that the world is in bad shape. And we have the power to change a lot of what's happened. But it seems like most people are so busy just trying to get by that no one is working the big issues. So maybe we are building something at a quantum level. With P, the big change came from pain. John is saying, collectively, the way into The Big Wide Calm comes from pain, from struggle, which on a smaller scale is certainly true. But it's such a dark view. There has to be another way that builds on what we already have.

"You want me to help the old system fall apart?" I ask.

"No. No. Trust me, there's no help needed in that area. I want you and your music to help people forward after the fall."

"But why me?"

"Because you can. Because you're talented and strong. Because if you accept what I'm saying, you'll be one of the few people when the darkness comes who will know what's going on and will have the means to move forward. All you need to do is finish what you started and keep making songs filled with emotion, with hope."

I'm not claustrophobic, but I need to get out of the cellblock after this last bit and get some air. Enough slides. Enough talk. For the first time since I've met John, he's scaring the Zep out of me. I mean, didn't he a short time ago tell me I shouldn't be living out Dad's dreams? Didn't he tell me I needed to figure out my own destiny? If I sign up, am I just replacing Dad with an older, richer version? I'm twenty-five years old. I want to be rich and famous. Create multigenerational art, yes, but the idea that I could somehow help through my music is, well . . . exactly what I've always wanted. But still unbelievable when it's right there in front of you.

"Want to go for ice cream?" I ask.

BLESSING

The blessing came at thirteen. We'd built a bonfire in the backyard of our house in one of those outdoor fireplaces Dad had purchased the year before. Just the two of us on a clear, not-too-warm New Mexico night, sitting around the fire in wooden rockers, drinking Mom's homemade lemonade, which, at the time I thought had too little sugar. Mom had fallen asleep early, as she often did at the turn of the century, and my sister, a true millennial, was out doing something somewhere with some boy, as she also often did around that time. The sky, clear and filled with wonder, let me glimpse the infinite for the first time. It wasn't the first time I'd seen a sky like that, but, it was the first time I could take it in, the first time I could hold it. That night, now that I think about it, is probably when science first showed up on my list of loves. Toward the end of the evening, Dad said, "The sky's your only limit, honey. You can do anything you put your mind to. Always remember how proud I am of you and how much I love you. Just listen to your heart each day, and the world will come to you."

I mean, every child should have a blessing. Today, sitting in my room in writing pose, which should be part of some yoga routine given how demanding it is to stay here, I write down "Blessing" in my journal. My new song. The sun is barely over the horizon and, hours earlier, I was wide awake waiting for it. Pregnant with this idea, which is not a phrase I use lightly, I barely slept last night. With song. Do male songwriters think about it the same way? A short time ago, I thought "Blessing" would be about Dad, and I guess in a way it will be, but mostly I'm thinking about John today. This is his song. After our talk the other day, we're going to be okay; we worked it through, and the forgiveness thing has stuck this time. Even though he'll never contact his family again, which I wobbly accept, I'm going to do it for him in this song. His kids never had a bonfire night with him, never heard the words that every child should hear, never knew how much he loved them as they grew. So I'm going to send his words out into the universe through this blessing, and, who knows, maybe it will reach them at some quantum level.

On my guitar, I finger-pick four chords where the bass note of each chord walks down a progression—E, D, C, B. At the end of the progression, I add a nice little bridging riff that gets me back to the top. I'll use this for the chorus. Best to make that simple, with beautiful harmonies. Maybe just the word "blessing" over and over again. Yeah, yeah, that will work.

You know, sometimes in great songs, the chords for the verses are the same as the chords for the chorus. They only thing that changes is the melody. That's what I'll do here. I'll have to add a B part between the verses and the chorus to mix things up, but that's easy enough. Maybe I'll walk back up a scale, though I'll drop the run down for variety. I mess around with the B part until it works, then put the whole thing together. I repeatedly sing "blessing" over the chorus until I get a melody I like.

What about the verses? I'll write them from John to his kids, from all missing fathers to their kids, from all missing mothers to their kids. At thirteen, just like I was—full of possibilities, of choices, of the infinite. I mean, John asked me to keep writing songs of hope, didn't he? Well, John Bustin, contemplate this: What would the world be like if all of its children had their fathers' blessings? Or their mothers'? Will that do? Let's make it part of the new constitution after the fall.

Just as I'm about to start writing, I do the FrankenJohnDad thing I did once before with John and Z, only this time I take all of the wonderful things Dad said to me that night, has said to me all along, and merge them with all of the things John never, but should have, said to his kids. My pen acts like my journal is an Ouija board. Over and over, it writes bits down, crosses them out, edits, rearranges. An hour later, with almost half the words on the page scribbled out, I play "Blessing" for the first time all the way through.

You are thirteen and just starting
You have your whole life in front of you
You are thirteen
I hope all I have seen
Will somehow help guide you through

I see a boy turning into a man full of possibilities
He is smart, honest, strong, vulnerable
He can still shed a tear

I see a boy who loves his life
He can do whatever he wants to do
A scientist, a poet, a sportsman, a father
All of these choices are in front of you

Oh, all I want you to know
Is how much I love you
Oh, all I want you to hold
Is this proud father's
Blessing, blessing, blessing, blessing

I see a world full of wonder
That sometimes seems hard and confused
Remember to listen to your heart each day
What you truly love will guide you through

Oh, all I want you to know
Is how much I love you
Oh, all I want you to hold
Is this proud father's
Blessing, blessing
You are thirteen and just starting

Lump in my throat swallowed, I phone John. "Hey, I wrote a new song. I can't wait the normal time to record it. Assemble the musicians. But first come down to the studio. I want you to hear it."

A short time later, John arrives at the studio. I'm waiting for him, guitar in hand. I don't waste any time and launch into "Blessing." After the first time through, John says nothing. Instead, he mics me up and asks me to play the song a few more times. Then we layer on some harmonies that seem to magically write themselves. Finally, after the fifth take, he says, "That's the one."

"What do you mean?"

"We'll play around with the full band when they get here later today, but my hunch is 'Blessing' is done."

"Really?"

"Really."

John goes into the kitchen and boils water. At the refrigerator, he pulls out the gallon of milk and fills three bowls. The dogs lap the milk down in no time, so he refills their bowls for round two. French press filled and plunged, he brings it over and pours my first cup. He leaves the studio without saying a word, dogs in tow.

I sip my coffee, which is particularly good, strong, European. What just happened? I mean, it's not like John to walk out after a song; we usually talk more. You know, I'm not even sure he liked it. Is there anything I could do to make it better? And where did he go?

After I finish my cup, I make my way out of the studio in search of John. I don't have to go far. On the ground, where the outdoor stage used to be before we tore it down, John is lying face up, hands behind his head for support, one leg crossed over the other, staring at the sky. The dogs are wandering around close by, sniffing every rock, branch, blade of grass, almost as if they know they're on sacred ground. John's face glistens, washed from fresh tears. I lie down next him, mimic his hand and leg positions. A gentle breeze blows over us.

"We should rebuild the stage," he says.

"Solly would want that."

"Thank you for writing the song."

"It's not done yet," I say.

"What do you mean?"

"I want you to sing the harmonies instead."

"I can't."

"I need you to, and no one else will do." I reach out and take John's hand. All of these years he's been walled off, playing the recluse. I don't think anyone realized, except maybe Solly, that he needs compassion, kindness, love, just as much as anyone does. Well, those days are behind him now. I've got him.

You know, there isn't a cloud in the sky. If I were flying, way up high looking down at a calm blue ocean, it would look identical to this sky.

Later that day, John sings the harmonies. He has a seraphic voice. High. Sweet. A cross between Marvin Gaye and Dave Matthews. The harmonies are beautiful, intricate, filled with so much emotion that I argue to bring them up in the final mix. But he argues against it. *The Big Wide Calm* is my album, and the emotion from the background vocals should be more subtle. Still, for the first time, I get the duet thing, and I find myself wanting to listen to every Civil Wars song.

I wrote and recorded "Blessing" so fast that I'm ahead of schedule. I could move on to the next song, but it's too soon. John and I are synced now; the hard stuff is behind us. And I think a little time apart for inspiration is probably a good idea. I've hardly spent a penny since I've been in Harton, well except for last-minute airfare, and instead have deposited most of my monthly stipend in the local bank. Without giving John any details, I tell him it's time for another road trip and that I'll be back in a week, hopefully with a few ideas for the next song. Or at least fully rested.

#

The café is large, right off of Piazza Maggiore in Bologna. In the back, there's a band-size stage where live folk acts play on the weekends. It wasn't that hard to find—not that many places in the city have live music. It's midday, sunny and warm, and the place is half-full. I'm sitting at a table outside, drinking a cappuccino that Grace served me a few minutes ago. It tastes just like John's cappuccinos. In fact, she has exactly the same machine that he has back in Harton, which can't be a coincidence. As she glides from table to table, she has no idea who I am, and I'm not sure if I'll tell her. For reasons I'm not sure I can explain, I had to see her. I mean, John's whole life is divided into before-Grace and after-Grace time.

As expected, she's beautiful. Maybe fifty-five years old, though she looks younger, except for a few strands of gray. She's tall with long blond hair, though for sure she was never a Barbie Blonde. Much more classy, with thick sixties glasses that make her look just as smart as John. She isn't wearing any makeup—she doesn't need any. She's wearing a sleeveless top that exposes an elaborate, colorful tattoo on her shoulder with a name I don't recognize— The Wides. There's a softness in her eyes, like she's cheering for everyone she meets to find their bliss, whatever that may mean. After she makes the rounds, she checks back in with me.

"Can I get you another cappuccino?" she asks.

"Yes, please. Do most of your acts do Italian songs?"

"Every now and then someone will pass through who does English songs. Do you perform?"

"Mostly my own stuff," I say.

"What kind of music?"

"Hard to describe, but I like The Civil Wars."

"Great harmonies. Be right back."

Grace wanders off to make my cappuccino. You know, my last little bit about The Civil Wars raised an eyebrow. Not to the point where she suspects anything, but enough to make a mental note. Best to have my second coffee and go. I saw her, and she's everything I thought she would be. I get why John loved her so much, why probably many men have loved her. I mean, who wouldn't? She's beautiful. She's strong. She's a singer-songwriter. A short time later, Grace returns with my drink.

"How long will you be in town?" Grace asks.

"Still trying to figure that out."

"Any interest in playing a small set to open for the main act on Saturday? I can't pay you, but I'm sure people would enjoy something different."

Okay, so this is an unexpected turn. I mean, I flew all of this way to see what she looked like, to get a feel for her life, to understand what all the fuss was about. I never expected anything more. Still, this is certainly one way for her to hear "Blessing." But no, it's too much.

"Sorry, but I didn't bring my guitar."

"You can borrow mine."

"You play?"

"I did." Grace points to her tattoo. "I was in this band years ago. We did a few albums."

"Anything I would know?" I ask.

"Probably not. They're out of circulation now."

I sip my coffee, do the nanosecond pros and cons thing. Playing "Blessing" for her is the only way I can really be sure she hears it, so the pros win.

"I guess I can do a few songs. Don't you want to hear me first?"

"No need. I'm sure you're talented."

#

The night of the show, the café is full. Everyone is speaking Italian; everyone is in their twenties; everyone is ready to judge. I'm sitting in this back room, which is filled with coffee supplies and isn't much bigger than a coatroom. The temperature must be one hundred, and even though I'm alternating an ice cube between each wrist, I'm sweating, which is a strange because I never sweat. The room smells like espresso beans, and for a moment, I'm sure the dark roast will seep in through my pores and stay in my skin forever.

You know, I'm going to play at least five of the new songs. But I'm not sure about "When John Fell from Grace." That might be too much, might give me away. I guess I'll decide last minute when I'm up on the stage. At least it's only a few songs—it will be over in thirty minutes. I hope she likes "Blessing." I mean, that's the key, right?

Before I go out on stage, I scan the room, gear up by letting The Big Flip go into full rotation. Heat flips; the air cools, the sweating slows, dries up. Judges flip to fans whose sole purpose is to help our hero hone her stuff. Grace flips to the unknowing receiver of the big blessing. In the front of the mic, with Grace's guitar strapped on like a bulletproof vest, I flip into a rock star.

A moment later, I'm strumming the opening to "The Gift." The noise in the room stays at about the same level. That's to be expected. These people came here to see the main act, but by the time I'm done, all they'll be able to remember is me. "I saw Paige Plant before she was anyone." "I knew her when." "I have her autograph from the now-famous café performance in Bologna." About midway through the song, the room quiets. People who previously had their backs to me turn their chairs my way. A few of them smile. I make out Grace, who has paused for a moment at a table to watch, empty cups in hand. She smiles. I relax. I haven't played out in months and, well, this is home. Yeah, yeah, this is home.

The room stays pin-drop quiet for the rest of my set, except for lots of applause after each song. At the end of the fifth song, "Talk," I say thank you a few times and unstrap Grace's guitar. Before I can leave the stage, the room has launched into *"Ancora, ancora,"* which causes me to rise out of my body and hover over the café. Italian men are so good looking. And Italian women. Right when I'm in the middle of scoping out a long brown-haired beauty, folk-singer-Paige launches into "When John Fell from Grace." Fuck. I try to jump back into my body, but I'm paralyzed in hover-land. At the end, folk-singer-Paige gets her first ever standing ovation. Except for Grace, who is sitting in a chair staring at me, I mean folk-singer me. Fuck.

GROWING DOWN

"Sex was never a big deal for me."

"Even with Grace?"

"Even with Grace."

"But you're good at it."

"Competence doesn't imply importance."

John and I are walking the dogs in the woods. I returned from Italy yesterday. I haven't told him anything about my road trip, and I probably won't. Best to move on. We're about a mile into the trail, and we're taking turns kicking a pinecone forward like a soccer ball. The dogs are busy fertilizing and ignore us for the most part. The morning sun has filtered everything blue like in all of those formulaic movie blockbusters.

Ever since "Blessing," I've had this feeling that there isn't anything else behind John's curtain. I pretty much know his story now. Well, except the details on this new bit about sex, but I will know that in a few minutes. You know, he has no more secrets, and I mean, that's probably the most generous thing he's ever done for me.

"Would you like to hear a story?" John asks.

"Always."

"Okay, here goes. When I was a boy, maybe thirteen, there was a girl, Serena, who lived on the first floor of our three-family in Worcester."

"You grew up in Worcester?"

"Yes."

"Any family left?"

"All gone."

"One summer day, Serena and I decided to picnic with only each other as nourishment. It was our first experience with sex, and we were both filled with anticipation. I think I showered three times that morning, and paraded in front of the mirror even more, before finally meeting her midday. Before I left my place, I grabbed a blanket from my bed. I spread it out behind the shrubs of our house and waited. A short time later, Serena and I were sitting cross-legged on the blanket, my knees touching hers. Dove soap, pine, and recently bloomed azaleas melded in the air. What a wonderful smell. The shrubs, dense, full, shielded us from the sidewalk and the road, which were only a dozen or so yards away. At first, only our knees were touching. Even through jeans, it was almost too much. After a short time, we were kissing; then our clothes came off piece by piece until we were completely naked and in the thick of trying pretty much everything inexperienced kids might try. We didn't know what we were doing, but the newness outweighed experience. We stayed there a good part of the afternoon, though, honestly, I lost track of time early on.

"Then it happened. The one thing we didn't account for was the view from the third-floor bay window. From above, I'm not sure for how long, my mother apparently watched everything. Right after a few awkward teenager false starts, right after I finally had entered Serena, my mother burst onto the front stoop, wooden spoon in hand, and started yelling.

"A moment later, back in my underwear with the rest of my clothes and sneakers in hand, I raced up the three flights of stairs. My mother, somehow tethered, repeatedly hit me with the wooden spoon, at least once per step, except for those moments on the landings where she hit and pulled my hair in syncopated rhythm. She sent me to my room and told me to wait there until my father came home. Hours later, after I had cried and paced back and forth into exhaustion, my father creaked on the wooden floor toward my room. He entered without a single knock, without a single word, and pulled off his black alligator belt. At first, as he whipped my back and my bottom, the pain was all consuming, though I didn't cry or scream. I knew it would last longer if I showed any signs of weakness, if I didn't toughen up and take it like a man.

"After a while, some kind of numbing mechanism kicked in, which honestly, at the time, saved me. The entire visit, he never said a word. Finally, he looped his belt back on, hand-combed his hair, and left me balled up on the bed. Later that night, I heard him laughing and having his way with my mother, as if nothing had happened. The next day my mother prohibited me from seeing Serena again, which was hard, given that we all lived in the same triple-decker, so the following month we moved to a different town. After that, I never saw Serena again."

I take John's hand, which has turned into my go-to move whenever we talk about something emotional. You know, touch is the only thing that will do in moments like this. I flash on my first experience with my schoolmate, Billy, which set the stage for all that has followed. What would the world be like if everyone's first experience of sex, of love, was a good one? I squeeze John's hand three times. He smiles just a bit. We stop for a moment at the brook so the dogs can water up midstream. They're no longer pups—maybe triple the size of when John first brought them home, strong and athletic, well raised. These woods belong to them. No, that's not right; they're part of these woods.

If only memories like John's weren't so sticky, more like running water, they would pass through without dragging weight. But we're not wired that way. I mean, maybe that's the one thing the universe got wrong. Or right, if this is meant to be the big struggle. I want to go back and scream at his mother and father, bring my own wooden spoon, my own belt. I want to break the spoon in half in front of her and shred the belt into lace.

"No wonder you feel that way about sex. When did you know?"

"About five minutes ago."

"Does anyone else know this story?"

"No."

Okay, holding his hand will not do at this point, so I reach over and put my arm around him. Yeah, yeah, much better. The vast majority of people in the world would not understand our relationship. He's my teacher, my mentor, my one-time lover, my creative partner, my friend. A true love, yes, but never again a romantic love. And that no longer has anything to do with age, ambition, Solly's death, or any kind of subtract. You know, the world holds up this idea that romantic love is the highest form of connection, the most intimate, that it's the best thing that can happen between a man and a woman, but it's not. This is the love we've chosen, and I mean, I don't think I could love another human being more than I love John right now.

"I have a little more. Okay?" John asks.

"Always."

"In some ways, Grace only really got to me by leaving. I would never have let her completely in as long as she was around. It's like she figured out that the only way in was out, and it was worth it to her to see the inside, even for a few moments."

"I'm so sorry, John. . . . What did she see?"

"I don't know. Back then, neither one of us had the words for anything other than songs. All these years, I held on to the affair, the betrayal with the other songwriter, as the thing that broke us up, but I drove her away long before that. And it had nothing to do with my work, my research. I couldn't let anyone in, so I constructed this labyrinth, most recently here in Harton . . . until you came along. In some ways, I let you in the first moment I saw you."

I slowly circle the palm of my hand on John's back, first clockwise, then counter-clockwise, waiting for the rest. When it doesn't come, I ask, "And?"

"In some ways, I didn't."

I kneel down and call to Shaman. He runs to me, and not fully aware of his own strength, he almost knocks me over. I give him a big hug, scratch his chest, look into his eyes. You know, this last bit is even harder to hear about than the beatings. In a way, John has been alone all of his life. Grace only saw him for an instant. His kids never really saw him. No friends. No family. Just Solly for a time. And now me. That was the sadness on his face I first saw all those months ago. Yeah, yeah, that was it. Fuck. How do you help someone heal from a lifetime of sadness?

"I have an idea," I say.

For the next forty-eight hours, we spend the entire time in John's bed, holding each other. There's hardly a word spoken between us, and a few times he breaks down, sobs like a thirteen-year-old who, on the same day that he touched limitless bliss, suddenly, violently, without any regret on his parents' part lost it for good.

#

The first thing we do when we get out of bed is eat and talk. John makes this mouthwatering frittata with just about every kind of vegetable, sausage, and bacon. I squeeze fresh juice. He makes cappuccinos. I make toast. When we sit down at the dining room table, we talk about every topic as if it's the most important one in the world. The Celtics. The *American Idol* judges and host. John's love of television shows about high school kids, especially *Buffy the Vampire Slayer*. And we eat like we've never seen food before. There are times when we both break out laughing at nothing, at anything, and those bouts would last for a bit. It's like we're passing a laughter ball; John takes it for a while and I follow his lead, then I take it and he follows mine. Overall, it may be the best meal I've ever had. Top ten for sure. We eat so much there are only two real choices afterwards—go back to bed for a nap or go for a long walk in the woods.

In the woods, everything seems more alive, more vibrant. Even the dogs seem to be in on our little secret. I mean, I've been walking these trails over six months, and I guess I know them pretty well, but today I can five-sense every rock, every tree, every stream, every animal. There is so much connected here. It makes me wonder why we do everything we can to separate ourselves, rise above, look down.

"I feel different," John says.

"How so?"

"Lighter."

"Lighter is good."

#

I'm back in Paige land, back in the studio. John is off running errands in town, hopefully restocking the refrigerator for our next feast. I've been staring at a blank page for the last week, and I have no idea what's going on. You know, ever since our bed-in, I've been so caught up in what's happening around me—so caught up in life, so happy—that I haven't been able to write a riff or a word. I mean, why create multigenerational art when it's right in front of you every minute of every day? Not that I haven't tried. I've sat here each day for hours just like this, waiting. But nothing comes. Not even my go-to blockbusters—swimming, walking the dogs—jogged lose a single word, a single note. And all John said was, "Don't force it, Paige. The songs will come when they come. Just enjoy where you are." Fuck. Even though we've abandoned our monthly deadlines, even though there's no external pressure to get the next song done, I need to get the album out there. If I'm great but no one hears me, well . . .

I go for a run; maybe that will help shake something lose. I sneak out of the studio with Shaman. Stillness and Talk, both sound asleep, dream of steak and burying bones to the hum of the air conditioner. A short time later, I'm heading toward a trail I've never taken before, one that goes up to Prehistoric Ridge, which I named because, even though raptors aren't partial to this climate, I'm sure there are few of them lurking there in the caves.

The movement, the warm summer air, Shaman running at my side are all helping me as I make my way up the ridge. The trail touches the edge of ridge, so occasionally I glance down at the twenty-foot-high ledge, at giant boulders that fill me with a sense of awe. Then two words come: *growing down*. That's what I've been doing this whole year. I had to before I could grow up.

At the top of the ridge, I stop to rest and look out into Harton Woods. About one hundred yards off, there's a black bear slowly making his way toward me. John and I discussed bears once. Play dead; don't do anything aggressive. Seek shelter if you can. Shaman sees the bear, too, and moves behind me. I've never seen him scared before. I don't think the bear has seen us, at least I hope not.

I start to run back toward the compound. I'm heading down the ridge as fast as I can when Shaman stops to bark in the direction of the bear. Without stopping, I look over my shoulder and yell, "Stop it, Shaman. Let's go!" He holds his ground, barks up a storm. I go back for him, try to push him along, quiet him. No luck. There's no time, so I forklift Shaman up, all fifty pounds of him, and resume running, which now that I'm weighed down, is more of a slow jog. I can't keep this up all the way back, but maybe Shaman will be okay after a little more distance. A minute or so later, I'm almost down the ridge. I glance over my shoulder; the bear's out of sight. Just a few more yards and I'll put Shaman down. We're going to be okay.

A step later, my ankle buckles on a rock in the path. Damn it! I fall toward the ridge, and as I tumble over the edge, I let go of Shaman. He lands on all fours.

Arms outstretched behind me, I hit the ground maybe eight feet later. Snap! My right arm gives way. I bounce right up, sling my arm with the other, and, Shaman at my side, race the rest of the way home.

#

John and I are sitting in the emergency room of the local hospital. When I told him what happened, he loaded me into his 750i and we raced here. I don't think I've ever seen him drive so fast, or look so worried. I guess the man doesn't like bears. My arm is casted and will be this way for ten weeks. Talk about a crimp in *The Big Wide Calm*. How do I get that look off John's face?

"Go get a magic marker. I want you to be the first to sign my cast."

John gives me a puzzled look, then a grin spreads across his face, then he bursts out laughing. After we pass the laugh ball for a while, he says, "I'll be right back." When he returns, he sits next to me on the bed and, with a purple magic marker, draws bears all over my arm. The laugh ball bounces a bit more between us.

"Right before this happened, I had an idea for my new song," I say.

"What's that?"

"Growing down instead of growing up. I feel like that's what I've been doing in Harton."

"Me too," John says.

"I only have the title. At least I can work on lyrics in this condition."

"You can do more."

"How?"

"You still have one good hand. I'll provide the other."

For the next few days, my guitar connects my left hand to John's right hand. I pick all of the chords, all of the voicings on the fretboard, and John either strums or fingerpicks using his right hand after I've told him what I'm going for. He's adamant that "Growing Down" must be my song, so my instructions must be precise. It's tough going at first, you know, like I'm a stroke victim and I've got to teach my right side how to walk again. And it's awkward with the cast, which I try my best to maneuver out of the way, but never really do.

John is a fast learner, and even with one hand, an accomplished guitar player. I use drop D tuning on this song and direct John to start with back-and-forth eighth notes between low D and D an octave up on the third string. The groove should be something like at the end of "Hey Jude," though "Growing Down" will be a guitar song with one main riff. And what about the riff? As John plays, I search for a bit to put over the Ds, something that's a working girl's riff, not too fast or too slow, like it knows that growing down takes time. After almost an hour of this, after John has taken to repeatedly, sarcastically, nodding his head and widening his eyes to the two notes he's been playing forever, the riff finds me. We both sit up a little straighter, and John's nod is replaced with an almost imperceptible smile. Then the first line of "Growing Down" comes and I sing it over the riff. "This year, I grow down, after years of growing up."

After we play the line mega-times, we reach a natural stopping point, and call it quits for the day. I have enough to work on the lyrics, and, besides, you can only do the left-hand-right-hand thing so long.

A week later, "Growing Down" is done and we're getting ready to record it in the studio. John is sitting in on guitar and will play all of the parts I normally would. The musicians are all buzzed—it's the first time they've heard John play and they're impressed. I'm standing at the mic. Someone in the control room is filling in for John and gives us a thumbs-up that we're recording. The drummer starts us off. Click. Click. Click. Click. The groove kicks in, and I do the slow bobbing head thing on the beat until I sing:

This year I grow down
After years of growing up
Below the surface
Toward the core
Plunging inward
Quietly

I do this alone, though you are the trigger
Just before I go, we acquiesce
We ebb and flow between separate and together
Generate strength from this slow dance

I unearth dark places
Turn them to pieces of light
No longer lost, unfettered
I am finally home

I do this alone, though you are the trigger
Just before I go, we acquiesce
We ebb and flow between separate and together
Generate strength from this slow dance

Everything I feel finds its way here
You're always there to help me through
I didn't know love could be this strong

This year I grew down
Finally found solid ground
No longer fear love's coming
Because of what I lost long ago

I did this alone
Though you were my trigger
Now as I go, we acquiesce
Though we'll be apart
We will always be together
In my thoughts, in my heart

THREE LITTLE NUMBERS

"It's time to try out your songs on a live audience. Are you up for it?" John asks.

"Always." When John focuses on something, he beelines. I mean, in no time, he's booked three dates in Cambridge—two at Club Passim and one at The Middle East—and the first one is only a week out. For someone who never leaves Harton, he's incredibly well connected. Or maybe it's just his money. Maybe they're the same thing.

To gear up, we bring in the session musicians to the studio. They're my backing band. Paige Plant and the . . . nah, just Paige Plant. First thing on the rehearsal agenda is to agree on the songs. After an in-your-face back-and-forth, the final set list contains all of the new songs spaced out for maximum effect, just as many old songs, and a few covers. A slow version of Cyndi Lauper's "Girls Just Wanna Have Fun." "Your Ghost" by Kristin Hersh. Aimee Mann's "I'm with Stupid Now." John's committed us to a ninety-minute set, and with me rambling a bit between songs, the set list will cover the night.

The rehearsal is maybe twelve hours, repetitive, mostly a blast, but occasionally fiery when I don't think a band member is pulling his weight. More emotion. You botched the lead. Pull back on the cello part. This is not normal, boys and girls, so notch it up. I mean, this is the world's first exposure to Paige Plant, its first exposure to a multigenerational masterpiece, its first exposure to fifty percent of *The Big Wide Calm*. Buckle up.

By the end of the week, we're grooved. The set flows, and it's hard to tell the new songs from the old songs. The covers sound like mine. The musicians are playing as one. Even the woman John brought in to play my guitar bits, given my arm thing, has nailed her parts. Radha is going to do just fine.

The day of the first show, I'm dotty. I shower. I stare at different clothes I might wear. I put on makeup. Take it off. Shower again. Prance in front of the mirror—even more than that time in high school when I was prepping for my first time with Billy. Finally, I settle on jeans and a T-shirt with one of John Lennon's paintings printed on it, you know the one with *come together* written off the side in teal and a bunch of colorful penis figures all watching a teal one float away. Best to never let one of those float away. After one more on-again-off-again moment, I settle on no makeup. This is about the music, right?

A few hours later on stage at Club Passim, I scan the audience. Z is in the first row; he'll be at all three of these. A red amulet. A quantum physicist. A probe. John is sitting with him looking, well, out of place in his suit, but like John. He's tapping his finger on his knee nippy beats an hour. Some guy is next to him with a tablet, typing something. There are lots of women sprinkled across the place in groups of two, three, four, apparently doing the girls-night-out thing. Three guys wearing red, white, and blue Patriots jerseys look out of place, like they thought they bought tickets to a Zep tribute band. The place smells like coffee and basement concrete.

Just as I'm about to launch into the first song, P slithers in and sits in the back of the room. Fuck. First time since. He waves in my direction like he still has a key up his ass. He looks exactly the same, though the smirk on his face I used to adore needs to be whacked off immediately. What's he doing here? Who invited him? My drummer snaps me out of whack-a-frack and into the first song. P fades from view, or maybe the energy from the rest of the room dwarfs him. Yeah, yeah, that's it. Dwarfed, shriveled P.

For ninety minutes, the spotlights are multiple suns, and I soak them up. Some artists shrivel on stage; the light scares them, makes them all too aware of what they aren't. But I'm not like them. I bloom here. Send out invisible lace tentacles into the audience until I've touched everyone, even P.

THE BIG WIDE CALM

This stage, any stage, is as much home to me as New Mexico, as Harton. At one point between songs, I head-jump back to John's story about touching Serena's knees. There's a connection, something like that, with an audience that's hard to explain, and, honestly, there's nothing better. Not even sex. Well okay, that's an exaggeration, but it's close to sex.

At the end of the show, the women in the audience applaud a lot. Some stand. The three football jerseys stand as well, hold up their beer bottles, whistle, and shout, "Killer set." A meet-and-greet line forms where I do the smile-autograph-hug-and-shake-hands thing. I could get used to this.

The guy with the tablet eventually makes his way to the front of the line. "Hi. I'm from *The Globe*. Great show. Can I ask you a few questions?"

"Sure. Shoot."

"I like your T-shirt. Are you a fan?"

"Of course."

"On 'Talk,' do you really think that kind of communication is possible on a global scale?"

"It has to be."

"Why?"

I take *The Globe* reporter in through my eyes, size him up, let him touch big strength. He's a good man. Just another member of the throng trying to figure out how to make a difference in this mess we've made. I place my hands on his shoulders and pull him a little closer. Then I whisper, "You already know why. We all do. I'm just saying it out loud."

#

The second week we don't rehearse as much. No need. A few times will do, given how well the first gig went. I'm happy. John is happy. Our routines take hold again. Walk the dogs. Cook. Ice cream. I still can't swim, but John has this elliptical exercise machine he bought ages ago but never used, which kind of does the job, though the thought crosses my mind that this contraption is no better for me than any of the much cheaper forms of exercise.

The real news is *The Globe* review. A couple of days after the show, my trusty reporter filed an article that, well, is the kind that changes everything. It started with a description of me that, I mean, I'm not even sure on my most *me* days I would write. "The stage presence of a goddess in full command of her powers." "Eyes that penetrate." "A voice that could start wars." Thank you very much, Mr. Globe, but enough already. Then he commented on the set list in the most flattering way, even the covers. Finally, he ended with this bit: "Run, and I do mean run, to buy your tickets for one or both of the next two shows. It's your opportunity to get in on the ground floor and see the next big thing, a future first ballot Rock and Roll Hall of Fame inductee, a future leader of the enlightened world. It's appropriate that Paige was wearing a John Lennon T-shirt to her first show. If John could have picked a single person to continue what he started, Paige would be a good choice. Maybe he already has."

The night of the second show, John and I BMW together.

"Only your second show of the last six months. Are you ready?" John asks.

Okay, there it is. Should I let it go or tell him the truth? After everything we've been through, after all he's told me, I can't lie to this man. I mean, sin of omission, no problem, do that all the time. But a direct lie?

"It's my third concert."

"Your third?"

"Yeah. I played out once on my last road trip."

"That's great. Why didn't you tell me?"

My seat belt tightens like it knows I need more support. Or wants to strangle me. I pat around on the door side of the chair for the eject button, I mean, there has to be one, but all I do is mess up my lumbar support. Fuck. I crack the window, hook one finger over the glass, touch the wind. Ah, just say it.

"I went to Italy. I saw Grace. I played a gig at her club."

John pulls the BMW over to the side of the road. With the car still running, he gets out and walks away. For a moment, I think he's going to go all the way back to Harton, but about fifty yards out, he turns around. He's storm-talking with himself. I have no idea what he's saying, but it can't be good. A moment later, back in the driver's seat, with the blankest expression I've ever seen, he says, "Tell me everything."

I tell him the Grace story. Met at the café. She didn't know who I was. Out of the blue asked me to play the gig. Got him to the end of the gig with all of the details of the new songs, including the last, "When John Fell from Grace."

"That's when she knew," John says.

"Yes. We talked after the show and I told her about you. I mean, at the end, it was pretty clear to me that she's accepted where you're at now. She only had one regret."

"What's that?"

"That the kids never got to hear The Wides albums."

"Oh."

The rest of the way, John drives in silence. We arrive a little early at The Middle East. There's already a line to get in, and pretty much everyone asks me to sign something—a paper, a shirt, an arm. Which I do. Best to practice these things now to build wrist strength. When I get inside, *The Globe* reporter is waiting for me.

"Thanks for the article," I say.

"I may be your first official groupie."

I smile, give him a hug, and make my way toward the stage. The band is already there, and everything is set up and ready to go. Next to the bass player, there's a guy that at first I don't recognize due to his lousy haircut. But then I do. Ian Asshole. I glance over at John, who's been silent at my side all the way in.

"Why?" I ask.

"What happened was my fault. He was just following orders."

"I didn't know he took them."

"After that review, you're going to need him. Hear him out."

When we reach the stage, at first I ignore Ian. Make the rounds with the musicians, you know, people who actually care about what I'm trying to do. Everyone is good to go. Finally, when I'm fueled up, I make my way to Ian.

"Hi, Paige. It's good to see you."

"I get a good review and now you want back in?"

"I never wanted out in the first place."

"Yeah, well, there's this word—*trust*."

"I can help you."

"Like you did last time?"

"Let me put a proposal in front of you. I'll have it to you before the third show. All I ask is that you read it. If you're not interested after that, I'll walk away."

Best to pause for a bit. I get fake distracted by the drummer, then the bass player, make it look like the conversations we're having are much more important than what Ian just proposed. Finally, I turn back to Ian and say, "I'll think about it. Now get back in line like everyone else."

Ian disappears like a good boy. There's still a spark between us, but what does that matter once the well's been poisoned? Toxic-spill Ian. He dumped billions and billions of gallons into Paige Ocean, though at least he seems to know I'm an ocean.

#

For the third show, at Club Passim, John surprises me. Mom and Dad are in the audience. John flew them in just for the show and set them up at a nearby five-star hotel, all dollars paid. Even though Dad can't be bought, not a bad move, Zen-master John. Mom and Dad are right up front, next to John and Z. My family.

Throughout the set, Mom and Dad beam. Occasionally, Dad leans over and whispers something in John's ear, which, you know, is a miracle in and of itself. During "Blessing," he wipes his eyes a few times. The show ends to thunderous applause. Three magical nights down. More, please.

After the show, we gather outside. It's relatively late, and Z has to work in the morning, so he does the hug-exit thing. As he walks away, I have this thought: he loves me too much. Is that even possible? How can I put enough space between us so he lives his life, but not too much? After thousands of years of male-female experiments, someone must have solved this one, right? At least we stopped having sex. Paige points for that. Mom is tired and wants to head back to the hotel, so we walk her there. The whole time my arm is hooked around hers, like best girlfriends, and we hardly say a word. Don't need to. Dad and John are talking up a storm about the music business, about the review, about next steps, about finishing *The Big Wide Calm,* which, I mean, unless I do soon, could zero out all this stuff. But I won't worry about that now.

At the hotel, Dad and John are still wired. Me too. It's a perfect time for ice cream, coffee, wine, beer, whatever. I know a late-night place in Inman Square. We can walk. It's only a mile with shortcuts. We head out. We're in speed-dialog mode. We cut each other's sentences off, the good way, the finishing-thoughts way. Music, sports, politics are dancing off our lips like we're ballet dancers in *Swan Lake.* Yeah, yeah, of course I danced as a little girl. You know, for sure John has won Dad over with the fly-you-in-all-expenses-paid thing. Or maybe it's more than that. As we turn onto a side street, I'm between the two of them. I reach out and take their hands. There's a charge that passes between John and me. Or a baton. Even with my cast covering my palm, Dad's hand is large, strong, the same as it's always been. No one deserves this much love. Or maybe few get it, so we knock it down with "deserve."

About halfway down the block, I hear a noise behind us. I glance over my shoulder. It's dark, so all I see is three disembodied Patriots jerseys rounding the corner. Hmm. Nah, couldn't be. We all instinctively pick up our pace and the conversation tightens a bit. I work at avoiding cracks on the sidewalk. Another twenty or so yards along, the footballers overtake us, turn around, block us.

"Hey, Paige, great concert a couple weeks ago. We tried to get tickets tonight, but the assholes wouldn't let us in. Want to party with us?" the tall one, number 87, asks.

"Thank you. I remember you guys. Sorry about the tickets. . . . I've got other plans right now, but another time," I say.

"C'mon, Paige, dump your two dads and let's go," the short, wide one, number 33, says.

"Hey, guys, that's enough. Have a good night," Dad says. He takes a step toward 87 and extends his hand.

Eighty-seven extends his hand, but just before accepting Dad's handshake, his hand fists and he bashes Dad in the stomach. Dad keels over, then before I know it, the two of them are fighting. John jumps in and tries to stop them, but things escalate when 33 jumps in. I take a step back from the four of them. I can't make out what's happening for sure; the four of them are tangled, fast-moving shadows in the darkness. Dad and John have to be winning. Have to. The third guy, number 12, clearly the one in charge, watches me calmly, like he already knows what's going to happen, like he's seen this movie a million times before. Fuck. A moment later, the shadow-tangle sorts and Dad and John are unconscious, both face down on the sidewalk. I can't move. I can't speak. I try to pop out of my body, but not even that works.

"Finish the job," 12 says.

Eighty-seven pulls out a gun and points it at Dad.

"Wait, wait. Please," I say.

"Sorry, we have a code. If you try to harm us, we hit you back hard. Bullets for fists," 12 says.

"Wait, wait. I have money."

"How much?" 12 asks.

"Eight hundred dollars. I'll take you to an ATM."

"You'll do that anyway," 12 says.

It cannot end this way. I refuse to let a bunch of thugs take the two men I love the most from me. Not now. Not ever. I take a step toward 12. "I'll take the bullets for them."

"What did you say?" 12 asks.

"You heard me. I'll take the bullets for them."

"You would do that for these two old faggots?" 87 asks.

"Yes. And they're not gay."

"Why would you do that?" 12 asks.

"You came after me, didn't you? Not them. You wanted a piece. I'll give you two."

"Sorry, we have a code," 33 says.

"Wait . . . you're one crazy bitch. Give me your phone," 12 says. Once in hand, he checks it out for a bit like he's calculating the street price, then smashes it on the ground. He says, "Let's go, guys."

Eighty-seven and 33 grab one arm each and follow 12. They're holding me so tightly that I'm afraid my forearms are going to toothpick-snap. They smell like beer pooled on the floor of a bar too long, stepped in too many times. As we turn the corner, I get one last glance at Dad and John, still unconscious on the sidewalk. They'll be okay. Someone will find them soon; someone will help. Has to.

A few blocks later, I'm shoved into a beat-up Ford Bronco and vice-gripped between 33 and 87 in the backseat. Twelve drives. Thirty-three's hands start probing. Then 87 joins in. As we drive, the car morphs into a red convertible that allows me to lift out of my body at last, hover. There, I count stars by the dozen, dream of the day when I finish *The Big Wide Calm,* replay my trip to the Hall. If we are all connected at the quantum level, how exactly am I connected to the goons below? I mean, enough. Sometimes assholes are just assholes. I look down. Covered-with-hands-Paige is softly singing the song Dad wrote all those years ago for her. Paige Plant. Paige Plant. Paige Plant.

Later, we pull up to an outdoor ATM. "Try anything and you die on the spot." Got it, 12. Eight hundred dollars in hand, I'm back in the car in a flash. Mister 12, who apparently didn't like what was going on in the back seat, has me sit up front. He asks me for my credit cards, my license, anything that can identify me as Paige Plant. I should be afraid.

"Why would you take bullets for them?" 12 asks.

"I love them."

"But they're old. And you're the one who *The Globe* says is going to be rich and famous."

"That doesn't matter," I say.

"Really? Most people wouldn't have done what you did."

"I'm not most people."

We reach an old house somewhere in Allston. Before we get out of the car, he glances my way and nods. The nod means this: because they're taking me to where one or more of them lives, my two bullets must be fatal. I nod back. It has to be this way; otherwise, they might get caught. In the house, they take me into the living room, sit me down on the sofa. Eighty-seven grabs three beers, hands them out. He and 33 sit on opposite sides of me. Twelve sits across from us in an I'm-the-boss armchair. The much-too-large flat-screen blasts *SportsCenter*. Twelve lowers the volume to a hum. The place smells like dust and leftover pizza.

"Let's do her," 33 says.

"Yeah, let's," 87 says.

"Was one of the men your dad?" 12 asks.

"Yes."

"And the other?"

"Mentor. Life-long friend. Chosen family."

Twelve goes off somewhere in his head. It's clear 33 and 87 want no part of this conversation. Sex and blood pronto, please. They've already downed their beers and are lubed up. Twelve frowns in their direction for the third time in the last couple of minutes. They'll do whatever 12 tells them, which, you know, is my only shot.

"I liked your songs," 12 says.

"Thank you."

"Not normally what I listen to. I like metal, but *The Globe* guy is right about you."

"Thank you."

"That's why we have to take it away." Twelve's face blanks as he glances over at an old color-washed photo on the wall. After a long minute, he says, "My old man's in prison. Killed a stranger on a dare, though he denies it. I never really knew him. He never taught me a thing."

"I'm sorry."

Thirty-three grabs my hand, pulls it over to his penis, starts to move against it. Eighty-seven does the same.

"Cut that out," 12 says.

"Why? Isn't that what we're here for?" 87 asks.

Twelve gives them the don't-make-me-say-it-again look, which instantly returns my hands to my sides.

"What's your name?" I ask 12.

"Tommy."

"That's a good name."

Tommy glances down at the floor. Then he scratches the arm of his chair while he slowly takes in every object in the room, like he wants to, needs to remember every detail before the big kill. A barbell loaded with weights. An almost-empty bag of pot. A stack of vinyl records with Mozart's *Forty-first Symphony* on top. Didn't expect that.

"It's time," Tommy says.

"I know."

"Do you want to stand or sit?" Tommy asks.

"Stand."

"We're not going to do her?" 33 asks.

"She's earned that much," Tommy says.

I stand up. Look around the room one last time. Everything is old, dilapidated, battered, you know, like somewhere along the way it lost its dignity, its bliss, its sense of why it was here in the first place. Time seems to slow and I calm, tap in. I mean, in the end, all the energy underneath is the same. I go through the tiny pinprick. I'm thankful for every moment of my life, every experience, even this one. I'm thankful I knew how to go through the pinprick when it mattered most. I mean, I played three perfect concerts. I loved. Dad. Mom. John. Z. Solly. Shaman. Even P. I created multigenerational art. I found my way into the big wide calm. How many people can say they packed that much in?

I swallow, taste strawberries. I swear they're real.

Even though it's my time, even though the world deems these guys monsters, and even though they are in a way, I want to reach out and hug Tommy, tell him there's a different path, tell him it's never too late, tell him I forgive him. The other two may be too far gone, but not Tommy. I can see it in his eyes.

"Any last requests?" Tommy asks.

"Got a cure for cancer?"

Tommy hairline smiles.

I rise out of my body one last time. I watch myself take one slow step toward him. Then another. Thirty-three and 87 cuff my arms, but Tommy nods them off. A few steps later, I reach him. There's this aura around me, my finest painting, which morphs between every possible palette color but settles on the reds. I mean, it's astonishingly beautiful; it's frackin multigenerational. As it engulfs him, bathes him, lets him touch the big wide calm for just a moment, I embrace him, cradle him like he's my firstborn, kiss his forehead. Thirty-three gives Tommy the gun and Tommy burrows it into my chest. Will I still be able to hover above when it's over?

I snap back into my body. If only all answers came that fast. Our eyes lock. One does not blink in this place.

"This is going to hurt."

"It's the deal I made."

Tommy points to a record on top of a pile, directs 87 to play it loudly. He scans the room again, though this time he pays particular attention to the same old photo framed and mounted on the wall. Who's the man? A moment later, "Kashmir" fills the room.

"Do I have your word?" Tommy asks.

At first I don't understand, but then I do, and I say, "Yes."

Tommy lowers the gun a few inches, pulls the trigger once, then again. "You won't die. Someone will find you on the street. You'll be okay."

I glance down at blood creeping out, soaking the side, bottom of my shirt. The two holes of pain are drama queens, burning, demanding every last bit of focus. I fall into Tommy, who catches me. As the room starts to fade, I hear someone say, "Thank you. You're a worthy man."

#

"Do you think you'll ever love another man?"

"You're asking me this when I'm about to give birth to our third child?"

"Sorry."

"I already love other men."

"I meant someone new."

"I hope."

"You hope?"

"Wouldn't you want me to have as much love in my life as possible?"

While sitting on the edge of my laboring bed, John zeroes in on a lever and pulls it. The bottom of the bed underneath him breaks off like one of those floating icebergs from a Discovery Channel special. He pushes off with his feet and rolls across the room.

Stirrups pop out of the remaining bed, like gray antennas in waiting, and startle me. "Why did you do that?"

John smiles. "Just curious. I'll put it right back."

I survey the rest of the birthing room as John reassembles the bed. You know, Mass General has done well. A framed black and white photograph hangs across from the bed, depicting a woman in the corner of a light-infused room; she might go off frame at any moment. A birthing chair faces a wall-mounted flat-screen TV where John and I watched Letterman the night before. Tucked away behind a row of cabinets on the near wall are medical supplies, which he'd cataloged during the commercials. Balled-up blankets and sheets cover a still-open sofa bed on the far wall. On the other side of the room, a nurse's station stands ready to monitor heart rates. A little farther away, a bed equipped with oxygen, a warmer, blankets, hats, diapers, and a nasal suctioner awaits Tommy. Running water gurgles into a large tub in the corner of the room.

The objects, the sounds, comfort me; at the same time, the restlessness I've experienced ever since arriving at the hospital remains. Tommy will be the last of our children, the culmination of a twelve-year phase of our lives. The smell of disinfectant, like ammonia and vitamins, permeates everything.

After John pieces the bed back together, I take in my body. Sprawled out on top of ruffled sheets and extra pillows, I've created a mare's nest. I'm covered in sweat, and my hospital johnny is twisted and pushed up to the top of my thighs. John loves me though, even like this, especially like this. His love has grown over the years, through children, through song, through simple moments together that struck chords deep down. He has nothing to worry about; no one else will ever get close.

He reaches out and strokes my forearm. "I guess more love is okay."

"Good. Can you put some essential oils in the vaporizer?"

"Which ones?"

"Bergamot, chamomile, lavender, patchouli, ylang ylang."

He goes over to the pregnancy bag he packed for me two days ago and pulls out five bottles of oil. At the vaporizer, he eye-drops in a bit of each.

"You know, I didn't scream at you during the first two of these because of that stuff, but it may not help this time," I say.

"Sorry. The question was on my mind. Not sure where it came from. Peace offering?" John asks.

"Your timing is normally better. Water therapy."

John helps me out of bed and into the Jacuzzi-style tub. He dims the lights in the room and pushes play on a portable stereo he's brought from home. "Blessing" pours through the speakers. Vaporized essential oils win the air battle with the disinfectant as he perches himself on the edge of the tub. He massages my hair with the tips of his fingers. Over the years, my color has morphed from dark brown, almost black, to a lighter brown striated with blonde. The same color that all women in their early forties have.

"Better?" he asks.

"Much."

"Last child."

"The end of a phase."

"Everything's right on track."

#

I open my eyes. John. Dad, Mom, Z. My version of heaven. Until their faces morph in relief, which I guess means I'm still alive. I raise my arm up until pain from where the IV is inserted pulls it down. Yeah, yeah, still alive. What a dream.

"Do you remember anything at all?" John asks.

"They dragged me to their car around the corner."

"Did you get a make and model?" Dad asks.

"No. It's a blur. We drove to an ATM in Inman Square. After I got them their money, I tried to get away. We struggled, and I guess that's when they shot me."

"You were very lucky. The bullets missed all the important stuff," Z says.

Everyone nods. Mom tears up, reaches down, and holds my hand for a bit.

"We need to file a police report when you're ready. Get their descriptions out. We'll get those bastards, honey," Dad says.

"I want to let it go, Dad."

"What? Absolutely not. They can't get away with this," Dad says.

"We're all okay, Dad. That's the important thing. Let it go."

Out of range, Dad talks to Mom and Z for a bit, who both seem to agree with him. They work themselves up until they've created some kind of closed-looped system that can't be anything but absolutely, positively right.

The whole time John remains close, silent, avoids the righteous indignation party, studies my face.

"We'll talk about it more in a few days. Mom and I want you to come back to New Mexico with us to recuperate."

"That's okay, Dad. I'm fine. The best thing for me is to get back to work."

"Absolutely not," Dad says.

I glance at John.

"She'll be okay, Alex. I'll take good care of her, and I'm sure Z will be out to visit often. Paige is right, we have a lot of work to do," John says.

"She'll be fine, Alex," Mom says. "She can take care of herself."

A DIFFERENT VOICE

After Tommy, the paintings stopped. You know, at first I didn't pay much attention to it. Best to let a block run its course. I mean, everyone knows trauma and blocks are ancient lovers. But after a few weeks, I came to accept that my urge, my itch to create with color had gone away. Just a phase. Done. Ended in the most beautiful red.

I'm on my bed now. Have spent a good portion of the last month here with John. John is fully dressed, tieless, jacketless, sleeves rolled up, holding me. I'm in jeans and a Janis Joplin T-shirt I bought at the Hall. Shaman is sprawled out on the floor, taking a long nap. The air is thick with sage. To be clear, the bed-in with John isn't about sex. The football numbers squashed my libido, and even though John and I have already ended that phase of our relationship, well, he is a guy, and he is in bed with me, so I figured I better spell it out. The bed-in is also not about words. John has been here for me in silence, exactly as requested. Overall, I'm a blob. Overall, I'm not sure anything will help, but today, I'm going to try confession.

"Want to hear the whole story?" I ask.

"If you're ready."

"I'll never tell anyone else." I replay the entire night from the knockouts forward. Every detail. Every sense. With few pauses and little hedging. It's my strength test—the more detail I reveal, the more it proves I'm cast iron. In my mind, I've done this test every day since the event, though the leap to out loud is, well, big.

The whole time John doesn't speak, doesn't seem to blink. He slowly, gently runs his fingers up and down my bare arm, outlining something. At one point, he tears up, switches patterns on my arm to different sized circles. After I finish, the circles slow, and he says, "You saved us. And yourself. Maybe even Tommy. You were incredibly brave."

"I don't know about that."

"You were. I have an idea."

"Shoot," I say.

"Nice choice of words. Ever do flash poetry?"

"No."

"One minute per poem. Just write whatever comes. Don't overthink it."

"Do you know you now hold the all-time record for a male in bed with me without getting an erection?"

John laughs. "What was the previous record?"

"Much, much shorter."

"Ready now?"

"You mean that didn't work?" I ask.

"Too late. I know them all."

"But it was such a good one."

John smiles, slips out of bed, and heads downstairs. A short time later, he returns with a fresh journal and this beautiful powder-blue pen. He hands them to me, then sits in the corner of the room, knees up to his chest, arms belted around his legs.

"Write in cursive and landscape."

"Why?"

"It will help."

"But why?"

"Just will. Trust me."

Cross-legged, I sit on the bed facing him. I open the pen, turn to a fresh page, begin to write. After a slow start, after two minutes instead of one, I finish the first poem. Guess he's not too rigid on the time thing. I reread what I wrote silently a few times, then go loud.

"What I regret is the time when I was a girl. And I used a magnifying glass to amplify the sun and fry a sidewalk ant. It was the first time I knew I was different from ants. Better somehow. It's taken years to unlearn that one. Time wasted when I could have been building farms."

"Read it again," John says.

"Why?"

"Twice is better. Trust me."

I read the poem again. He nods, smiles, tells me to keep going.

A couple of minutes later, I read him my second poem.

"I want someone to break in. Fight the good fight to the inside. Lay next to me face-to-face until I get it, until I absorb the piece about holding peace inside after violence, about not fucking up love when someone is face-to-face."

These are kind of cool. And easy. I could do like a hundred of them. Best to jump into the next one right away. You know, with all the high-tech gadgets out there, I don't write in cursive very often—pretty much autographs only—but there's something about connecting all the letters into words, into sentences, into poems, that works. Must be a quantum thing. Chalk up another one for Zen master, my Zen master.

After several minutes, I put my pen down and read out loud, "I had this black circle of a balloon once. It floated up into the sky. At first, I thought it just covered the sun, but soon after I realized it replaced it. When the rain came, it tried to spread life, but couldn't without the sun. So it rained more and more, trying to spread life on its own."

Instant art. Not multigenerational, but not bad.

John is perfectly still in the corner; I'm sure he's going to start snapping his fingers after one of these things. Or light a match. But he does neither, so I go back to work.

Poem Four. "Kindness came in through the window and wrapped me in a powder-blue blanket. The blanket sprouted wings that carried me back to this place before the violence, before the sadness. There I was happy, laughing all the time, full of hope and joy. But I didn't know a thing, so I asked Kindness to bring me back to the sadness, to the place I was just passing through."

John gets up, comes over to the bed, kisses me on the forehead. "I'll make coffee. Keep going while I'm away." He heads for the door. Before he leaves, he pivots around, loops his thumbs into his pockets, and gives me the I'm-not-going-anywhere look.

That much I do believe.

Temporarily charged up, I go to work. Can't stop. All of this stuff is pouring out of me. The Big Release, I guess, which after all of this time in bed is, well, titanic.

Poems later, he returns, pours me a cup, resumes his corner position.

"I'm going to read you four in a row," I say.

Poem Five. "Pull my hand please, like my life depended on it. Because when you dream awake at the bottom, sometimes the undercurrent is too strong for one. And the only way back is through your pull."

Poem Six. "After the fall, when you're alone, time slows like in one of those action movies. Only it's not bullets or knives or fists or penises coming at you. It's nightmares of friends, relatives, past loves who you somehow hurt or who hurt you. Mostly you try to forgive or ask for forgiveness, though sometimes you think it would be easier to endure a bullet, knife wound, or a couple of cocks."

Poem Seven. "Sometimes when the sadness is thick, I see you through a glass wall doing a crossword puzzle. You're using no letters, only mysterious symbols that can be touched but rarely understood."

Poem Eight. "Once, when I was sleeping, I saw your eyes, deep blue, in a dream. They went through, past all of the broken things, until they found the black marble. Then a strange thing happened: the marble turned into a pair of blue eyes and looked back."

John grabs a fresh bundle of sage from the nightstand and resumes his corner position. There, he lights it and holds it above his head with one arm. He reminds me of a male version of the Statue of Liberty, minus the green stuff. John Bustin, you've created a monster. A big, bad, broken monster who vibes on flash poetry. Who would have thought?

#

I've had this book on my nightstand for months—*In a Different Voice* by Carol Gilligan. John gave me it to me, told me it was worth reading. I started it a few times, and it was okay, but it always stalled out. Today is different. Today, it's caught hold and won't let go. There's lots of stuff in it, but the main bit is about how boys and girls play. For boys, it's the rules, the competition. Sports rules. War rules. Business rules. Music business rules. Compete for everything, and someone must win. For girls, it's about harmony. Keep the peace at all costs. Smile when angry. Say yes when you mean no. Take care when you're in need. You know, I've sided with the boys over the years. I mean, coy I'm not. Men's rules make things more direct, more honest, but now I realize also more violent, where the winners win too much, and losers, well, why bother after the big fall.

Today the girls are running wild in my head. They're saying, "Enough already! We have a better way." They're saying, "Get the fuck out of bed, Paige Plant." I call Z, tell him to come for a visit. I call John, who's gone back to his own bed the last few days at my request, tell him to stop down later for a walk. My first in thirty-seven days.

I push out of bed.

Shaman, who's abandoned his brothers the entire month to be with me, wags his tail. I kneel down, let him lick my face a few times, give him a kiss on the snout. He smells like cherry incense. In the bathroom, I check myself out in the mirror. My hair is a mess, the dark circles under my eyes sandwich my nose, and my eyes are so bloodshot that the red bits outnumber the white bits two to one. All of that doesn't matter though. What matters is underneath that surface stuff, I'm strong, calm, ready. The football numbers have not won. They never will. All kinds of women hologram out of my head and dance to music I write on the spot. Poets. Doctors. Teachers. Architects.

Mothers. Scientists. Each one has a different colored aura morphing around her. Red. Blue. White. Yellow. Green. They're beautiful. The song is a rock anthem, a takeover march—no, a partnership march, for now without lyrics.

There's also one in army fatigues, with guns and knives strapped all over her body. She pulls out a machine gun and is about to fire it into a throng of football players hovering over the toilet seat. Before she does, she glances over at the others and signals them to follow her. In unison, they all say, "Not like that." She hesitates, re-aims her gun, but the poet comes over to her and gently lowers the weapon. The different auras from all of the women surround the soldier, embrace her. She starts to cry. Then a strange thing happens—the auras combine together, rainbow-like; they pulse, morph, to the music. Not like the chintzy ones you see in clubs or at concerts. This combination is much more intricate, like lace, like every color is represented, no matter how subtle, how minutely different. For the first time in my life, I can see *and* hear my music at the same time.

A few hours later, Z, John, and I are on the trail with the dogs. There's such natural beauty all around us. The giant oaks. The rocks covered with moss. The brook. The forest bed of pine needles. I love these trails, these dogs, these men. I love the smell of pine in the morning.

"I've missed these walks."

"Me too," John says.

"Me too," Z says.

We walk for a time in silence, you know, just take it all in. Stillness, Talk, and Shaman crisscross often on their way to new trees. This is more than enough to take in on my first day back. Really, it's more than enough for any day.

"I gave up painting today. For good," I say.

"Really? Why?" John asks.

"My next song."

"What?" Z says.

"I can already see it and hear it."

John stops walking, goes over to the stream we've been walking along. He crouches down, pulls out, like, ten small water-polished rocks and stacks them in a perfect pyramid about a foot from shore.

"So you don't need to paint it."

"I could never see both before at the same time. The songs will be more whole, more fluid from now on."

"Calm?" John asks.

"That too." I join John next to the stream, pull out my own polished beauties, stack them next to John's pyramid. The pyramids look like twins. "By the way, I've been thinking about Bono. I want him back for the rest of TBWC. The songs will be better with him."

John pops up, dries his hands on his suit pants. He gently places both of his hands on top of my shoulders, smiles, and says, "Of course."

#

I'm sitting on the magic piano bench, slowly pressing middle C over and over. It's been forty days and forty nights. Not even a manual go, which, you know, would be astonishing if it wasn't so depressing. At least I'm thinking about it now, which has to be a good sign. Even though, strictly speaking, nothing happened with the football numbers, with the combined one hundred twenty—even though I talked my way out of gang rape, out of dying—in a way, I didn't. I mean, I'm an artist. I visualize. For those guys, sex with a blood chaser, well, there's nothing better, and thoughts of that combination crushed me, shut me down. But not for much longer. I just need to figure out with who. Not John. Not Z. Bono? Nah, it was never really like that with him. Someone new? Maybe, though the gun-shy thing is working full tilt.

I start to play, improvise. Simple chord voicings with my left hand hold together a nursery rhyme of a melody I'm playing with my right hand. In a few, I take the bit as far as it can go. It's in the same key as the "Paige Plant" song Dad wrote all those years ago, so I morph into that, start singing "Paige Plant" over and over again, just like my dad did when I was a girl. When I finish, I move right into a piano version of "Stairway to Heaven" I used to play as a teenager. Dad loved it, but the boy I was dating at the time, a grunge electric guitar player named Todd, thought it was an abomination. I liked that boy. He was my third. Or maybe my fourth.

When I was with P, when it was still good, he made me playlists all the time of songs, mostly love songs, that he liked. Of all those songs, the one I liked best was "Answer" by Sarah McLachlan. I start to play it from the top, but skip right to the chorus, which I sing like I'm putting it on my own CD. "Cast me gently / Into morning / For the night has been unkind / Take me to a place so holy / That I can wash this from my mind / The memory of choosing not to fight." The second time through, I change the last line to "The memory of men lost in rage." Many loops later, I'm done with "Answer."

I rise up from the magic piano bench, make my way to the control room. I find the playlist John used that day we first danced, queue it up, go back into the studio. At first I barely move. I thought it would be more like riding a bike, but it's not. It's more like wading in mud. Trudge on, soldier, trudge on. One by one, my holographic female friends join me, teach me new moves, freer moves. There appear to be dozens of them, like I've been subconsciously recruiting since last we met, like I knew ahead of time only dozens would do. I shut my eyes, lose myself in the music, dance for a long time, until I'm dripping wet with sweat, until I'm floating above the quagmire, until I shed the combined weight of one hundred twenty. When I open my eyes, the women one-by-one hug goodbye, fade as they came. When they're all gone, holographic Ian presents right in front of me. He smiles and extends his hand.

\#

Radha Hanlon steps inside the studio wearing a black English derby. She has short red hair, large blue eyes encircled by black mascara lashes, and so many freckles that she appears tan. A vibrant red lipstick matches her hair. She doesn't need makeup, but I like it on her. A brown skinny-strap tank top exposes the freckles on her shoulders and confirms they're all over her body. She's wearing jeans, sandals. Her toes are painted red with a gold toe ring on one foot. Five-feet-something and well shaped, she's about the same height and build as me. What's the perfume? Like red azaleas in bloom. The sex-tingle stirs for a bit, then goes quiet.

"I thought I'd check in on you," Radha says.

"Thanks. I'm heading out in a little bit to get this cast off," I say.

"Guess this is goodbye then."

"Guess." I haven't seen Radha since the last concert. She really did a boffo job filling in for me on guitar. Turns out she's not only a player; she does the singer-songwriter thing, too. She has a solid voice and only a few early stage songs, but I mean, she's young, like twenty or something, so she has a little time.

I boil water. She's a tea drinker, so I let her pick a bag from a box of infinite tea. English Breakfast. A moment later, we've rearranged two foldings in the studio so they're facing each other. She crosses one leg over the other, bobs her sandal. It's going to slip off any second now. You know, I liked her from the first moment I saw her, but the flash sex-tingle caught me off guard. Last time I was with a woman was, well, a long time ago, during my freshmen year experimentation phase. A robotics engineer.

"I'm working on a new song," I say.

"That's great, Paige."

"'In a Different Voice,'" I say.

"Like the Carol Gilligan book?"

"Yeah, yeah, you know it?"

"Yeah. Mom's a feminist. Made me read it at thirteen."

"Ah." Okay, there it is. What are the chances? I mean, I haven't seen Radha in over a month, she checks in derby and all, triggers the sex-tingle, and knows the book. After my little holographic dance, I thought of Ian, but now I'm not so sure.

"I'm so sorry about what happened, Paige."

"Thank you."

"You're strong. Looks like you're almost back."

"Almost."

"What's left?"

"Sex."

Radha lifts her head up just a notch so her eyes line up a little better with mine. Her face, her arms blush red, almost to the point where they match the color of her hair. She lifts the guitar off the stand next to her, pulls it close, and begins to perform an old Jane Siberry song I haven't heard in years, "Love Is Everything." When she's done, she rests her hand on the curve of the guitar body, strokes the wood with her index finger. What is it about me and redheads? Every time I'm broken, well, they're healers.

"I love that song," she says.

"It's beautiful, and honest."

"Do you have a verse part for 'A Different Voice' yet? If so, I'll play it for you."

I go over to the piano bench and work out the part I heard with my holographic sisters earlier. Just simple stuff, mostly with my right hand because the cast makes anything intricate with my left difficult. In no time, Radha picks it up.

"It's good," she says. "Do you have any words or a melody yet?"

"Still playing with both." As Radha continues the verse groove, I play around in my mind with a few lines, a few melodies, until I land on something I like. I never share an idea this early in the process. Even with John, I'm normally much farther along. But it seems okay with Radha, so I sing, "When I was young I learned those girl rules / Stayed in relation, rarely argued / I smiled when angry, took care in need / Said yes when I meant no / looked pretty but never seen."

"That's fantastic, Paige. I love it," Radha says.

"Thanks. Still a long way to go."

"Let me take you to get your cast off. Then I'll buy you lunch."

A couple of hours later, my arm is floating in Radha's car, weightless. I love the sensation, like I'm about to lift off and my arm is running point.

This happened once before when I was a girl. I'd broken my other arm in two places after falling off my bike and onto a curb. When that cast cracked off and my arm lifted, it was the first time I knew I was going to be famous, the first time I believed I could change the world. Anyway, Radha is driving and we're headed for Great Brook Farm State Park for a picnic. We just made a stop at Whole Foods to stock up on goodies.

At the trunk of the car, she pulls out a large blanket and a few bags of picnic food. She hands the blanket to me. We trek into the forest. A warm fall day, the temperature drops to ideal under the tree canopy. A floor of pine needles seems to part in front of us as we head off-trail. There isn't another soul anywhere.

Radha takes my hand. Her hand is soft, gentle, warm, like a slow wake-up caress after sleeping in on Sunday. A mile or so later, at a large flat rock overlooking a pond, she spreads out the blanket, slips off her sandals, and floats down.

"What a perfect spot," I say.

"It is." Sitting cross-legged, she reaches for a bag and pulls it close. She feels around inside and removes two glasses, two bottles of Guinness. She twists open the bottles, pours two glasses, generates way too much foam. "I love Guinness."

"I've had it a few times."

"Really? It's my favorite."

Next she pulls out a plate with different cheeses, nuts, and grapes. She smiles as she pops a grape in her mouth. "I love grapes." Then a piece of cheese. "And cheese." Then a few shelled pistachio nuts. "And nuts. Pretty much, I love food." With beer in one hand, she feeds me a grape like she's Hippocrates with the other.

"I miss performing with you," she says. "I know it was only a temporary gig, but it was so much fun."

"It was."

Radha moves a little closer.

I close my eyes for only a second. I don't want to miss anything. Her lips are soft, gentle, like she instinctively knows she has to go slow. Her tongue, supple, probing, carries peace and lust at the same time. With her eyes closed, I study her freckled lids. They cover her, protect her.

"First kiss in a long time."

"It was great."

"Hungry?"

"Not for food." In one fluid movement, she straddles me and pulls her tank top off over her head. Then she helps me pull my top off. She kisses me gently, expertly, careful not to go too fast or too aggressive. After a time, she works her way down my body, stops for a long time on my breasts. Finally, she unbuckles my jeans.

"Should we check to see if anyone's around?" I ask.

"I'm okay giving them a show if you are."

"I'm sorry."

"Why?"

"This is going to be one-sided."

"I'm okay with that. It's an honor, really."

For a time, all thoughts subside except this one—I'm so thankful. Each time after I come, I sob, do the thankful-thought thing. Each time, Radha makes her way up my body, wipes the tears, gently kisses my eyelids, and says, "I've got you, Paige."

Afterwards, clothes back on, my only confirmation of where we've just been is the glow on her face, the taste on her tongue, eyes that know. I go into the blues in wonder, like a girl who's found treasure, or a woman who's found peace. All this time, so much was waiting there.

Radha fills our glasses with more Guinness. She dips her fork twice into each of the Whole Foods containers, which are spread out in a semicircle around us. First time she samples the food like she's checking for poison. Second time she feeds me.

"How do you feel?" she asks.

"Safe."

#

The next morning I'm by myself, in my room, in my bed. Sleep was peace—first time since the event. Someone is tiptoeing up the stairs. I'm still half-asleep and Fred is blurry. Nine o'clock, I think. I have no idea who's coming. Radha? Z? John? The footballers? There's a light knock on the door.

"Paige, you awake? It's me, Bono."

"Bono!" I pop out of bed and race to the door. I'm only wearing a T-shirt, but it's okay. I've waited too long to worry about showing too much. I fling open the door. Up on the balls of my feet, I kiss him on both cheeks, hug him for a long time. He smells like fall, like leaves and burning oak. "Go put some water on for coffee. I'll be down in a couple."

After I wet my hair and brush it straight back, I slip into some jeans and, barefoot, make my way toward Bono in the studio. With each step, the wood floor tickles the balls of my feet. I've missed Bono these months. John was in control back then, and I mean, part of me disagreed with his decision, but part of me just let it go. I should have done more to keep Bono in the game. He's a friend and we're good for each other; he's going to circle around me for a long time, and I'm going to circle around him. In the studio, we sit facing each other on a couple of foldings. Just like me, he's lost twenty pounds and is too thin. Need to fix that.

"How have you been?" I ask.

"Okay. Working a lot. Trying to save some money."

"And music?"

"Not much. I was surprised when John called."

"I told him I could use your help finishing the album."

"You don't need my help."

"It will be better with you. And Radha."

"Who's she?" he asks.

"Another singer-songwriter. You'll like her. She's great. She's been helping me heal from the event."

"John told me. I'm so sorry."

"Old news. I'm stronger now, more determined, calmer. Want to hear my new stuff?"

For the next hour or so, I catch Bono up musically. I play each new song twice. First on acoustic guitar, then the final full-band mix really loud through the monitors. When I shut my eyes, the studio monitors are so accurate that it almost sounds like the band is right there with us. Bono is a fan all along the way, and even uses some of the same lines that Dad did when he first heard the songs. "Fantastic!" "Artistic!" The universe, I guess. Finally, we get to "A Different Voice," and I play him what I have a couple of times.

"Nice. Maybe spread the melody out a bit so there's less space."

"Yeah, I was thinking the same. Before we dive in, let me call Radha. I'd like the three of us to work on it."

While we wait, Bono and I play dueling guitars, trading leads over a made-up progression that Bono came up with while in exile. It's good, like we haven't missed a beat during all of those months. He's right in the middle of some nice licks when Radha walks in, guitar case in hand.

"Don't stop for me," she says.

We both rest our guitars on our knees. Radha walks over and kisses me on the cheek. She pulls up a folding, opens her case, and pulls out her Martin. Wearing jeans, work boots, a black Dublin Luthier T-shirt, and her now-famous black English Derby, she's made quite the entrance. Bono is clearly interested; I'll need to pull him aside in a few.

"Nice guitar," Bono says.

"Yours too," Radha says.

They guitar-talk for a bit until they're both impressed. Bono catches Radha up on how he knows me. Radha does the same, minus the biblical piece. We start up a new jam. Blues this time. You know, you can tell a lot about a musician by how she plays the blues. Best not to trust one who doesn't play them well. I mean, it's the source. Both Bono and Radha's leads are full of old-soul loss, the kind where there aren't too many notes, but the sum total leaves a lump in your throat. Was there ever any doubt?

After the blues have run their course, I say, "So here's what I'm thinking. I'd like the two of you to help me with 'A Different Voice.' I'd also like you to become part of my band when I go out on the road in a few months."

"Really?" Bono says.

"That's generous," Radha says.

"Also, I'll need an opener. Maybe the two of you can work something out together?"

"Absolutely," Bono says.

Radha looks at me and smiles; something passes between us. It's not a sex-tingle, though it could lead there. It's more like kindness, like my offer just closed the circle. Yeah, yeah, that's it. What a feeling. What would the world be like if the kindness loop were always closed?

Anyway, time to get to work. I play the first verse of "A Different Voice." Radha already knows it, so she plays along. Bono picks it up right away.

"Let's work on the melody a bit."

We launch off Bono's idea to extend the melody, to spread it out. Much better. Best to always have something going on melodically in a song, with as little empty space as possible. You can pass the melody from a vocal to an instrument, or to anything really, but you have to keep it going. Bono also changes a few notes that make the melody a little more mainstream, but Radha pushes back. She's more from the same atonal school that I am. I do the arbitrator thing and pick a final version somewhere in between. You know, I like this way of working. I write the first pass of everything; they refine.

Next, we move on to the chorus. When writing an anthem, the chorus has to stand on its own. Think "We Are the Champions" or "I Love Rock and Roll." Or "Give Peace a Chance." Sometimes the song isn't even about what most listeners think it is, like in Springsteen's "Born in the U.S.A.," but there'll be no room for misinterpretation on "A Different Voice." I've worked out lyrics for the chorus, but I don't have a guitar bit yet. I recite the lyrics. "Now I've found a different voice / Full of strength, full of choice / You better watch out because I'm coming back your way / And when I get there, what I say will be in a different voice / A woman's voice."

"Love it," Radha says.

"Bono?" I ask.

"Still processing."

Okay, there it is. If I'm trying to write an anthem for women, does it really matter what Bono thinks? Best to limit his involvement to the music itself. Radha and I will work through the lyrics. I glance over at Radha, who appears to have already written Bono's feedback off before he's given it. Patience, dear, which I know you already have in abundance.

"For me, if the chorus portrayed strength and kindness at the same time, I think it would work better," Bono says.

I eye-dart over at Radha, who is in the middle of a frown-to-smile morph. Bono is right. I don't want the song to just show women as strong. I want the women of "A Different Voice" to be strong and kind. That's the piece that so many men have missed, the piece that led to so much conflict, so much suffering. I change the last line to "a kinder voice," and my two bandmates raise their guitars up like giant lighters, hold them by the neck, and each gives me a single nod.

"If ever there was the need for a Zeppelin power chord chorus . . ." Radha says.

"Yeah, yeah," I say. I start playing around with power chords, piecing bits of the lyrics on top. Bono pulls the melody a little more toward pop. Radha pulls in the other direction. For the next two hours, we do nothing but work on the melody until we've got one that is, well, the best thing I've ever written. Or the best thing we've ever written. Bono pulls a Goldtop Les Paul off its stand, plugs it into the Marshall amp in the corner of the room, dials up just the right amount of distortion, which is, well, a lot. Radha puts a harmony over parts of my melody. The three of us are so good that I'm tempted to call up the drummer and bass player right away.

But I don't. For the next sixteen or so hours, well into the night, we work on the remaining verses and the bridge. Verses: *For those who speak but are not heard / For those who play it safe / For those waiting to be saved / It will never occur until we do it ourselves / I stood under for so long that I understand those rules / Let's write new ones for all of us where we live honestly.* Bridge: *There will be some who don't believe in change / There will be some who try to strike us down / There will be times when you will wonder / If what you lost is better than what you found.*

When we're done with my first anthem, it's too late for Radha to go home. And while Bono could easily go up to his room in the main house, he doesn't. Like we're back in high school, we decide to have a sleepover. I bring down pillows and blankets from my room, Radha pulls some cushions off of the control room sofa, and Bono goes to the house to scoff up much more wine, beer, and snacks than we could conceivably consume. We set up camp next to the magic piano bench. Faces up, like we're staring at the stars instead of the ceiling, in our separate little makeshift beds, we crunch on chocolate and sip beer, wine. We talk until the sun comes up. About everything. Politics. Sports. Music. John. You know, when you choose your tribe, there's nothing better. Even though I'm still adding members, I like saying the names of the current line-up in a row—Z, Bono, Radha, John.

Over coffee and tea in the morning, Bono asks, "Do you think men and women will ever really understand each other?"

"Probably not," Radha says. "There's too much of a gap."

"I don't know. It's possible. A lot of work, for sure, but possible." What's John up to today?

#

I've had this proposal from Ian on my nightstand for the last month. He gave it to me at the last show, but I never got the chance to thumb through it. Ever since my time with Radha a few days ago, I've had this feeling I should call him. I skim his stuff just enough so that I'll sound like I read it, then dial his number. After the great-to-hear-from-you and I'm-so-sorry and your-proposal-has-merit bits, I ask him to meet me at Bukowski Tavern in Inman Square to further discuss his plan. I sound so businesslike that I almost believe that's really why I'm going. I mean, why not, right?

In Cambridge a couple of hours later, I park a good distance from Bukowski's, the place I was planning to take Dad and John before the football event. On my way, I retrace our path from that night, stop at the exact spot on the side street where I left Dad and John unconscious, bullet-less. Nearby, two young girls are drawing a fresh hopscotch board on the sidewalk. "Do you want to play?" one asks. I join Emma and Mia. I hop for a bit, spend extra time in the "safe" semicircle. When I was a girl, Mom, a New Yorker, called the game Potsy. She watched us play from the front porch, had an uncanny knack for bringing us drinks and snacks at just the right time. After a few games with Emma and Mia, I say my goodbyes like we're best girlfriends, continue on my way, take a mental note to call Mom soon. You know, the street is quite beautiful in daylight. Old Victorians line both sides, and young families are sitting out on their porches drinking iced tea, lemonade. Occasionally, Paige-on-the-porch holds up a cardboard sign, painted in rainbow colors, that says, "Someday."

As I approach Bukowski's, Ian is waiting for me, perched on a stool at the front of the tavern. There's no front door to the place; it's more like a front wall that completely opens up to the sidewalk. I beeline to Ian's table, give him a hug, a quick peck on the cheek. The sex-tingle skyrockets.

"Thanks for coming," I say.

"No problem. Why did we come here?"

"It's where I was headed the night of the event."

"Oh . . . brave."

"I guess."

Ian orders a glass of red wine. I order a Guinness and couple of heavy-on-the-salt appetizers. You know, the man does it for me. I mean, he's just sitting across the table, overdressed as usual, saying something about how he hopes we can work together. Then he smiles. Cut the words, get off of your bench, and kiss me. Now. Better yet, leave a fifty on the table, whisk me back to your place, get on with the rose petaling. How I've missed rose petaling.

"So what do you think?" Ian asks.

"About?"

"About my proposal."

"Oh right."

The waiter serves us our drinks and appetizers. Ian sips his wine, waits for my response. I sip my Guinness, which really is much better on tap, glance at the appetizers. Salt is one of the great pleasures of life, but I seem to have lost my appetite. I'm sure his proposal is fine, and if not, we'll work it out as we go.

"I like it," I say.

"I'm glad. Not hungry?"

I smile a non-answer, count to three, slip my hand into my jean pocket, and pull out a couple of twenties. After I place them on the table, I get off my stool, take a step toward Ian, kiss him, well, like I've never kissed a man before. He tastes like strawberries.

"Let's get out of here," I say.

We take our separate cars to Ian's place, which I was against at first, but, well, give the man big-time points for knowing how to fuel the tingle. As soon as he opens his door, the room blurs. All I can see is his face. Eyes open, I'm kissing him. My lips, my tongue, my eyes, my taste are a collective doorway. Come in now, please. We propel forward through the apartment, toward his bed. Rose petals trail behind, provide a way back in case we get lost, though I have this peaceful feeling that there's no way back.

On his bed, both naked, I reach down, cradle him. He's thick, just like I remember him. I start to slowly move up, down, but 87 and 33 in their jerseys, helmets, with denim-covered erect penises, freeze me. Twelve smiles, just before he shoots two burning bullets through each side of my abdomen again. I pull my hand away. Fuck.

"Don't stop," Ian says.

"Eighty-seven and 33."

"What?"

"I need to tell you something."

Ian notches down for a bit, then gets out of bed. He reaches down to help me up. After he pulls back the covers, we slip under them and assume cuddle position. This has never happened before with any boy, man, woman, when either of us is this far gone, when the sex-tingle has ballooned into a full-blown rock anthem, when we've already crossed the must-come-soon point. Did all of that happen a short time ago? Will the numbers ever get out of my head? Nestled up against Ian, fetal position, one side of my face on his chest, he wraps his arm around me and rests his hand on my shoulder. Even though he's warm, even though he's holding me, I start to shiver, shake. A full-blown 9.7 on the Richter scale.

After I slow down to an occasional aftershock, I calmly tell him everything that happened that night. I mean, the floodgates open. He has to see it all, and right away. Best to not press pause for too long while naked in bed with a guy who floats your boat. When it's all out there, when all of the pieces are undressed and in view, when they're ready to be puzzled or ignored, then we'll see. Ian asks a few questions along the way, but mostly there are no words. A kiss on the forehead. A gentle squeeze of my shoulder. A finger streaming up and down my arm. When I'm done with the not-so-brief history of the event, I glance up at the cobalt blues. A single stream from each of his eyes makes its way toward me. Didn't expect that. A short time later, one thousand puzzle pieces spread out on the sheets. I ask, "Are you okay?"

"You're so brave."

"Thank you."

"Thank you for telling me," he says.

"Thank you."

"For what?"

"For helping me."

With long strokes, I tickle Ian's thigh, take in his smell, which is, well, intoxicating. A tingle builds, but not of the sexual variety, the kind that floats me out of my body. From above, I study the two of us in bed. We're laughing. Tickle wars have begun. And a pillow fight. I'm winning, of course. It's good to laugh.

I glance over at the corner of the room. John is sitting on the floor, knees up to his chest, encircled by his arms. He looks up at me, smiles, and nods once. He knows. He's always known. He mouths, "Go through." Just as I'm about to respond, he half-waves and fades away. I swallow dryness, love.

Okay, enough already. Time to go. One. Two. Three. I uncoil myself and straddle Ian. In no time, he's thick, inside of me. I've brought all of my past stuff to this moment, all of my experience, all of my songs, my paintings. I begin finger-painting Ian's body, inking bodies entwined, trust lost, Stillness, Talk, Shamans of Movement and Light, A Different Voice, Growing Down, When John Fell from Grace, violence, forgiveness, trust regained.

When I come, I come loud. A giant sound wave spreads out like a mushroom cloud toward Allston. When it reaches the numbers, it engulfs them, makes it clear what they will never have, sends them back into the throng for good. I sob from release, from weightlessness. After forty-seven days, after Z, John, Radha, Ian, I've gone through the tiny pinprick, through the knothole. Thank you, thank you. I'm so calm.

"What are you thinking?" Ian says.

"It's time to write 'The Big Wide Calm.'"

THE BIG WIDE CALM

John and I are sitting on the magic piano bench playing Schubert's *Fantasy in F Minor*. It's a little bit beyond my skill level, but I hang in there. Best to make John comfortable before I pop the big one. The dogs are under the piano, which doubles as their doghouse, apparently watching John work the foot petals. At one point near the end of the piece, Shaman, in a YouTube moment, starts to howl along.

A week has passed since I finished writing "A Different Voice." We recorded it yesterday with Bono, Radha, the full band. After the session, John told me it was the easiest song he'd ever produced; he just sat back and let us do our thing. You know, that may be my favorite John compliment of the last nine months. Well that and the bit about being brave.

After we finish, I whirl around on the bench, lift off, make my way into the kitchen. Milk and coffee time. I fill the dog bowls, press a pot. A bit later, I return with two cups of coffee, hand one to John, sit across from him on a folding. Legs outstretched and crossed, I say, "I've been thinking."

"About what?"

"It's time to write 'The Big Wide Calm.'"

"I thought you would do that one last?"

"It will be the last one."

"Ah . . . weren't you going to write twelve songs?"

"Yeah, yeah, that was the plan. But with a 'A Different Voice,' I have six. Also, I've been thinking about the P song I wrote before I came to you. That one belongs on this album. We can rerecord it for sure, but it belongs. And there are a few more old songs that played well in Cambridge. So I'll have eleven."

John scratches the back of his ear while he stares into his coffee cup. He crosses one leg over the other, then a second later apparently changes his mind about which leg should be on top. "Are you sure this is what you want?"

"Yeah. After these last couple of months, it feels like it's time to finish."

John nods, studies my face, tries to figure out if I mean what I just said. He pushes off the piano bench, walks over to the window, stares for a bit at the oaks, the maples.

After he must have counted all of them twice, he says, "You're right. Let's finish."

"One more thing."

"What's that?"

"Will you write the song with me?"

"That's not going to happen."

"Why?" I ask.

"It's your work. I'm only here to help."

"Writing the song with me would be a big help."

"I can't, Paige."

"Let's take the dogs for a walk. They need to go out."

For the next hour, the dogs and the woods are one, part of something larger, something old, ancient. John and I don't say a word to each other the whole time. Even though John said no, it's best to let him percolate for a bit before I move in for round two. I've given this a lot of thought and, well, I'm not writing "The Big Wide Calm" without him. We've come too far not to do this last piece together, and, you know, I'm not into ultimatums, but, I mean, it's for his own good. Though he doesn't understand that yet. And here's another reason: When two people are in a big love, sometimes they need to show the world by doing big stuff. Wedding vows. Children. A house in the suburbs. Dancing. Except for dancing, we're not going to do any of those things, so for us, to paraphrase that famous Clinton campaign slogan that Dad loves, it's *The Big Wide Calm*, stupid.

At the end of the walk, just before John's about to head up the path to the house, I say, "Well?"

"I already told you."

"Do you love me?"

"Of course. They aren't linked."

"I need you to do this for me, John."

"Why is this so important to you?"

"It just is."

John turns away and starts walking toward the house. Fuck. This may be harder than I thought. What do I have to do to get him to come around? I mean, there has to be a way in. About halfway up the path, he spins around, and while continuing to backpedal says, "Let me sleep on it."

#

When I open my eyes, Fred says 10:00. Radha's arm is wrapped around my waist, and I can feel her breath on the nape of my neck. Her taste, salty-sweet, is still in my mouth, and the room is still thick with sage. A single sheet covers us, and the breeze through the crack in the window has settled the room to crisp sleeping temperature. For a moment, I convince myself I could stay here for a very long time. I mean, Radha has been so generous. Along with Ian, she's done the heavy lifting these last weeks. And for that, I'll always be grateful, even after she moves out of my bed and into someone else's who can truly give her what she deserves. I told her about Ian from the start, about Bukowski's, about the float-the-boat thing. And she kept coming here anyway. You know, extraordinary kindness like hers may save the world yet, or at least bring me fully back.

Still no word from John. We haven't talked about the song since the let-me-sleep-on-it bit a week ago. I mean, it is a big one for him, maybe the biggest, so it's best to let him have space. I've been filling my slots re-recording the P song, or helping Radha and Bono with their songs. I never knew what a rush it could be to work on someone else's stuff. Good to give back, I guess, especially to your tribe. Individually, they both have big talent, but together, well, they may be the ones headed for the Hall. Wouldn't it be something if we all got in?

Creak. Creak. Creak. There's someone tiptoeing up the stairs. Bono, I'm sure, though he's a little early for our practice session. Best to put him on coffee duty while Radha and I shower, dress. A moment later, the door cracks open.

"Hi, Paige, thought I would surprise—Oh, I'm sorry, I didn't mean to . . ."

"Hi, Ian. This is Radha."

"Ah."

Ian enters the room, closes the door behind him. He has a bouquet of white long-stem roses in his hand. He does the traditional bit well, which normally amps me up, but not today. His face droops despite his best effort to hold firm. I mean, I told him all about Radha, but it's one thing hearing it and another thing seeing it. Still, he's a smart man. He'll get it soon, if not right away, that all of us need a tribe bigger than two. Especially when broken.

After a moment, a slow smile builds on Ian's face. That's unexpected. He pulls out two roses from the bouquet, comes over to the bed, hands one to each of us, then bends over, gently kisses me just a bit.

"Okay for me to slip in with the two of you?"

I glance over at Radha. She smiles, nods, somehow knows this is the right next step. How did the universe know to send me these two? How does the universe always know? I mean, of course two is the perfect antidote for 87 and 33.

"Are you sure, Ian?" I ask.

"As long as you are."

Ian undresses and slips into bed with us. He's warm, ready. Okay, I'm not exactly inexperienced or anything, but this is the first time I've had two people under the sheets who are completely dedicated to my well-being. There's something about getting the sex-tingle in stereo, that's, well, hard to explain. My heart races; I swallow dryness; I scratch the top of my foot with my toes; I hold back a tear swell. Together, we're about to go much deeper than either of them could have taken me on their own. I know it; they know it. I can see it on their faces—a peacefulness, a confidence, like they're sure that they can get the black marble out once and for all.

For a long time, a blur of hands, fingers, sweat, tears. We're all in. A few times, just when they're about to extract the black marble, it slips back down deep again. Like surgeons, their tongues, fingers, eyes patiently reach in, begin again. Finally, when the marble is securely out, when we're sure it's been expelled to the edge of our solar system, we start to laugh, roar really, at the tangle of bodies and sheets intertwined. Think nude Twister with occasional patches of Egyptian cotton.

I float up above the bed, shut my eyes, listen to the continuous roar. Sounds from The Big Wide Calm. This was exactly what I needed; this was the last piece.

#

An hour or so later, someone tiptoes up the stairs. Okay, this time it has to be. A light tap on the door.

"Paige, you awake?" Bono asks.

"Yeah, I'll be right down. Can you put coffee on?"

The three of us stealth out of bed, try not laugh, though our grins are threatening a big eruption. We jump into the shower together because it will be faster, except it turns out not to be. On the brink of being really late, we parade down to the studio. Ian first. Radha second. Me last. Bono's eyes widen a bit. Of course they do. Best to leave it at that. He probably wouldn't believe me if I told him. The smile on my face must be a mile wide.

"I'm glad we're all here. It's time to start planning the tour," I say.

"Any progress with John?" Bono asks.

"Not yet."

We set up the foldings. Ian sits on the magic piano bench, which causes Bono and me to have an anxiety pang at exactly the same time, but we recover. Bono pours coffee, passes around a box of pastries he's brought down from the main house that John apparently bought fresh only an hour ago. Whenever John isn't sure what to do next, he turns to Italian pastries, which has turned out to be quite okay with me. And to think where I started.

"So in a month I'll finish *The Big Wide Calm.* Ian, can you book us around the country? Small venues. Maybe east and west coast to start."

"Already working it."

"Radha, Bono, can you be ready with five to eight songs?"

"Yes," they say in unison.

"Ian, are you going to travel with us?" Radha asks.

"Wouldn't miss it. What about John?"

"I don't think he'll leave Harton. Maybe we can record the shows and send them to him?"

"We can," Ian says.

I snatch another cannoli, take a bite. There's something about working with people you care about. We're so efficient, but it doesn't seem like work, more like connection. Connected work. The working world could use more of this. I mean, John and I have always done the work thing well, but for this last song, we need to step it up a level to a new place, a blissful workplace. Yeah, that's a good name.

"Which brings me to another thing. If John and I have any chance of writing 'The Big Wide Calm' together, we need to do it completely alone. So until it's done, I need you guys to go away. Bono, maybe you can stay with Ian."

"Do you think that's the only way?" Radha asks.

"Yes."

"Are you sure?" Ian asks.

"Yeah. For these last few weeks, every ounce of my energy has to go toward the song, toward John."

#

Crunch. Crunch. Crunch. It's three weeks later, I'm heading up the gravel trail to the main house, all of the instruments I need in hand, for my umpteenth attempt to get John on board. The trip is taking longer than usual, and my work boots are losing the battle to pulverize the stones. John has no idea I'm coming, which may or may not improve my chances. I mean, I'm flat out of ideas if it doesn't, so . . . I slip in through the front door. The dogs scurry up to greet me, give me away. I kneel down, play with them for a bit, take a few deep breaths before moving in.

John is at his usual dining room chair, in his usual suit, sipping his usual cappuccino, occasionally pausing to pop a Hole. He's reading the same Stephen Hawking book he told me about the other day, *The Large Scale Structure of Space-Time*. "Paige, you have to read this." Right.

I place my instruments down on a free chair, sit at the opposite end of the table, fold my hands, smile. John puts his book down on the table, asks me if I want a cappuccino. "Yes please, a triple." A moment later, he places a cup in front of me along with the box of Holes. I pop a few.

"I have an idea," I say.

"What's that?"

I lift the instruments off the chair—two fresh leather-bound journals and two Mont Blanc pens. Best not to spare any expense when going for the big one. I place one journal, one pen, in front of John, and the other journal, pen in front of me. I open my journal to a fresh page. John is even-faced as he taps the pen on his journal in perfect rhythm.

"Do you remember when you asked me to write flash poems?" I ask.

"Yes."

"It did a world of good."

"It did."

"I thought we could write together now," I say.

"More about the event?"

"About The Big Wide Calm."

235

"Oh." John opens his journal to a fresh page, gently strokes the paper with his fingertips. He takes the cap off his pen, places it on the other end, starts to doodle some repetitive cube-like symbol over and over. Finally, after the page is almost full, he says, "I didn't forget about your request. It's just taken me longer than expected to decide."

"Maybe this will help."

"Maybe. Slide the Holes back this way."

I smile, slide the box toward him, thank the universe for sugar, for poetry. "So same rules as last time. Write for a minute in cursive, landscape. We'll each read back what we wrote twice. . . . Okay?"

We dive in. It's hard to concentrate on my stuff—I keep glancing over at John. He's propped his notebook up against the edge of the table and is writing incredibly fast. For a second, I wonder if he's just drawing cubes. At roughly the minute mark, we both put down our pens.

He nods once in my direction, says he'll go first. Round One, John: "At the bottom, the core, when I'm most free, I shake for the sons, for the fathers, who, despite good intentions, great love, lost their way. Listen to me. Come home now."

That's heartbreakingly beautiful. Maybe, just maybe.

Round One, Paige: "Go through the great shiver, the tiny pinprick of a knothole into The Big Wide Calm. I wish you nothing but peace. May your truths set you free, as mine have me."

John nods, smiles approval. He seems into this. We agree to move on to round two. A couple minutes later, we place our pens down at the same time.

John takes a deep breath and says, "If you could love me under the weight, the wrinkles, through the thick, fogged distance, the arrogance, the intellect, that would be okay. I'm actually quite handsome and sometimes funny."

"I do love you," I say.

"I know. That one wasn't about you."

"Ah. Here's my round two. . . . Ride a wave of confusion, of fear, in until it settles to a glass sheet. Then you'll see all the way to the bottom, or all the way to the top."

John nods approval again.

We resume writing at the same frantic rate. It's like as long as I give him structure, constrain the space into one-minute chunks, he moves forward. Maybe he doesn't consider it songwriting yet. Maybe I'm in the middle of my first Zen master trick with the Zen master.

"Round three turned out okay," John says. "There are no books here, no concrete rooms. This is a place where thought will not do. Just Grace playing a new song we wrote. And children laughing."

"That it did. Here's mine: There are doorways, all of them illusions. Because once you're in, you know you've always been. Here, magically, pain flips to peace, loss to gain, violence to love, sadness to joy. They're all the same in a way; everything is a way in."

After three rounds, we stop for more cappuccino, more Holes. Silently, we both reread what we've written. Then John starts to write again on his own. This is unexpected but promising. When he's done, he says, "I hope you don't mind. I did a few more on my own."

"Not at all."

"Here goes. Sometimes a man gets confused. Works his whole life as a carpenter when he was meant to be a painter. Then one day his brush touches an unexpected canvas and changes everything. All of the wood in all of the structures he built over the years turns to sawdust and rides the wind to its rightful home. And here's the next one: I am sad. I am lonely. I am too old. I am too young. I am shame. I am fear. I am too smart. I am dumb. I am love. Now replace *am* with *feel*. Stir and add sugar."

I raise my hand, snap my fingers three times. These last two really get to me, like he's not only writing about The Big Wide Calm but has tapped into it using some strange cursive loop. Or maybe a Möbius strip. I nod a few times, then say, "How do you feel?"

"I feel like we're going to write 'The Big Wide Calm' together."

#

Right away, we move to the studio. As soon as John enters, he adjusts a few knobs in the control room, hits record. A moment later, we're sitting at the magic piano bench improvising. Ideas flow; we ride them for a bit, then switch to fresh ones, seamlessly, without comment. You know, it's like one of those brainstorming sessions you sometimes see in schools with different color stickies, where there's no judgment of the ideas. Except we're using musical notes, chords, riffs instead of words. Sometimes we do the four-hand thing. Sometimes we play with nursery rhyme melodies, of which we're both particularly fond. Sometimes I switch to guitar and John stays on the piano. I'm amazed at the strength of the sync. He completes my riffs, adds to them; I complete his. The synergy is, well, exponential, like we've spent all our months in the Harton Woods practicing for exactly this session.

Hours pass. We order Chinese takeout, extra hot peppers. As we're eating Schezuan chicken and Peking ravioli, sipping plum wine, we listen back to what we've done. In no time, we agree on the bits we like, throw away the rest. I've never worked this way before. There's a palette of words, a palette of sounds; we dip often. I pick up a pepper, study it, pop it in my mouth. Then another. Hot! Makes me sweat. John follows my lead. Makes him sweat. We both zero in on one of the nursery rhyme melodies, start playing around with the flash poems to see if we can fit word fragments into it and form a chorus. In no time, we rough something out, let her sit for a bit.

I get an idea. Why not do the song as a real duet? I'll sing a verse, then John will sing one. We'll do the chorus and bridge together, add soaring harmonies. John agrees, doesn't put up an ounce of fight. Then John gets an idea. The song should be about how the two singers help each other find The Big Wide Calm. Make the song intimate and specific to them, then let the listeners generalize on their own. I agree, don't put up an ounce of fight. For a moment, I drift to John and Grace years earlier, writing on this very piano. How did he give this up? How does anyone give up something true?

Next we settle on an overall structure: verse, verse, chorus, verse, verse, chorus, bridge, verse. That's a lot of moving pieces, but we're okay with it.

There's much to say. I settle on guitar as my instrument; John settles on piano. We spend hours building the pieces, dipping into the flash poems, the improvised music, writing some new bits until we have a first pass of "The Big Wide Calm." When we're done, we don't say a word. We both know. Instead, John disappears into the control room, sets up the record, grabs a remote. A moment later, back at the piano, he hits record again, counts us off. One. Two. Three. Four.

> *Paige Verse:*
> *Look in my eyes*
> *What do you see?*
> *I am strong. I am calm. I'm at peace*
> *You know, we did this*
> *We did this*
>
> *John Verse:*
> *Take my hand*
> *What do you feel?*
> *I'm all these parts changing constantly*
> *You know, we did this*
> *We did this*
>
> *Chorus Together:*
> *We came home to the big wide calm*
> *Walked in together, palm in palm*
> *We came home to the big wide calm*
> *Tapped this magic place*
> *That turns all to grace*
>
> *John Verse:*
> *I come close now*
> *Take in your scent*

Like lavender wildflowers near the sea
Like a woman content
You know, we did this
We did this

Paige Verse:
I touch your lips
What do I taste?
Italian pastries, good coffee
Something I can't replace
You know we did this
We did this

Chorus Together:
We came home to the big wide calm
After all the pain, after all the wrongs
We came home to the big wide calm
Tapped this magic place
That turns all to grace

Bridge Together:
We didn't know the doorways in
Were just illusions
We were always here
Thick with fear, full of confusion
Now that we've set ourselves free
We can finally see
Love is you
Love is me
Love is we

Together Verse:
Listen now
What do you hear?
So many people knocking
Into thin air
Don't follow us
Just find your tribe
And your kindness
You know, you can do this
You can do this

John hits rewind on the remote, plays the song back. Pretty good. As the song plays, I hear all kinds of harmonies in my head, start humming a few. John glances over at me, smiles, adds his own bits on top, underneath, around mine. His stuff is amazing. It's like the harmony gods in the sky have chosen us to flaunt their stuff, and we're happy to oblige. You know, there's something about a duet. The back-and-forth lyrically for sure, but it's more than that. When it's working, the back-and-forth musically builds on the back-and-forth of the lyrics, and together, they create something, well, multigenerational, something that takes us through the tiny pinprick.

We run through the song a few more times until our harmonies are solid, then John hits record again. In a few passes, we add second, third parts, each one intricate, synergistic. We've been at it for many hours, each only a minute. You know, there's nothing better than the feeling of losing yourself with partner, in song. Now, we rest, listen back for the first time to the harmony version of "The Big Wide Calm." I know I say this a lot, but this one really is the best song I've ever written. Co-written.

"What do you think?" I ask.

"What time is it?"

"Close to four in the morning."

"I'm calling in the musicians. Call Radha, Ian, and Bono."

"Don't you think we should sleep first?"

"No. This is too good. We have to get it down right away."

A couple of hours, two pots of coffee, and an early morning run to Dunkin' Donuts later, the full band arrives at the studio. It's good to see my tribe; I've missed them. Over coffee and Holes, we play the harmony version for everyone. Loud.

"Paige, John, it's other-worldly," Radha says.

"The harmonies are so intricate and melodic," Bono says.

"We need to get this out there like *now*," Ian says.

All the band members echo Radha, Bono, and Ian. We set up and start to rehearse. Bono and Radha learn the harmony parts in no time. The string players come up with the most Kashmiresque part. The bass player and drummer find the groove. Normally, we rehearse a song for up to a week, but everyone picks up on John's bit about trying to capture the moment, and they compress their learning curve. By mid-afternoon, we're ready to record. We do three takes just to be safe, though we all know we nailed it on the first one.

After we all listen to the first take, I place my guitar down on the floor, send a silent thank-you to Dad, tear up. A moment later, on the floor next to my guitar, hands behind my head, I stare at this lace-like spiderweb in the ceiling corner. It's incredibly large, like it's taken decades to build. After my admiration for spiders skyrockets, the floodgates open. You know, I can't stop crying, no matter how hard I try. Fuck. Bono, Radha, Ian, John, Z—who arrived mid-morning after I sent him a text saying I needed him here—sit down and form a circle around me. John takes my hand, strokes it with his thumb. Radha's eyes are welled up, but she holds the tears back. Ian swallows a lump in his throat, doesn't do as well on the suppressed tear front. Z and Bono apparently decide the best thing to do is get it all out, so they join me full-throttle. My tribe at their best.

As the group-cry bit slows, John, in maybe his ultimate Zen-master move, starts to sing the song my Dad wrote for me when I was a girl. Over and over again, "Paige Plant. Paige Plant. Paige Plant. Paige Plant." Radha and

Bono add the most loving harmonies on top. Z and Ian join John on the main line. They're good in an endearing we-can't-sing kind of way. I try to join in at some point, but my sobbing acts up again.

A long time later, when the song has done its work, John asks, "What are you thinking?"

I know exactly what I'm thinking, but for some reason, I'm having a hard time getting it out. Finally, I say, "We did it."

#

I'm here in my room, in this bed probably for the last time, trying to get in a few hours before I head out in the morning. Fred says 4:00. I can't sleep, don't really want to. I need to take in as much of this place as I can, store it up for the rough spots that are bound to come. In the morning I'm leaving. For the last few weeks, we've prepared. Printed CDs, T-shirts, built the website, done the Facebook and Twitter things. I don't much like the social media bits, but Ian convinced me they're necessary. He booked about a hundred shows over the next six months, which is a big wow. John was right about Ian business-wise. Well, not just that.

We'll be away from Harton for a long time. I'll miss this place, the dogs, John. All the studio musicians wanted in on the tour, and along with Radha and Bono, agreed to become my official backing band. We've rehearsed every day these last weeks until we nailed every detail of the set. We're ready, which is good because my hunch is the hard part is just beginning.

After the black marble bit, Ian and Radha slowly settled back in as tribe members. Best not to have a steady lover, or two, when you're about to unveil multigenerational art to the world, when you're about to build a loyal audience one person at a time. Who knows, Ian and I may start up again sometime. I mean, no one is smart enough to predict the future, right?

John and I have been in such a calm place. It's like we both knew the big goodbye was coming, so we got in our favorite bits every day. We walked the dogs. He cooked for me; I cooked for him. We consumed ridiculously expensive bottles of wine. We went for much too much ice cream, downed way too many donut holes with our cappuccinos, did the pastry thing. One day, I helped him empty the concrete room, which took no time, but still. Another day, I treated him to a Patriots game. There were so many numbers in the stadium; they made me smile.

I am a little worried about leaving John behind, about leaving this place—it's my home. We even talked about it during an extra-long walk the other day. John said he'll be okay. We'll stay in touch by phone. He'll send me feedback on all the concerts. He has plenty to keep him busy. And he has the dogs. Still.

Creak. Creak. Creak. Someone is coming up the stairs. Good. I could use some company. I mean, if I'm not going to sleep, might as well be with a tribe member. I have no idea which one it will be, which I guess is the definition of a connected tribe. Creak. Creak. Creak. Whoever it is is going back down the stairs. Should I get out of bed? No. They probably had a change of heart and didn't want to interrupt my sleep. My tribe members are also considerate. I turn over on my side. Maybe a different position.

A few moments later, not an inch closer to sleep, I get out of bed, pee, look in the mirror. Maybe I won't have the tooth fixed after all. Just as I'm about to get back in bed, I take a quick detour, open up my bedroom door. There are two envelopes resting against the top stair. I pick them up. Both are in John's handwriting. The one on top says *Read this one first*. What the—? I flick on the overhead light, sit down on the top stair, open the first envelope.

Dear Grace,

Paige told me she came to visit you. I'm glad you got to hear her music. She's quite something, isn't she? We finished her album recently, The Big Wide Calm, and she's going out on tour to promote it soon. Believe it or not, we wrote the title song together. It's the first thing I've written since the last Wides song we wrote all of those years ago. I hope you get a chance to hear it, and I hope you like it.

Paige also told me that your one regret is that our kids never got to hear our music. It turns out that while I thought I bought and destroyed all the copies of our CDs, one of our old acquaintances, Jacob, contacted me recently and said he had one of each of our five albums. After an offer he couldn't refuse, he sold them to me. I'm going to have them shipped to you by special courier. They should arrive some time in the next week.

Do you remember the first song we wrote together, "Wide Open"? I forgot how much I loved that song, especially the lines, Do you remember the first time you cried in my arms? / You said you felt completely seen / Do you remember my darkest time? / You held me close and said / I love you / I love you.

Take care,
John

Okay, there it is. This swell from the base of my spine rises all the way up to my head, then down to my toes. John did a good thing. The kids may never know him, but at least they'll get to hear his music. I return to bed, read the letter a second time. Round two of the swell. I smile, run my fingers through my hair, scratch the back of my ear. Some things you can't get enough of. . . . I place the letter on my nightstand for safekeeping, open the second envelope.

Dear Paige,

I thought it was best to say goodbye this way. I have some CDs to deliver to Italy. I'm not sure how long I'll be gone, so I asked Z to watch the place while I'm away. Don't worry, I also hired a live-in dog sitter. :-) I'll see you in six months when you return.

I know you're going to do great things out there. The Big Wide Calm is fantastic, multigenerational, a work of art! It will get you into the Hall someday. I can't tell you how proud I am of you, both in terms of the music you've created and the woman you've become. Just remember that everything you need to connect with your audience you already have. Actually, everything you need you already have, though this point is a little harder to hold for all of us. On those days when you slip a little, trust your tribe. That's what we're here for.

I also wanted to thank you for being yourself. You are an incredible woman, my closest friend, my witness, my teacher, the catalyst for what I'm about to do. You did save me. Twice.

I love you.
See you soon.
John.

P.S. I lied about the CDs. There's a second set, which I left for you on the magic piano bench. I hope you like them.

#

I'm in the 335i heading out of Harton Woods. The sun is shining through the trees, which are full of color. Reds. Oranges. Yellows. Greens. Browns. An infinity of color, really. When I reach the fifty-foot rock formation, a doe and her fawn dart out from behind a rock cluster and cross the road twenty yards in front of me. They're beautiful.

At The General, I stop for a cappuccino, even though I've already had two at the house. On the way out of the store, cup in hand, I take in the streets, the green, the fields. The sidewalks are filled with people, children are riding their bikes, town soccer games are at a fever pitch, a few girls are playing hopscotch. Just as I'm getting back in the car, an older woman I've seen many times waves, tells me to have a good day.

"You, too. By the way, my name is Paige Plant. I don't think we've ever formally met."

"Aimee Jenkins. Nice to meet you. I see you have a guitar in your backseat. Are you a musician?"

"I work as a singer-songwriter. Leaving town for a bit to share my stuff."

"Ah . . . I'm sure you'll do well. Good luck, honey."

As I accelerate up the I-495 ramp toward my first gig in New Haven, I pop The Wides's first CD into the car stereo. John and Grace pour through the speakers, fill the space with love, with connection, with hope. Their harmonies are like no other.

In the end, I may never change the world. I mean, at best it's a long shot, right? But I did help John. I did witness his truths set him free. I do fully see him, fully love him. And I know it's a big ditto for him. Paige sees John. John sees Paige. It's pretty simple, really. I mean, how many people can say that, say they found The Big Wide Calm together?

Now take what we have, multiply it by a few billion, and imagine. Yeah, yeah.